THE
MILLIONAIRE'S
WIFE

SHALINI BOLAND

Bookouture

Published by Bookouture in 2018

An imprint of StoryFire Ltd.

Carmelite House,
50 Victoria Embankment
London EC4Y 0DZ

www.bookouture.com

ISBN: 978-1-78681-598-9
eBook ISBN: 978-1-78681-597-2

This book is a work of fiction. Names, characters, businesses,
organizations, places and events other than those clearly in the
public domain, are either the product of the author's imagination
or are used fictitiously. Any resemblance to actual persons, living or
dead, events or locales is entirely coincidental.

For my beautiful mum xx

CHAPTER ONE

3rd January 2017, Barbados

He watched her hasten down the stone steps, slightly ahead of him, her bare, tanned legs lithe and slim – a combination of good genes and regular dance classes, more like a teenager than a woman in her late twenties. For a moment, he felt as though he were watching a memory, a video on his laptop of someone he used to know. He gave himself a shake and followed her.

'Come on, slowcoach!' she called, dark ringlets bouncing around her shoulders. She threw him a glance over her shoulder, a teasing grin. He smiled back and put on a spurt of speed, scooped her up in his arms and jogged down the remaining steps with her until they reached the arc of pristine sand which curved around the turquoise bay, its backdrop of trees swaying in the breeze. The sand sifted pleasantly beneath his soles, warm and soft. Later it would become a white-hot furnace, impossible to walk on with bare feet, and he'd have to dig out his flip flops from the beach bag.

Katie wriggled out of his arms and pulled him along by the hand to their favourite spot under the morning shade of a benevolent palm, far enough away from the manchineel trees with their poison fruit and deadly sap.

A cursory glance left and right showed two other couples already on the beach, stretched out on bright towels, and one older woman on her own, nose buried in a paperback. It was a weekday, so no sign of the weekend yachties and speedboat owners who would moor up in the bay often staying until sundown. No. Today the view was of empty ocean and sky. Perfect.

Dropping her towel and bag onto the sand, Katie twirled her hair up into a makeshift bun, fixing it in place with a hairband from her wrist. 'You coming in?'

'Later. I think I'm going to relax for a while.'

'Lightweight,' she teased. 'The woman in the villa next to ours said she saw whales in the bay yesterday. I'm going to swim out and see if I can spot them while it's still early enough.'

'Don't go too far,' he said, knowing she'd most likely ignore him.

He'd never been on holidays like this before he'd met Katie. Yachts, mansions and ski slopes had not been for the likes of him. Katie, however, had been born to it. While he'd been skinning his knees learning to ride a second-hand bike at the local skateboard park, she and her parents had been gliding across virgin snow, flying to far-flung continents on safari, or watching prima ballerinas twirl on famous stages. She had led a charmed life.

Surely, the parents of a girl like this should have been horrified when she brought home a nobody like him – a dirt-poor, classless loser with no career to speak of. But he had been proven wrong. The Spencers were nice people. Warm and welcoming. Non-judgemental. Nothing like his own family. To give himself credit, he did have a decent sense of humour and a beautiful face. He had always been admired. Charm was his gift.

And so, it had been an easy thing to become absorbed into this family. He and Katie. The golden couple. Shining wherever they went. He had shrugged on her privilege with ease, taking it for his own. Long-haul flights to distant lands, skiing, safari-ing, visiting the ballet, the opera. Moving in dizzyingly high circles without once losing his balance. They were a pair. And she loved him without reserve.

Peeling off his t-shirt, he began applying sun lotion to his torso, watching as Katie walked across the beach in her skimpy bikini towards the gently lapping ocean, its water the perfect temperature. Not like the English Channel back home which would steal your breath, needle your skin and finally give your stomach an icy punch. No, Barbados seas were warm yet refreshing. Already up to her waist, Katie struck off away from the shore, her arms powering forward. He watched her for a moment and then lay back, gazing at the palm fronds and blue sky above, trying to let his mind go blank for a while.

It didn't do to overthink things.

He lay there for some time before he heard the noise. Faint, at first, like a lazy bumble bee or a neighbour's lawnmower. Then, growing louder. An engine, determined, fast, the random crashes of its hull against the ocean's surface. He imagined himself sitting up and looking at the sea, searching out the source of the noise, but his body was locked in place, too tense to move. He couldn't stop staring at the impossibly blue sky. Could barely breathe.

A scream jolted him from his brief stasis and he jerked upright before springing to his feet. As his senses sharpened, he saw the other sunbathers running towards the ocean, their hands raised against the glare of the sun, pointing, shouting. Beyond them, a white speedboat bounded out to sea, its wake contaminating the glassy, blue ocean. His eyes scanned the water for Katie. No sign. Maybe she was hidden by the chop from the boat.

He sprinted down to the water's edge, shielding his eyes from the sun, trying to locate her.

'Did it hit her?' a woman with a German accent cried out to him. 'Did you see?'

'What?' he replied, panting.

'The boat out there. I think it might have hit your friend.'

'Are you sure?' he questioned, his voice slow and stupid, his mind frozen. 'The boat? It hit my wife?' He didn't wait for further confirmation, but dove into the water, powering through the ocean to reach Katie.

He felt the company of another swimmer beside him – a concerned sunbather wanting to help. The boat was already a pale dot in the distance, its motor a receding hum. He didn't know where to look for her. Stupid. He should have been looking out for her instead of staring at the sky. But the man ahead of him knew where he was going, his long, powerful strokes propelling him towards a fixed point. He would follow that man.

A crimson stain like a beacon spread out before him, already losing its bright hue, turning pink and dissolving into wisps. Soon it would be absorbed into the ocean. But still no sign of Katie. This is where it must have happened. Where the speedboat had collided with his wife. He took a long gulp of air and dove down. He couldn't let the other man reach her first. The crystal water showed him what he needed to see.

Her body was whole, but had been mangled, torn up beyond repair. One side of her head was missing, ribbons of red following her descent. He looked away briefly, noticing the blurry shape of the man from the beach next to him. Then he turned back, swam towards his wife, took hold of her slippery body and kicked up to the surface, gasping for air.

The man rose up with him, clapping him on the shoulder. 'Jesus,' the man gasped. 'Let's get her to shore. That fucking speedboat, man.' A South African accent. 'Shall I help you… with… her?'

'No. I've got her.' He knew how to tow an inert body. Remembered it from his life-saving classes. The South African swam alongside him as he carried his dead wife, the smell of sun and salt and blood in his nostrils, a strong desire to vomit, a blank void in his brain, a trail of blood in their wake.

Back on the beach, one of the women was shaking her head and crying, the other two had mobile phones clamped to their ears, no doubt calling the emergency services. The other man on the shore took Katie's legs and they carried her between them, up the beach away from the shoreline towards his and Katie's favourite palm tree. They laid her on her towel, where she'd been standing less than an hour earlier. A numbness overtook his body and he realised he was shaking.

Someone placed a warm towel over his shoulders, but the shivering only increased.

'He's in shock.' A woman's voice, loud and authoritative.

'It was his wife,' the South African said.

'Do you think they'll catch them? The people in the speedboat?'

'I gave the police a description of the boat over the phone. Didn't see who was driving it, though. Surely they can track it on radar?'

'No chance. They'll be long gone.' An English voice.

'Irresponsible bastards.'

'I can't believe it. Poor woman.'

'Poor guy.'

The crush of words wove through his consciousness, but he didn't respond. He closed his eyes and clutched at the towel around his shoulders, desperately trying to stop the shivering and act more coherently. React. Respond. Cry. An arm slid around his shoulder – the South African. 'The police will be here soon, mate. Don't worry. They'll catch them. Those bastards will get what's coming to them. Don't you worry about that.'

CHAPTER TWO

7th January 2017, Bournemouth, England

The trouble with revealing secrets is that you never know how the other person is going to react. A secret is like gravity, pulling everything inexorably towards it in a deteriorating orbit. The bigger the secret, the bigger the pull. The people around you can feel something tugging at them, an unexplainable curiosity drawing them closer. But, until you choose to reveal that something, everyone is still just spinning in ignorance. Dizzy. Oblivious.

As I stand on the table hanging silver streamers from the ceiling, trying to keep my balance on the slippery, polished surface, I realise I don't want that for me and Will. I don't want to keep secrets any more. I love him. Our life together is so perfect, I've been terrified of opening my mouth and wrecking everything. Of pulling him out of his perfect orbit too fast. But we're strong enough to endure it. I trust Will to understand why I left him spinning in the dark for so long. Anyway, it wasn't just for him that I've had to stay silent. I had to bide my time. Wait until the danger passed. And now, finally, I think it's safe to tell my husband what I should have told him at the start.

But I won't be revealing any secrets to him tonight. It's his thirtieth birthday. It's not quite the right time. Not yet.

The thing is, now I've made the decision to tell him, I can't wait. I'm nervous, excited, all those things. But I'll have to keep it in for just one more day.

After all, timing is everything.

*

'Happy birthday, dear Will. Happy birthday to yooooou!'

I'm not the world's greatest singer, but what I lack in tone, I make up for in enthusiasm. We let off our party poppers and cheer my husband who's making a valiant attempt to blow out all thirty candles on his cake.

Will's dad, Steve, rises to his feet and dings his glass several times with a pastry fork. He sets the glass back on the polished wood table and runs a hand through his wavy salt-and-pepper hair while he waits for us to quieten down.

'I'd like to say a few words if that's okay,' he says. 'Don't want to embarrass Will, but, what the hell, I'm going to anyway.'

The room rumbles with laughter, and Will's best friend, Remy, elbows him in the ribs.

'My son…' Will's dad clears his throat and gazes around the restaurant. 'My wonderful son William Blackwell turns thirty today, and I'd like to tell him, in front of all you good people, that I couldn't be more proud of him.'

I can feel the collective melting of hearts around the room.

Steve turns to look at Will, his eyes glistening. 'Your mother would have been so proud of you. She'd have loved to see the man you've become.' He holds his son's gaze for a moment then retrieves his glass and raises it high, waiting for us all to echo his gesture. 'Happy birthday, Will!'

'Happy birthday, Will!' We begin to clap and cheer and stamp our feet, but Will's dad holds his hands out for quiet once more.

'I'd also like to say a big thank you to Anna for organising this evening, managing to keep it a secret, and for making my son pretty much the happiest man alive.'

I flush at my father-in-law's glowing praise, uncomfortable in the spotlight. Will turns and beams at me, his lips meeting mine briefly before he, too, rises to his feet.

'Thanks, Dad. Thank you. And you're right, Anna is responsible for *this*,' he says, pointing to the expanding grin on his face. Then he raises his glass. 'To Steve, the best dad a man could wish for, and to my beautiful wife, Anna, for making me the happiest man alive.'

'To Steve and Anna!' The room erupts into more cheering.

As everyone toasts us, I take my husband's hand and squeeze it, a glow of happiness spreading throughout my body. A feeling that I still can't get used to. That I still don't feel I quite deserve the life I have.

We're celebrating Will's thirtieth at Blackwell's, a charming French bistro that belongs to Will and his dad. They must have the magic touch where food is concerned because Blackwell's is the place to go in Westbourne. They're always booked solid – and that's no mean feat considering there are around two hundred cafés and restaurants in this small, affluent suburb of Bournemouth. Good job I blocked off this Saturday in the bookings diary months in advance, or we wouldn't have been able to hold his party here. We filled the date with bookings under fake names so Will wouldn't find out about the party.

One of the waitresses, Louise, comes and takes the birthday cake away to cut up into slices. My phone buzzes on the table, but I ignore it, slipping it into my handbag on the back of my chair.

'Thanks for arranging this, Anna,' Will says. 'It's an absolutely brilliant night.'

'Your dad's speech was lovely. I thought I was going to cry.'

'Me too. Who knew the old man could be such a softie.'

Will's mum died from a brain tumour when he was nine and he rarely talks about her, so I'm not surprised he got choked up hearing his dad mention how proud she would've been of him. I love how close he and his dad are. I wonder if Steve will ever meet anyone else, but he once told me that Helen was the love of his life and could never be replaced. He seems content with his son, his restaurant and his friends from the tennis club. Maybe that's enough.

'There's something else.' I say. I take Will's hand and then nod at his dad.

Will gives me a quizzical look.

'Okay, guys!' Will's dad calls out. 'Follow Will and Anna out the back door please.'

I give Will what I hope is an enigmatic smile, and lead him out through the restaurant, past the bar and through the set of swing doors which lead into the kitchen. The waiting and kitchen staff all wear big grins.

'I feel like the Pied Piper,' Will says as everyone follows us.

'Close your eyes,' I say, as we reach the back door.

He does as I ask. Steve comes and stands on his left side, while I'm on his right. We each take one of his arms and lead him outside into the chill night air, making our way carefully through the small patio area and out through the gate into the car park beyond. There are gasps and sighs from our friends when they see what's on the tarmac.

'You can open your eyes now, Will,' I say.

'Happy Birthday, son,' Steve adds.

Will opens his eyes and blinks a couple of times. Remy is standing to the side, videoing Will's reaction to the immaculate 1969 cherry red Ford Mustang sitting in the car park, done up with a huge, white bow.

'Wow,' he whispers.

'Do you like it?' I ask.

'*Like* it?' He straightens up and grins. 'It's a beast. I love it.'

It was my idea to get him the car as a birthday present as I know Will has a thing about American classic cars. But I'd spoken to his dad about it first to see what he thought. 'I think it's a great idea,' he'd said. 'As long as I can borrow it!'

'It's the 429 Boss model,' I say to Will, 'Had it shipped over from The States. Sorry I couldn't manage to get one with right-hand drive, but—'

'It's perfect,' he says, dark eyes gleaming as he turns to kiss me. 'Thank you, thank you, thank you.'

I hand him the keys and he walks towards the car, shaking his head. My heart fills with joy to see him so happy. He runs a hand along the bonnet before opening up the driver's side door.

'Gonna take her for a spin, mate?' one of our friends calls out.

'He's probably too pissed!' someone else cries, and everyone laughs.

Will gets into the driver's seat, but leaves the door open, his muscular frame filling the small space. He slots the key into the ignition and starts up the engine, revving it, letting the engine growl and roar. We stamp our feet and cheer, laughing at Will's schoolboy glee. But, whoever called out a moment ago was right – Will is most definitely over the legal limit to drive. He reluctantly slides out of the Mustang and closes the door. Then he kisses his palm and touches it to the car roof.

Sloping back towards us, he hugs his dad, then wraps his arms around me and whispers, 'I love you, Mrs Blackwell. You're incredible.' We kiss, hard, almost forgetting the world around us. I reluctantly pull away, remembering what I've got planned for the rest of the night.

'Later,' I promise.

He sighs and runs a thumb down my cheek.

I check my watch. They should be ready by now. 'Okay,' I say, taking his hand once more. 'Let's go inside. It's chilly out here.'

'That's a point,' he says. 'We probably shouldn't leave the car out here overnight. It's too cold. The frost will damage the—'

'Already thought of that,' I say. 'One of the lads is driving it home in a minute. It'll soon be back in our nice, cosy garage. You can tuck her up later.'

'Brains *and* beauty?' He smiles. 'I lucked out.'

I give him a wink. And I have another surprise for my husband as we re-enter the bistro. While we were outside in the car park, the waiting staff have moved the tables and chairs against the walls, and a top London DJ has set up by the bar. The lights have been dimmed further, and the chilled restaurant music has been replaced by a loud, low beat.

'This is so cool,' Will says. 'Best birthday ever. Did I tell you lately that I love you?'

'Um, maybe once or twice,' I reply. 'Happy birthday. Here's to an awesome night.' I tilt my head up to kiss him again, but we're interrupted by someone clearing their throat.

'Right, then.'

I look up to see Will's dad hovering beside us.

'I'm off now,' he says. 'Leave you youngsters to it.'

'You don't have to go, Steve,' I say. 'Stay. Have a dance.'

'Thanks, Anna,' he replies, patting my shoulder. 'I've had a great night but I need to be up early. Got to get to the quay by seven if I've any chance of getting some decent fish for tomorrow's specials board.'

'Why don't you ask Paul to go to the quay,' Will says, knowing very well that his dad will never ask his chef to go in his place. Steve loves gossiping with the fishermen down there. It's part of his daily routine.

'No, I'm off. Have fun,' Steve says shaking his head, ignoring our pleas.

'Thanks, Dad. That Mustang… thank you. It's—'

'I already told Anna I'm first in line to borrow it.'

'Any time, Dad. Just, maybe not this week.'

'Hmm.' Steve ruffles his son's hair. Then he leans across to kiss my cheek.

Will and I watch him for a moment as he goes to say his goodbyes, working his way around the room. It will probably take him half an hour at least.

'Hey, guys, come and dance!' My best friend Sian bounces over. She scooches in between me and Will, loops her arms through ours and drags us into the middle of the room. Remy joins us, body popping for our amusement. As well as being Will's best friend, Remy is also Sian's boyfriend, so the four of us are like family. We're drunk enough to not mind being the first ones on the dance floor.

Pretty soon, the floor is packed with our friends, and Will and I are at the centre of it all. It reminds me of our wedding a little over a year ago, only now I know Will's friends so much better. They're *my* friends, too.

After twenty minutes or so, I wriggle out of Will's arms and make my way over to the bar for some water to dilute the alcohol in my bloodstream. Glass in hand, I make a quick detour to check the message I received earlier. My phone's in my bag, still hanging off my chair.

Tugging at my dress which I now realise has ridden up my thighs to an almost indecent length, I sit and open my message folder. It's from an unknown number. My head is nicely fuzzy and I hum along tunelessly to Bruno Mars. Gulping down some more water, I tap the message to open it and an image pops up on the screen.

I'm horrified. It must be junk mail. It's sick. The photo of a dead woman. My head swims with the faint traces of nausea. She's youngish. Her face smashed in on one side. Why the hell would anyone send me an image like that? Talk about an instant buzz kill. My finger goes straight to the delete icon. But then I pause, suddenly noticing the line of text above the photo.

My blood turns to ice as I read it.

Hello Anna. Your turn next x

CHAPTER THREE

June 2007

'Put your tongue back in,' Sian said with a smirk.

'Hm?' I watched as Fin threw his board up and down the tiny wave, getting the most out of the short ride. He was definitely the best surfer out there. No one else was catching anything. Just bobbing up and down on their boards like forlorn black seals waiting for fish.

'You've got drool on your chin, Anna.'

'What!' Mortified, I wiped my mouth and chin with the back of my hand before I realised Sian was teasing me. Now, she was doubled over laughing. 'Cow,' I said, grinning.

Being the first warmish day of the year, the beach was crowded. A group of us had come down after school to swim, surf and get away from our parents for a few more hours. We always hung out at the same spot – just east of Boscombe Pier because it was usually the best place for decent surf. Sian and I weren't really "in" with the rest of the group, so we sat slightly apart. It wasn't that they didn't like us or anything, just that we weren't into the same things – drinking, smoking, pushing the boundaries. Sian and I were too square.

'You like him, don't you?' she asked.

'Who?'

'Shut up, you know who I mean.'

'Don't know what you're talking about.' I looked away so she wouldn't see my cheeks turn scarlet.

'Fin Chambers,' she needled. 'You like him.'

I didn't reply. Tried to think of something to change the subject, but my mind came up blank.

'Come on, Anna. Admit it. You like him. I tell you all my dirty secrets so it's only fair you tell me yours.'

Fin held court over everyone. You could see it in the set of his shoulders and the tilt of his chin. He would accept no dissenters. All the boys wanted to be him, and all the girls wanted him. Including me. As usual, my best friend was spot on. Trouble was, I didn't stand a chance so I was reluctant to add my name to the ever-growing list of the Fin Chambers fan club.

'He's okay,' I said.

'*Okay?*' Sian raised an eyebrow. 'He's bloody gorgeous is what he is.'

I tilted my head in acknowledgement.

'Look…' Sian crossed her legs and faced me, adopting a more serious tone. 'You're hands down the hottest girl in our school. I know we're not part of Leah's little gang, but Fin would have to be mad or blind not to want to go out with you.'

My heart gave a skip. 'Do you think?'

'Duh.'

We laughed.

'You're prettier,' I said. 'You've got cool hair and your eyes are really unusual – grey and sexy.'

She grinned and shook her head. 'Ha! Thanks for trying to make me feel better, but I can't compete with that natural blonde-haired, blue-eyed Swedish thing you've got going on.'

'Back in Stockholm, I'm just normal. Like everyone else. Nothing special.' I'd moved to the UK from Sweden with my family two years earlier.

'Well here you look like a goddess or something, so you better get used to it.'

I'm not sure I believed her, but it was nice to be complimented. Sian and I had bonded last year in PE over shared hysteria during a "country dancing" lesson where we'd almost wet ourselves laughing at the lame music and the moves. She'd been a bit of a loner before that, having nothing in common with the other girls who were either totally nerdy or into getting wasted all the time. So, I guess it was inevitable that she and I would become friends.

'Want to go for a swim?' I asked. We'd already put our bikinis on under our uniforms before we left school, but it had turned out too chilly to sunbathe.

'No way,' Sian replied, looking at me like I was crazy for suggesting such a thing. 'It's freezing.'

'Come on. I don't want to go on my own.' I had spent every summer previously with my family at our dilapidated forest cottage in central Sweden. Part of our daily ritual had been to sweat in the sauna, followed by a flamboyant leap off the crumbling wooden jetty into the icy lake. So, the cold English Channel didn't bother me one bit. In fact, I loved it at any time of the year.

I noticed the already pathetic wave swell was diminishing down even further to almost nothing. Pretty soon the sea would be a millpond. Perfect for swimming. Fin was coming out of the water, his broad-shouldered walk almost a swagger as he headed towards our scattered group, pushing his wet, blond hair back off his face. I wondered if he'd look my way or even if I might get to talk to him. Of course, we'd spoken the odd word before, but always in a group, never alone. I peeled off my school uniform and stood up, feeling mildly self-conscious in my bikini.

'Watch my stuff. I won't be long.'

'Nutter,' Sian replied, blowing me a kiss when I turned to go.

As Fin walked up the beach, I made sure our paths didn't cross, keeping twenty yards or so to his right, and avoiding eye contact. I didn't want him to think I was purposely trying to talk to him. My heart hammered just to be in such close proximity. I was usually confident around boys, but something about him made my knees go soft. I focused straight ahead on the ocean. I'd have to go in far enough away from the surfers that they wouldn't collide with me. The tide was still pretty far out so it was quite a trek to the shoreline. As I walked, I enjoyed the faint warmth of the sun on my shoulders.

'Hey, Anna.' Fin appeared by my side. He must have altered his course to talk to me.

'Hey. Hi,' I replied, my voice coming out like a strangled croak.

'Going for a swim?' he asked.

'Yeah.'

'It's cold out there – and I'm wearing a wetsuit.'

'I don't mind the cold.'

'Let me dump my board with the others and I'll come and join you,' he said.

'Oh. Okay.' My voice sounded less than enthusiastic, but inside my heart raced.

'Only if you want?' he asked, less confident.

'Yeah, sure. That'd be cool.'

He tipped his head to the side and bashed at his ear with the heel of his hand, his fair curls spraying droplets everywhere. 'Water in my ear,' he explained. 'Annoying.'

I nodded.

'Okay, see you in a sec,' he said.

'Okay.' I nodded again and continued my walk to the ocean. Fin Chambers was coming swimming with *me*, Anna Karlsson. He'd purposely come over and asked if he could join me. Did this mean anything? Was this the start of something? Or simply an innocent swim? I glanced up the beach to see Sian grinning. Then she pretended to snog the back of her hand. Heat flooded my face and I transferred my glance to Fin, praying he hadn't seen my friend trying to embarrass me. But he was talking to his mates, thank goodness. I pulled a face at Sian and then jogged the rest of the way down to the sea.

The only way to enter cold water is to fully submerse yourself instantly. Otherwise, it becomes a long, tortuous process of inching down bit by painful bit. The only problem being that the bay here was so shallow I had to take a run at it and part-dive, part-belly-flop. As I launched myself in, I felt someone else splash in beside me. Fin must have sprinted back down. He rolled onto his back and gazed at me as I emerged and stumbled upright. The sea still only came up to our chests.

'Want to race out to the buoy?' I said impetuously.

'It's pretty far,' he replied.

'We don't have to…'

'Three, two, one, go!' He rose up and dove into the water like a porpoise before I could finish my sentence. I took a breath, diving after him.

I caught Fin up easily, realising it would have been no effort to overtake him. But I had the feeling it wouldn't go down too well if I beat him, so I fell back a couple of metres. I watched as he triumphantly grabbed the buoy, waiting for me to arrive. We both bobbed there for a moment, catching our breath and grinning at one another. The water lapped around us, a few curious gulls surveying us from a safe distance.

'You're fast,' he said. 'I thought you were going to overtake me at one point.'

'You were too quick,' I lied.

He tipped his head in acknowledgement. 'I swim a lot.'

'Saw you catch some waves earlier,' I said. The instant I'd spoken, I realised he'd now know I'd been watching him.

'Ugh, the surf was crap today.' He wrinkled his nose. 'I can't wait until they build that artificial reef. Next year apparently.'

'My parents don't think it will work,' I said.

He raised an eyebrow.

Why did I say that? Talking about my parents wasn't the coolest start.

'How do your parents know if it'll work or not?'

'Apparently, the company building it, they've built two reefs before and neither of those worked, so…'

'Really?' His expression darkened, but I couldn't tell if he was annoyed with me or with the news I'd given him. 'So why don't the council get someone else to build it?'

'Money,' I replied. 'This company were the cheapest.'

'Typical.'

I nodded in agreement.

'We're going into town to get a burger after this,' he said, brightening. 'Want to come?'

I thought about saying yes, but my parents were expecting me home by seven. And there was no point asking to stay out later because I knew what their answer would be: *No. You're fifteen, Anna. England isn't like Sweden. Blah, blah.*

'Sorry, I can't,' I replied.

'No problem,' he said with a shrug. 'Some other time, yeah?'

'Sure.'

He turned and launched himself off the buoy, heading back to shore with a splash.

I followed behind, my heart pounding with possibilities.

CHAPTER FOUR

January 2017

The noise from the party recedes, and everything shrinks down to these five stark words on the screen. They blur out of focus and suddenly I'm back there, in that cold, one-bedroom flat, where I once thought I was so happy. But now, the thought of that place makes me cringe. The memories of that time are ones I've tried to bury, but it looks like they're about to bubble to the surface. I only hope they don't pull me under.

I shudder, blink, try to push the memories away. It has to be a joke, surely. He can't possibly have… he can't possibly think… I thought all that was over and done with.

'Anna!'

I look up, startled, suddenly remembering where I am. Will stands in front of me. I shove my phone into my handbag and plaster a smile on my face.

'Everything okay?' His eyebrows quirk upwards. 'You looked freaked out for a minute there.'

'What? No, everything's great. Come on let's boogie.' I let him pull me to my feet and we return to the dance floor, but everything has changed. My champagne buzz has gone. The music is no longer a happy celebration. It's manic. Too loud. The beat is a war drum. Our friends' laughter is brittle, harsh, distant, like hyenas closing in.

Will throws his arms around me and pulls me close, his hands on my lower back, his mouth nuzzling my ear, his comforting presence already a fading dream. I cling onto him like I'm drowning and he's my life raft, wishing it was just the two of us, far away, somewhere safe, insulated from the rest of the world. But the image of the dead woman has imprinted itself on my retinas. I'm going to throw up, and I know I won't reach the ladies' in time.

I pull away from my husband, claw through the other dancers and barge my way outside onto the pavement. The cold air hits me, but it's not enough to stop me vomiting into the icy gutter by the wheels of someone's brand new Audi TT.

'Ew, gross.' Women's voices behind me, their footsteps echoing away down the street. But I have too much on my mind to feel ashamed or embarrassed.

'Hey.' I feel a hand at my back. 'You okay?' It's Will.

'Too much champagne,' I gasp.

'That's not like you,' he says gently. 'You can normally drink me under the table.'

I retch again.

'Shall I get you some water?'

'No.' I cough and wipe my mouth with the side of my hand, straightening up. I look him in the eye. 'Don't leave me.'

'Never,' he replies, pulling me into his arms.

I hug him back. Tighter. Scared to let go.

'Feeling any better now?'

I nod, although my whole body is shivering, my teeth chattering.

'Maybe you're coming down with something.' He rubs my arms, trying to warm me up.

'Sorry, Will. I'm ruining your party.'

'No.' He smiles. 'Don't worry. Think of it as a funny story we can tell our friends.' He's trying to make me feel better, cheer me up.

'Ugh. I think they might already know.' I see Sian and Remy's faces pressed up against the glass, looking at us.

Will turns and gives them a wave. They shrug and frown, probably wondering what we're doing out here.

'Do you feel up to going back in, or shall I take you home?'

'You're not taking me home! It's your birthday. Honestly, I feel much better now. Let's go inside.'

'Sure? We can get a taxi now. No one will notice.' His voice is so soft, so full of concern, it rips at my heart.

'Yes, totally sure. I'm fine.'

He takes my hand and leads me back inside, his hand already like a stranger's. Luckily, no one saw me throwing up and Will tells them we were just getting some fresh air. I somehow manage to fake happiness for the rest of the night, to pretend I'm still just Anna Blackwell, Will's beautiful wife. But inside, my stomach churns and my heart is twisting and shrivelling. Aching with the knowledge of what that text means…

CHAPTER FIVE

June 2007

I kept my eyes down on the worn linoleum and headed past a row of battered lockers towards Mr Williams' History class, the pungent aroma of sweaty socks and bleach making me hold my breath and wrinkle my nose. I hadn't been targeted by any of the older girls yet, but it was a rough school compared to the one back home, and Sian said I was as likely to get my head kicked in for being too pretty and from a foreign country (even though I had no trace of an accent any more), as I was for being too fat, or too weird, or whatever else the school bullies thought deserved their attention. But today fear wasn't the thing that had me preoccupied. No. History was the first lesson of the day that I shared with Fin. My stomach turned over at the thought of seeing him. Would he acknowledge me after our swim last Friday?

I had spent the whole weekend going over every word he'd said at the beach, every look he had given me. Was it because he was interested, or was I simply another friend, another hanger-on? Did he see me differently? I hoped so. I hadn't been able to eat or sleep, and I hadn't wanted to listen to anything my parents or brothers had to say. All their boring talk had dragged me away from my thoughts of Fin. Couldn't they see I needed to be alone? To think. To dream.

I finally reached Mr William's class with my pulse racing, smoothed my hair and walked in. A quick scan of the room showed only a handful of students had arrived before me – Fin not among them. I slouched over to my usual spot, about a third of the way from the front, and sat down before hauling my textbooks out of my bag, trying not to look up every time someone else walked in. Fin normally sat a couple of seats across from me, over near the window, so he'd probably pass right by me when he arrived. Sian was in a different academic set, so I didn't share any lessons with her, apart from PE.

Mr Williams sat at his desk, engrossed in his marking. Few of the teachers at Shelborne looked like they enjoyed their jobs, and Mr Williams was no exception, his face set in a permanent scowl. When my parents moved here, they hadn't realised there was such a huge difference between standards of schools in the area. Unfortunately, I'd ended up in the one with the worst reputation in the whole of the South of England. It was safe to say I had no love for the place, but at least I found the work easy. Plus, I had my best friend, and I was quite possibly on the verge of acquiring my very first boyfriend. Education was a frequent topic of conversation between my parents, though, and I lived in fear of them yanking me out of a school I knew, to enrol me somewhere else where I'd have to start all over again.

'Hey.' A soft voice to my right made me jump.

I glanced up and bit my lip as Fin gave me a lazy smile, his blonde waves obscuring one eye.

'Oh. Hi.' I tried to sound nonchalant.

'Good weekend?' he asked.

I shrugged. 'It was okay. You?'

'Same.'

'Mr Chambers…' Williams' Welsh accent cut through our conversation.

We both looked up at the teacher.

'Sorry to interrupt your social life,' he continued, 'but will you zip it and SIT down.'

'Twat,' Fin murmured under his breath. I'd become familiar with this well-used English term over the past year, as it had been applied to most of the teaching staff and more than half the kids at school. Sian had explained that it related to a part of the female anatomy.

I stifled a smile.

'Did you say something?' Williams was on his feet, now, eyes narrowed, glaring at Fin.

Fin shook his head.

'Because if you did, then you should know that I am on detention duty this week and I'd be thrilled to have your company, Mr Chambers. Thrilled and delighted.'

'I didn't say anything, Sir,' Fin snapped. Then, under his breath, I heard him utter the word "twat" once more.

I inhaled sharply. This wasn't going to end well. The whole class was totally silent now, all eyes flitting from Fin to Williams, waiting to see how this was going to play out. I realised he was getting into trouble for talking to me, but I didn't know what I could do to help.

'You know,' Williams continued. '*You*, Mr Chambers, you think you're a big shot in this school. You think you're "cool".' He raised his fingers in air quotes. 'But, let me tell you, Boyo, I've seen it all before. I may be a History teacher, but I can also predict the future. And I can tell you exactly how your life will play out. Do you want me to be your fortune teller? Because I have a ninety-nine per cent accuracy rate.'

Fin stayed silent by my side, the anger radiating off him in waves. I willed him not to say or do anything else stupid.

'Here's how it goes.' Williams smiled and cast his eyes around the room, his gaze finally coming back to rest on Fin. 'You, Boy, are a waster, a loser, and you'll never amount to anything. Do you hear me? Everyone, pay attention. If you want your life to end up down the toilet, this, right here' – he pointed to Fin – 'is how you behave. Now *sit* down in your seat and I don't want to hear another word come out of your pathetic mouth.'

Silence hung in the air for the briefest of moments before Fin kicked over a chair and stormed out of the classroom, slamming the door behind him and raising his middle finger at Williams through the glass door panel.

'Right! Everybody, open your Tudor textbooks to page 57,' Williams boomed, his face red, his jaw now tightly clamped. We all did as he asked, heads down, mouths closed. I was surprised Williams hadn't gone after Fin, but I guessed he couldn't leave his class unattended.

The whole lesson passed by in a sickening blur. I couldn't concentrate on anything. Thankfully, Williams didn't single me out to answer any questions. What was going to happen to Fin, now? Would he get detention? Suspension? Expulsion? I hoped not. Had he left school for the day? Would Fin blame me for getting him into trouble? No, surely not. He'd been the one to come over and start talking.

I'd never felt so relieved to hear the bell go for break. I needed to tell Sian what had just happened.

'That must've been horrible.' Sian linked her arm through mine as we walked around the English block – a familiar loop we always did at break time. We weren't cool enough to hang out by the music block, and all the juniors played their childish games on the playground so we wouldn't be caught dead there. Walking around the English block was the only place we didn't get hassled.

'It was awful,' I said. 'But at the same time, I was sort-of happy because he'd come over to talk to me. Do you know what I mean? Only now I don't know where he's gone. Do you think he'll be expelled?'

'No. Don't worry.' Sian squeezed my arm. 'He'll definitely get detention though. Maybe a week's suspension if he's bunked off.'

As we passed by the school fence at the back of the building, a long whistle made us look up. Sian nudged me in the ribs and pointed. Fin stood on the opposite side of the road, partially obscured by a red van.

'Hey, Anna,' he called.

Sian and I came to a stop and my heart began to race.

'Come over here.' He was asking me to leave the school premises. To skive – something I'd never done before.

'Don't go, Anna,' Sian hissed. 'You'll get in trouble.'

Fin smiled a lazy smile that made me catch my breath. He jerked his head, indicating that I should join him.

'Come with me, Sian,' I begged, scared of doing this alone.

'Joking, aren't you.' Sian's eyes widened. 'I'm not getting in trouble just so I can be a gooseberry. Three's a crowd.'

'Okay. Well, I'm going to go.' I glanced left and right, my pulse racing.

'But—'

'I'll be fine. Tell the office I'm not well. That I had to go home.'

'You're mad,' she said, shaking her head. 'Okay. Well. I suppose you need a bunk up over the fence?'

I nodded so she looped her fingers together. 'Will you be okay on your own?' I asked.

'I'll go and find the film nerds,' she replied. 'They won't mind me tagging along.'

I tossed my schoolbag over the fence, stepped into her hands and pulled myself up and over the warm metal fence, my face hot as I landed on the dusty pavement.

'Have fun, you rebel,' Sian teased.

'I'll call you later. Don't forget to tell the office for me.'

She nodded and then disappeared around the side of the building, leaving me feeling suddenly quite alone and wondering what on earth I was getting myself into. But then I turned to see Fin give me a wink and my stomach flipped. For months I'd wanted him to notice me. Well, it looked like now he had. Only this wasn't quite the scenario I'd been imagining.

I snatched up my bag from the ground and ran across the empty road to where Fin stood waiting on the pavement.

What now?

He took my hand in his and led me around the back of the van where we were hidden from view of the school. I chewed the inside of my cheek, hyper-aware of our hands locked together, his other hand sliding around my waist, his face coming level with mine. The minty smell of his breath. Before I could say anything, he kissed me.

It happened so quickly.

I'd never kissed a boy this way before. Not this hungry type of kiss with tongues. A kiss which connected with every part of my body, a deep pull inside. There was no question in my mind about what it would lead to. When you kissed Fin Chambers you were his. Special. Our kiss was a pact. Sealed with the thrust of his tongue and the press of his fingers. He was in control and I had no say in the matter. He was Fin, and I was lucky to have been chosen. I truly believed that. Finally visible. The luckiest girl in the world.

He broke away first, leaving me breathless, my lips raw, my brain spinning. 'I like you, Anna,' he said. 'Let's get out of here.'

I nodded, swept away by the force of him. At that moment, I would have followed him to the ends of the earth.

We walked a few blocks in silence, my hand in his. I couldn't think of anything to say. Nothing witty or smart came to mind. Cars passed by, and the occasional pedestrian. My eyes darted around, thinking any moment we could run into someone we knew – a parent or teacher. But I kept my fears to myself. Eventually, I couldn't bear the silence between us any longer.

'I hope it wasn't my fault you got into trouble today,' I said.

'What? No. Course not.'

'It's just that you were talking to me when Mr Williams—'

'He's such a knob.' Fin stopped walking. He let go of my hand and turned, levering himself up to sit on someone's brick wall. 'I mean, who the fuck does he think he is, anyway? Does he think he's something special? He teaches at Shelborne for fuck's sake – probably the worst school in England. Telling me I won't amount to anything. Yeah, well watch this space, Mr mortgage, two kids and a boring hatchback.'

'He's an idiot,' I said. 'I can't believe he spoke that way to you. They'd never be allowed to talk to students that way in Sweden.'

'They're not supposed to talk like that here, either. I should report him.'

'You should.'

'Thanks.' He dropped his scowl and drew me closer, dipping his head to kiss me again. 'Want to come back to mine?'

I wondered if he expected me to sleep with him. Either way, I knew then I couldn't say no. There was something irresistible about Fin. I was drawn to him like a wave to the shore. I wanted to be as close to him as I could get. Fin made me feel reckless, in a way I'd never felt before.

'Where do you live?' I asked.

'Not far. Just to warn you, our house is a dump, and my dad is worse than Williams.'

Fin must have noted the look of worry spreading across my face.

'Don't worry,' he continued. 'We'll hang out in the shed – it's cool in there, with cushions and stuff, not like a regular shed. I spend most of my time in there. So we won't have to talk to my dad. He'll be getting stoned with his mates, anyway. He won't notice us.'

At this, I bit my lip, determined not to wimp out and ruin my chances with him. 'Hang on,' I said, fishing my phone out of my bag. I called my mum's number. She'd be at work now. It rang three times before she picked up. 'Mamma?'

'Anna. Are you okay?'

'Yeah. I mean, no, not really. I've got a stomach ache. Can you call the school and tell them I've gone home?'

'Oh no. Do you want me to come home, too?'

'No. It's okay. I'm going to try and get some sleep.'

'Have you vomited?'

'No, Mamma. Don't worry. I'm just going to get some sleep. Can you call school?'

'Okay. But call if you need me. I'll try and be home by five thirty.'

I could hear the stress in her voice, but I shrugged off my guilt. I was always well behaved, always doing the right thing. This was a one-off, to be with the boy I'd wanted since the first moment I saw him.

'Thanks, Mamma. See you later.'

'Bye, darling.'

I ended the call and slipped my phone back into my bag.

'You were speaking English,' Fin said. 'I thought you'd speak Swedish with your family.'

'No. When we got to England, my parents said we had to speak English all the time – even at home.'

'So that's why your English is so perfect.'

'Thanks.' I dipped my head and smiled.

An angry banging made me look up to see a woman thumping on her bay window, pointing to Fin sitting on her wall and making a shooing motion with her hand.

He turned to look, blew the woman a kiss, then hopped back down onto the pavement. 'Come on,' he said, taking my hand once more. 'Let's go to mine.'

My throat was dry, my head whirling with everything that was happening between us. I had wished so long for this moment, and now, at last, it seemed my wishes were coming true.

CHAPTER SIX

2017

No matter how late I go to bed, I always wake early. It's annoying. I wish I could lie in, but once I'm awake, I'm awake, and that's that. Will's still in bed, out for the count. The house is silent as I pad down the stairs, my dressing gown loosely tied, my feet bare – the wonders of underfloor heating. I rub at my face; my skin papery, eyes raw. I forgot to take off my make-up last night, only managing to give my teeth a quick brush before sliding under the covers. I don't know why I bothered even trying to sleep. My brain was so wired, I barely snatched twenty minutes. It's a miracle I slept at all.

Everything that was only recently so comforting and familiar about our house seems different this morning. Even the air smells tainted. I have to keep my panic at bay. Have to think of a way out of this. I can't let that text message change my life. I can't. This is all too precious to lose.

In the kitchen, I head straight for the Nespresso machine. I don't trust my stomach with proper food. Not yet. I run the tap and fill the jug with water, slotting it back into its holder and pressing the start button. Normally, we get great sea views from up here in our clifftop arts-and-crafts house, but this morning a sea mist has rolled in, pressing itself up against the bay windows, blanking everything out. The huge room seems somehow smaller, like the walls are closing in.

Will grew up here, and when we married, his dad gave us the house as a wedding present. He said the place never felt the same after Will's mum died. That it needed a family, kids, dogs and all of that. So, he moved out and now the place is ours. We love it, despite the fact that half the garden has crumbled away down the cliff. Will's dad now lives in a brand-new mews house – a bachelor pad, easy walking distance to the bistro. He says he feels much happier there.

The aroma of coffee soothes me for a second or two and I lose myself in the ritual of pouring milk into a tall glass, warming it, frothing it, then pouring the coffee over the top. But my hands are shaking and I'm trying desperately not to cry. I must pull myself together before Will comes down. This was the day I was going to tell him everything. But how can I tell him now, after getting that text? I had thought the danger had long-since passed. But I was wrong. It's all got worse. Much worse.

Part of me wants to check my phone again to see if the message is really there. That it wasn't a figment of my drunken imagination. But the thought of seeing that girl's body again… I shut off that train of thought. Push it out of my head. I'm not looking at my phone this morning.

We're supposed to be meeting Sian and Remy later for brunch followed by a walk on the beach. So that's what we'll do. I'm not going to let a text message ruin everything. *You can't just ignore it*, the voice in my head says.

I take a sip of coffee, pick up the TV remote and press the power button. The mundanity of breakfast television should take my mind off things. I let the local-news presenter's voice wash over me as I make Will a cup of tea. I'll take it up to him in bed. Probably need to grab some paracetamol for him, too. I bet his head's in a delicate state after last night. Beer and champagne don't mix too well.

'Morning,' a voice says behind me.

I give a small scream before spinning around. 'Will! You scared me. I didn't hear you come down. I thought you were still asleep.'

He stands in the doorway dressed in grey jogging bottoms and a red hoody, and gives a small smile. 'Sorry. I know it's early for me, but I needed tea.'

'I was just about to bring you some up to bed.'

'You do know, you're quite possibly the best wife in the world.' He comes over and kisses the side of my head, takes a sip from the mug I hand him, and points at the window. 'Foggy.'

'Yeah, I know.' I give a small shiver. 'It's creepy out there. How're you feeling this morning? Not too hungover?'

'Not bad. Hangover'll probably kick in later. Such a great night. Thank you, Anna.'

'Glad you had a good time.' I reach out, attempting to tease down a stray lock of his hair sticking up at a funny angle.

'And that car.' He brings his hand up to try to help me smooth his hair down before giving up. 'Leave it. I'll take a shower in a minute. I can't believe I own a Mustang. Shall we take it out today?'

'Yeah, why not. Better be careful in the fog, though.' I take another sip of my coffee and lean back against the counter top.

'Didn't think of that.' He frowns. 'We'll have to wait until it clears.'

'Probably a good idea,' I say. 'You don't want to end up crashing it into a lamppost.'

'I was worried about you last night,' Will says, his brow creasing. 'Do you feel any better this morning?'

'So much better. It must have been a weird bug or something.'

'Or maybe a touch of champagne-itis.' He wraps his arms around me and gives me a gentle hug. 'We can take it easy today, if you like. Shall I cancel Sian and Remy?'

Will is still speaking, but suddenly I don't hear him any more. Instead, I turn to the TV where the news presenter is talking about a boat company based in Poole. My blood freezes when I hear the company name, all thoughts dragged from my husband's gentle concern to the fresh horror that's encroaching on my life.

> *The daughter of Martin Spencer, owner of local luxury yacht company, Blue Swift, was killed while holidaying with her husband in Barbados. Eye-witnesses say her death was caused by a reckless speedboat driver. The investigation by Barbadian and British police to find and bring the culprit to justice continues.*

'Anna? What do you think? Should I cancel today?'

'Hm?' I ease myself out of his arms and turn to stare at the screen on the wall, at the image of a massive yacht moored at Poole Quay. Then at the image of the victim. *It's her.* But in this photo, she's smiling at the lens, not lying dead with half her face missing. The reporter is still talking, but my mind can't latch onto the words, and now they're onto a new story about how it's set to be the coldest January on record.

Will is talking to me. Asking a question. I need to focus. Breathe. Calm down. But the words from the text: *Your turn next* keep replaying over and over in my head, sending shards of ice down my spine.

'Anna?' His voice breaks through again.

'Sorry. Sorry, Will. I got distracted by the TV.'

'Yeah, it's going to be the coldest January on record. They always say the same thing every year, and it never is. I just wondered if you wanted to cancel our brunch today. To be honest, you do look a bit pale.'

My legs are jelly. I walk over to the navy, velvet sofa and sit, perched on the edge, gazing at the fog, its tendrils swirling, silently tapping at the window. Normally, I'd love this weather – the spookiness of it would thrill my Scandi heart. But not today. Today it unnerves me even more. An omen of ill-tidings.

'No. No, don't cancel,' I reply, even though I honestly don't feel like going. How will I manage to act normally? But what's the alternative? To stay at home chewing my fingers wondering what to do? To reply to the text? To ditch my phone and run away?

'You sure?' Will comes over to the sofa to join me. 'You really don't look so good.' He sets his tea down on the coffee table and puts a hand to my forehead. 'Clammy. I'm going to cancel.'

'No,' I snap. 'Please stop worrying.'

He raises his hands in surrender. 'Okay. I just—'

'Sorry, Will. Sorry.' My shoulders slump and I put a hand on his arm. 'You're just being sweet and lovely, and I'm being a grumpy cow.' I force a smile onto my face and lean into him. 'I really want to go.'

'If you're sure.'

I nod. I have to pull myself together. I just need to put all this out of my head for a few hours. Be the new, better version of myself. The person I am when I'm with Will. I can't give in to the fear. The news report only told me what I already knew from the text, so why is my heart hammering and my vision blurring? I take a breath, hold it, and slowly exhale. I have to keep calm. This is all fixable. Of course it is. The alternative is unthinkable.

Had I really believed I could move on with my life and forget about the past? Back then, my mind was a jumble, a dark mess. Until last night, I'd pushed that period of my life aside. Hoping it would all simply go away. But it hadn't. And now the background hum of fear has amplified. Has become a roaring monster that's here to collect its dues.

But I don't want to pay. And I don't think I have enough strength to face it.

CHAPTER SEVEN

August 2010

The butterflies in my stomach weren't just to do with the fact I was collecting my A-level results today. The nerves were kicking in hard because if I got good grades, it meant I would be going back to Sweden. It meant I would be assured a place at Stockholm's School of Sport and Health Science. It also meant I would have to leave Fin.

Fin now worked part-time in a local surf shop, which he loved. So far, we'd had the perfect summer together. Lazy days on the beach, partying with his new friends, staying up until dawn. We were in love. Had been inseparable since we'd first got together three years ago. I still hadn't told him I was leaving, but I couldn't put it off for much longer.

'Are you sure you don't want us to take you in to school?' Mum asked as I nibbled on a piece of toast.

'I'm walking in with Sian.' I dropped the toast back onto my plate, too antsy to eat.

'Okay. Well come straight home after, won't you. Don't keep us in suspense.'

'Don't worry,' Dad added. 'I'm sure you'll do well enough to get into college.'

The sports course had been my parents' idea. Their work in the UK had come to an end, so they were moving home to Sweden next month, and they'd automatically assumed that I would be going with them. My older brothers, Theo and Elias, had already moved back a year ago, which meant I would have no place to stay in England.

The doorbell rang. I scraped my chair back, stood up and wiped toast crumbs from my t-shirt. 'That'll be Sian.'

'Good luck,' my parents said, standing to give me kisses and hugs. I finally managed to shrug them off, grabbed my bag and made my escape.

'Hey,' Sian said as I pulled the front door closed behind me.

'I'm not looking forward to this,' I said.

'You'll be fine. You always do well in exams.'

'That's what I'm afraid of,' I replied.

She gave me a puzzled look, but I just shook my head and smiled.

The roads were quiet, the pavements empty, the mid-morning sun already hot on our arms and faces. But, despite the blue sky and the mounting heat, I had a creeping sense that summer was already over.

'I don't know what I'm going to do without you, Anna.' Sian stuck her bottom lip out and blinked. She'd already been given an unconditional place to study Beauty Therapy in Bournemouth, so today's grades didn't really matter too much to her. Whatever her results, it wouldn't change her plans.

'Promise you'll come and visit me,' I said as we sauntered across an empty road.

'I'll try. It won't be the same without you here. I won't have you. Or Marco. I'll be a nobby-no-mates.' Marco had been Sian's boyfriend for the last two years, but they'd split up when he'd gone travelling.

'Do you miss him?' I asked.

'A bit, I suppose.' She hadn't seemed too upset when it happened, but you couldn't always tell with Sian – she didn't open up about her feelings easily.

'You'll make loads of friends on your new course,' I told her.

'Yeah, just like the "loads of friends" I made at school.' She rolled her eyes.

'School's different,' I said. 'On your course, you'll meet people who are into the same stuff as you. It'll be way better.'

'I hope so.'

As we neared school, we spotted other students heading in the same direction, some chattering non-stop, others silent and drawn. I felt like I was heading to the executioner's block. If I failed my exams, my options would be zero, but if I passed, I'd still end up doing something I didn't want to do. How could I stop this?

'Anna? Anna!' Sian's voice startled me as I stood in the middle of the pavement lost in thought. 'You okay?'

'I don't want to go back to Sweden,' I said.

'Do you have to go?'

'What else can I do? It's not that I don't like it over there – I do – but I don't want to leave you or Fin, or the beach… I love my life here.'

'Come on,' she said, pulling at my arm. 'Let's get this over with, then we can talk about it after.'

We followed a set of printed signs which led us into the sports hall where a queue had already formed. It was strange to be at school, knowing this would be the last time I'd ever be here again. The once impossibly tall climbing wall at the far end already looked smaller, more childish. The familiar smell of bleach and old socks took on an alien, nostalgic quality.

Sian and I stood together waiting our turn, the stale air chilly, making goose bumps prickle my arms.

Fifteen minutes later, I finally had the white envelope in my hands, my name printed on a sticky label on the front. The answer to my future. Most of my other classmates were tearing theirs open before they'd even left the hall, celebrating and laughing, or being comforted by friends. Sian and I were quieter, our heads bowed. We left the sports hall, nodding at a few familiar faces on our way out.

'Shall we open them now?' Sian asked.

I nodded, my heart racing.

'Let's go in here.' She jerked her head towards an empty class-room and we snuck in, balancing our backsides on the teacher's empty desk, our legs swinging.

'You first,' I said.

'Okay,' she replied. 'I don't know why I'm so nervous, it doesn't even matter what I get.'

I gave her arm a comforting squeeze as she opened the envelope and pulled out the folded sheet of paper. She opened it out and cleared her throat: 'C in English, B in Art and B in Design Tech,' she read out her results in a soft voice. I couldn't tell if she was pleased or not.

'Well done!'

'Thanks,' she said. 'I guess two Bs and a C is okay, isn't it?'

'You got three really good A-levels,' I said. 'I think you've done brilliantly. Loads of people would kill to get those results.'

She flushed. 'Thanks, Anna. Okay. Your turn.'

I slotted my finger into the gap at the top of the envelope and tore along the crease. Now the moment had arrived, I felt strangely calm and unconcerned. I looked at my results without reading them aloud:

A* for Maths, A* for Biology, A* for Sport and A for Physics.

I had exceeded my own expectations, but I didn't want to rub Sian's nose in it.

'Well?' she asked.

'I did okay.'

'Let's see.' She took the sheet of paper from my hand and read out my results. 'Wow, Anna. You aced them. Three A stars and an A. You could probably get into somewhere like Oxford or Cambridge with those results. But you'd probably have to wait till next year.'

'Shall we go?' I said, sliding down off the desk.

'Aren't you going to say anything?' Sian raised an eyebrow. 'You must be pleased, right?'

'I suppose so. It feels a bit weird, to be honest.'

'Your parents are going to be over the moon.'

'And yours.'

'Yeah, well, they'll be happy I guess.' She curled her lip.

'Come on,' I said, taking my results sheet back as she got to her feet.

'We should celebrate,' Sian said with a grin. 'Do something crazy.'

I couldn't tell her that all I wanted to do was climb into my bed, curl up and go to sleep. I didn't want to think about a new college and a new country. I envied Sian, staying here.

We left the classroom and stepped out of the school building into a completely different day. Black clouds had gathered in our absence and I felt a dusty raindrop on my cheek, sensed the static electricity of lightning in the air just before it forked across the sky. A deep rumble followed.

'It's going to pour,' Sian said. 'Let's go back to mine.'

I shoved my results into my bag and we ran along the pavement arm-in-arm as plump raindrops splattered us, and puddles formed at our feet. Pretty soon, the drops became sheets which soaked us right through to our skin. As our feet skimmed the ground and droplets of water flew around us, I came to a sudden decision – one which made my shoulders lighten and my mind clear. A laugh bubbled up from my chest to my throat, escaping into the sodden atmosphere. Sian caught my altered mood and turned to me, an eyebrow raised.

I slowed to a walk and Sian fell into step with me. 'What's funny?' she asked.

'I'm not going!' I yelled above the drumming rain.

'What? Not going where?'

'To Sweden. I've decided – I'm going to stay here.'

'Really?'

I nodded, grinning so widely my cheeks hurt. I realised that the results in that envelope shouldn't determine my happiness – I was in charge of my own future. I didn't know where I would stay or exactly how I would manage it, but I'd figure something out. Within seconds we were both laughing hysterically and jumping up and down together. I knew without a doubt that I was making the right decision.

Now… I just had to tell my parents.

'What do you mean, you're not coming with us?' My mum's smile froze on her face before melting into disappointment, then progressing to something approaching anger.

'I'm sorry,' I said, facing them over the kitchen table as the rain lashed down outside. It was early afternoon and I'd just got back from Sian's. I hadn't wanted to keep my parents waiting, but I'd been too nervous to come home straightaway. I'd known I was in for an almighty row. After their initial jubilation at my outstanding grades, this was a slap in the face for them.

'You're sorry?' Dad said, running his hand over his almost-bald head.

'Is this because of Fin?' Mum asked. 'Because it's not fair of him to put pressure on you like that.'

'Fin doesn't even know,' I said, pushing the tips of my fingers against the white melamine table and taking a deep breath.

'Okay,' Dad said. 'So if you're serious about staying here, we need to sort you out a university place, quickly.'

'She's not staying here,' Mum cried.

Dad shushed her. 'They'll all be falling over themselves to accept you with your grades.'

'I'm not going to uni, Pappa. Anyway, all the places will have been allocated for the year.'

'What do you mean you're not going to uni?' My dad never got angry but, in that moment, I could tell he was trying hard not to lose it, his jaw tensing, his face turning a deep shade of red.

Mum, on the other hand, was freaking out big time, wagging her finger at me and yelling. 'You are coming with us, Anna, and that's that. I'm not leaving you here on your own.'

'I'm sorry, but I'm staying,' I snapped. 'I'm eighteen. An adult.' Desperate to stay calm, I took a breath and clenched my fists. I didn't want to argue. They were in shock, that was all.

'Anna,' Dad said. 'You have four As, you can't throw away this opportunity. Let your mother and me help you get a university place in England, if you won't come with us. You can see Fin at the weekends and come home in the holidays.'

But my plans didn't involve universities and weekend visits. They involved me and Fin being together, every day. Even as it was, I could barely go a few hours without seeing him. It was a physical ache when we were apart. So the thought of being separated by hundreds of miles, unable to see him for weeks at a time was not something I could contemplate.

'And where do you plan to live?' Mum asked. 'You have no money. No job.'

'I can get a job. And I'm sure I'll be able to stay with Fin.'

'Does his father know?' My mum got to her feet and started pacing around the table. 'That man is a drug addict and he has all kinds of people at his house. I've told you before! You can't stay there. It's not safe.'

'It'll be fine. They have a garden shed that's weather proof. It's almost like a little Swedish cabin. We can make it homely.'

'You're giving up a place at a prestigious school, to live in a shed with a shop assistant?' My mum threw up her hands in anger. 'Anna Karlsson, you may have got outstanding A-level results, but you have no brains! No brains at all!'

'Britt, calm down.' My father placed a hand on her shoulder. 'We all need to calm down and talk this through rationally.'

'She's throwing away her future for a boy.' She turned to me, reached for my hands across the table. 'Don't you understand, you can do anything. Be anyone.'

'Mamma, I'm already exactly who I want to be.'

She let go of my hands and banged both fists on the table. Then she stood and left the room. I heard her march upstairs. Heard her bedroom door close with a loud click.

'Give her time,' Dad said. 'She's disappointed.'

Thankfully he didn't say he was, too. But he didn't have to – I could see it in his eyes.

They both blamed Fin, thinking he had persuaded me to stay. He hadn't. It was my choice. But part of me knew that if I'd told Fin about returning to Sweden, he wouldn't have wanted me to go. He would have tried to keep me here. Maybe that was why I'd delayed telling him. I'd had to make the decision for myself. And I didn't want us to have any reason to fight. I couldn't risk losing him.

*

Knowing what I'd given up to be able to stay in the UK with Fin, I was determined to do everything in my power to make this work. First on the list, was finding a place for us to live. Granted, it wasn't the most beautiful studio flat in the world, nor was it in the nicest location. But it was the only place in our price range that didn't smell of cat pee or have mould growing up the walls.

'What do you think?' Fin asked as we stood on Florence Road outside a former Victorian hotel that had recently been converted into flats. The developer had squeezed as many units as he could into the building, without too much thought for its potential residents. But the smell of fresh paint had seduced us. As we'd looked around the tiny bedsitting lounge/kitchen with its separate shower room, I'd squeezed Fin's hand, knowing this flat was definitely the one, picturing us ensconced within its walls.

'Yeah,' I said with a skip of excitement. 'I think we should go for it.'

'Me too. Shall we tell him?'

I nodded. Fin kissed me, his fingers creeping up my bare thigh beneath my dress. I laughed and pushed his hand away. 'Not here,' I whispered.

The agent was yammering away on the phone, but as soon as he'd finished talking, we'd tell him we wanted to sign the six-month lease.

After trying everything they could think of to change my mind – bribery, reverse psychology, threats – my parents had finally accepted that I wasn't going back to Sweden with them, and neither was I going to university. At least they were going to help us out with the deposit and two months' rent up front.

It would be a struggle to afford the rent and bills, but Fin had managed to get a full-time contract working at the surf shop, and I had just passed my life-guarding course and been offered a job at a local leisure centre, starting the following week.

As Fin and I stood waiting for the estate agent to finish his call, I took a breath, excited about all that lay ahead. It felt as though we were embarking on an adventure. Just the two of us.

CHAPTER EIGHT

2017

Bundled up against the cold, I'm sure we must be the only people mad enough to be out walking when we can't even see two feet in front of our faces. The mist hangs thick and damp, seeping into our clothing and clinging to our hair.

Sian and I trail behind Will and Remy, our arms linked. They've been swallowed up in the fog. We can't see them any more, can just hear odd snatches of laughter, snippets of words rolling back towards us. Our feet crunch over shells and honey sand, its soft granules like demerara sugar.

'I ate too much,' Sian says, groaning. 'I thought fried breakfasts were supposed to be good for hangovers.'

'Poor you,' I reply. 'The walk will help.' I was barely able to eat two mouthfuls this morning. Worry always takes away my appetite. Give me contentment and I can eat for England.

'You were quiet in the café,' Sian says. 'You okay?'

Should I tell her about the text?

'Anna?' she prompts.

'Yeah, I'm fine. Just a bit tired, you know?'

She looks sideways at me, slowing her pace. But I keep walking, pulling her along, thinking of how I can change the subject.

'Did you have an argument with Will?' she says. 'I noticed you hardly said two words to each other earlier.'

'No, course not. You know Will and I don't argue.' I give a small laugh.

'Well, you can always talk to me if there's anything—'

'Thanks, honestly, I'm fine. There's nothing wrong between me and Will.'

'Really?'

'Yes. Really. Now how about you? Excited about the wedding? Settled on a date yet?'

Sian gives me a suspicious look that lets me know she's aware of my sneaky subject change. But she answers me anyway. 'No, not yet. We're trying to find a venue, but Remy's so busy he never has time to come and visit the places on my shortlist. I'm worried everything'll get booked up.'

'Do you want *me* to come with you?' I ask, thinking it could be a good distraction. 'We could narrow it down further, then all he has to do is visit one or two places.'

'Would you?'

'I'd love to.'

She starts squealing and jumping up and down. Normally, I would laugh and jump around with her. But today my feet are made of lead and my voice is weak. I manage a smile and a hug.

'What's going on?' Remy and Will have slowed their pace to see why we're making so much noise, bemused smiles on their faces.

Sian explains and Remy grins.

'So I'm off the hook. Thanks, Anna.'

Sian gives him a playful shove. 'What do you mean "off the hook"? You're the one who asked *me* to marry *you*, remember?'

'Joking!' He raises his hands in surrender.

My phone pings and my equilibrium evaporates.

'Was that yours?' Sian asks.

'I'll check it later.' My bag suddenly feels heavier on my shoulder, like there's a bomb inside it.

'Don't know about you guys, but I'm freezing,' Will says. 'Shall we go? Come back to ours if you want?'

'Thanks, but I need a kip,' Remy replies. 'Last night's catching up with me.'

'Getting old, mate,' Will teases.

'Excuse me, I'm still in my twenties. You're the old fart around here.'

'Hilarious.' Will rolls his eyes. 'Not for much longer, though. Your thirtieth is coming up, too, Rem. No getting away from it.'

'This,' Remy points at himself, 'never gets old.'

Sian and Will groan as Remy does a little dance.

I wish I could join in with their easy banter, but it's as though there's a vice around my chest and a hand around my throat, choking off speech. Last night's text buzzes around my brain like a living thing, a wasp in a jar. As the winter mist thins, and we say our goodbyes, my head is elsewhere, running through all the *what ifs*, the limited options I'm faced with. Maybe Will and I could get away for a while, buy some time. Or maybe I should pluck up the courage to reply to the text. Will throws an arm around my shoulder and we start back along the beach towards home.

'You were quiet today.'

I've already had Sian interrogating me, now it looks as though it's Will's turn. I know they're only concerned, but I can't deal with it today. I restrain myself from snapping. It's not his fault. 'I'm fine,' I say. 'Just a bit tired.'

Thankfully, he accepts my answer, kissing the top of my head. We walk in companionable silence, lost in our own thoughts.

Back home, I can bear it no longer. As Will stretches out on the lounge sofa with the Sunday papers, I make my way upstairs to the bathroom, my bag still over my shoulder. I need to look at last night's text, and I also need to see if that ping I heard on the beach means I've received another one.

'Going for a bath!' I call down the stairs.

'Okay!'

I head into our bedroom, through the dressing room, into the en suite, locking the door behind me. With trembling hands, I lean over the claw-foot bathtub, twist the dial to close the plug hole and turn on the taps, adding a splash of my favourite Prada bubble bath. I don't feel like taking a bath, but I need privacy. I need time to myself. To think. To process. Once the water is running, I drop down onto the grey tiled floor and lean against the outside of the tub. Next, I plunge my hand into my bag and draw out my phone. It feels strangely hot, as though it could burn my skin. But I know that's ridiculous.

The message icon shows three new text messages. Two are from friends thanking me for last night's party. And one is from an unknown number. The same unknown number as yesterday. A pulse beats in my ears, echoing in my fingertips.

I open the message.

I read it:

Did you get yesterday's text? I need you to reply.

Sweat prickles on my back, my neck, my palms. I can't reply. What would I say? *Think. Think.* The air in the bathroom thickens with steam, its perfumed scent catching in the back of my throat.

I still can't believe a woman has died. It's horrific.

Part of me wants to reread the first message, but that would mean seeing the image again. And I'm just not up to it.

He's not going to let me walk away. He's not going to leave me alone. Did he really do it, or was it an accident? A coincidence? What can I do? There's no one I can talk to. Not Will, not Sian. It's not safe. My parents? No, they've already done so much for me – I can't worry them any more. Maybe… I have an idea. A long shot but it's worth a try, surely. And it could kill two birds with one stone.

I need to get out of this room. The heat is too much. I jump to my feet and turn off the bath taps, unlock the door, open it, and take a few deep, steadying breaths before heading back downstairs.

'That was a quick bath,' Will says as I walk into the lounge.

'I changed my mind. I'll have one later.'

He reaches out his hand to guide me onto the sofa next to him.

'Do you want anything?' I ask. 'A drink? Lunch?'

'No thanks. This morning's brunch will probably last me till Tuesday.'

I give a small, fake laugh, wondering how best to broach the subject that's on my mind.

'Will?'

'Mm?' He sets the newspaper down on the wooden coffee table.

'What would you think about us visiting Sweden for a bit?' I turn to face him, trying to look as though I'm excited at the thought.

'Sweden?' He frowns. 'But you're always putting me off the place, telling me I'd be bored stiff.'

'I know, but I've changed my mind. I thought it could be fun if I showed you around.' Will never usually joins me when I go back to visit my parents, but I think the time has come for him to really get to know my family. I think it's the only place we'll be safe.

'Sure,' he says. 'If you want to. I'd like that. We could book something for the summer.'

'I was thinking a lot sooner than then.'

'We're already going away over Easter with Sian and Remy – you remember – we're taking the Sunseeker over to The Channel Islands.'

'Yes, yeah, sure, I know. I was thinking, though, why don't we be spontaneous and see if there are any flights next week. Tomorrow, even? It would be fun to do something spur of the moment, don't you think?'

'Tomorrow?' Will sits up straight and looks me in the eye.

I give a closed-mouth smile and tilt my head. 'Yeah, why not.'

'Umm, the bistro? I need to be there next week. Dad can't cope with double shifts any more, and Malcolm's away.'

Shit. He's not going to go for it. 'Don't you think the bistro is getting to be a bit of a bind?' I say. 'I mean, it's not like you need the income.' As soon as I say the words, I wish I could unsay them.

Will's eyes darken and his face closes off.

I don't blame him for being angry. Blackwell's is about more than money. In fact, it's not about money at all.

Back in the eighties, Steve and his late wife, Helen, built up a successful bakery business which they subsequently sold for millions to a multinational company, meaning Will and his dad are mega-wealthy. So, the bistro has always been more of a passion, a hobby, than a business. It was Will's brainchild – something to keep his dad busy, stop him missing his wife so much. And it was a great idea. They both love it, and normally so do I.

'Sorry.' I put a hand on his arm. 'I didn't mean that.'

Will shakes his head.

I can tell I've made a hash of things. I try again. 'All I meant was, it's a shame that we can't just take off when we feel like it.'

'*You* can go if you like, Anna,' Will says, rising to his feet. 'I mean, there's nothing stopping you.'

'Don't be like that.' I stand next to him, desperate to make amends. Will is the most easy-going, lovely man until you say anything negative about his family. And Blackwell's counts as a member of the family. It's almost like it's his surrogate mother. 'It was just a daft idea that came out wrong,' I say. 'I don't know what's wrong with me today. Sorry.'

Will's jaw clenches and I brace myself for a full-blown argument. But, just like that, the fight goes out of him and his shoulders slump. 'It's okay.' He sighs. 'You just caught me off guard, that's all. I've got responsibilities. I can't just take off, much as I'd like to. But there's nothing to stop us planning a trip soon. Maybe even next month?'

'Yeah? That would be really good,' I say, sitting back down and running a hand through my hair.

But I know by next month it will all be too late.

CHAPTER NINE

February 2012

'How was your day?' I asked with forced brightness, dreading the answer.

'Pretty much the same as yesterday, and the day before that,' Fin replied, shrugging his coat off and draping it over the arm of the sofa. It slithered off onto the ratty, brown carpet, but instead of picking it up, he just flopped onto the sofa with a sigh. 'I'm sick of working Saturdays.'

'Want a cuppa?' I asked.

'Like that's going to fix my life.'

'I…' There was nothing I could say or do when Fin was in this kind of mood. But if I didn't say anything, he'd accuse me of not being supportive. 'I'm sorry you had a crap day.' I stood by the tiny kitchen table, pushing my fingertips against its scarred wooden surface.

'Yeah, well, it's not like it's a surprise that I had a crap day. Working in a shop for minimum wage isn't exactly how I imagined my life panning out.'

'Maybe we could change things.'

'How exactly?' His lip curled into a sneer.

I took a breath. 'What about going to college? You could study something you enjoy.'

'Fuck that shit. I hated school – no reason why college would be any different.'

'But you'd be doing something you liked.'

'Like what?'

'I don't know. Maybe we could have a look online and see what—'

He rolled his eyes. 'Look, Anna, I know you're trying to be helpful, but I'm knackered and I really don't want to talk about this right now.'

'Sorry. I just thought—'

'I mean, if you really wanted to help, maybe you could pick up some more shifts at the leisure centre.'

I currently worked part time as a lifeguard and studied part-time at the local college. The idea being that if I got better qualified, I'd be able to apply for a management job which would (hopefully) pay more. But I knew Fin resented my time at college. He hated the fact I was mixing with other people he didn't know, and he also hated the fact I now brought home even less money than before. I'd tried to explain that it was only temporary, that it would be a couple of years of struggling for something better at the end of it, but he didn't want to hear it.

'If I pick up more shifts, I won't have enough time for my college work,' I said. I was already studying until past midnight most nights. And I didn't mention the fact that he'd gone and spent our council-tax money on a new surfboard, trading in his old one for a pittance.

Fin didn't reply.

'Maybe I could squeeze in a couple more shifts,' I said, regretting the words as soon as they left my mouth, and wondering where I was going to make up the time. 'I know they need more people to work on Sundays.'

'Cool. That would be good,' Fin said, his face softening. 'Maybe I will have that cup of tea.'

As I turned to fill the kettle, an idea came to me. It was probably stupid as I didn't have much free time in the first place, but if I was going to be working more hours from now on, I thought one last day of fun couldn't hurt. 'I was thinking... how about we do something different tomorrow? A change of scenery. All we seem to do these days is work, eat and sleep. So maybe we could go to the New Forest. It'd be lovely. We can walk and get some fresh air.' I picked up a couple of mugs from the draining board and began drying them with a damp tea towel.

'Hmm,' Fin replied. 'Thing is, there's surf tomorrow morning.'

I could tell he was about to dismiss my idea, so I tried my best to sell it. 'We could go after you've been surfing. I used to go there with my family all the time when they lived here. There are wild ponies and deer. It's so beautiful. And it won't cost us anything – apart from a bit of petrol money.'

After a couple of seconds, he surprised me by agreeing. 'Yeah, okay, why not. Sod it. We deserve to have some fun. Come here.'

I set the mugs down, walked over to the sofa and sank onto his lap.

'I'm so glad we've got each other,' he said. 'It makes up for all the other crap we have to deal with. You know, I'm going to punch the next smug bloke who comes into the shop with his perfect family and platinum Visa card.'

I leant in to kiss him, winding my arms around his neck. 'It's not so bad,' I said. 'I bet those smug blokes have problems, too.'

'Yeah, probably tough decisions like whether their next car should be an Audi or a BMW, or whether to go snowboarding in Aspen or Courchevel. Bastards.'

I shook my head, letting him get it all out of his system.

'I promise you, Anna, this shit isn't going to last. I'll get us out of this dump soon. We'll get married and have beautiful kids and live in a fuck-off big house, okay?'

I laughed.

'I'm not joking.'

'I know.'

*

It was the perfect day for a trip to the forest. Diamond bright, crisp and fresh. After Fin's early-morning surf, he thawed out with a hot shower, and we bundled up in thick jumpers, coats, hats and gloves in preparation for a long walk. Our ancient Vauxhall Corsa rattled along empty stretches of road bordered by tracts of forest and open swathes of heathland as we chatted about silly things and sang along to cheesy songs on the radio. I'd almost forgotten what it felt like to have fun. The past few months had been swallowed up in a blur of work and household chores.

Fin drove, and the road signs were clear, so there were no arguments over which route to take. We'd already decided on the area we'd visit – an out-of-the-way section of forest with a choice of several trails to follow.

Finally, we pulled into a shady car park which already had around a dozen cars parked up.

'Is that a ticket machine?' Fin asked, his shoulders drooping.

'Oh. Yeah. Looks like it.' I hadn't factored in the price of car parking.

'I've only got a five-pound note,' Fin replied, feeling around in his coat pockets.

'I've got change,' I replied. 'Shall I put five hours on?'

'Yeah, okay.'

'Hang on. I'll check how much it is.' I opened the car door and crunched across gravel and mud to the machine, scanning the board for prices. I winced when I saw the cost and turned back to the car. Fin had got out and was leaning against the driver's side.

'It's £4.80,' I called over, a tug of disappointment in my belly. 'Do you want to go somewhere else?'

'It's already half eleven. How much is it for four hours?'

'£3.90,' I called, having checked the board. Still a lot of money, but we'd come all this way…

'Yeah, let's do it. Four hours should be enough, anyway.'

'Okay.' I turned to slot my coins in and waited for the machine to spit out a ticket. Every pound coin we had was precious, but I hoped a day in the fresh air surrounded by nature would lift our spirits. Sometimes there was more to life than money.

Despite the sunshine, the icy air took our breath and stung our faces. But we walked briskly and soon our bodies warmed up. Finally, we were deep into the forest, away from the roads and the houses, away from work, people and problems. I had been so right to suggest this. I felt more relaxed than I had in months. The sun threw shafts of light through the branches, while patches of frost glimmered in the shade.

A crackle of branches made me turn my head. 'Look, Fin.' I pointed up ahead to our left. Through the trees came a couple of brown forest ponies. We stopped to watch them. They didn't seem fazed by our presence, but simply walked on by, a few feet from where we stood. Seconds later, half a dozen more appeared through the trees following the same route as the previous two.

Fin took a few steps back.

'They won't hurt you,' I said.

'How do *you* know?'

'I've seen them before. They're not interested in us.'

I didn't think Fin believed me and he was happier once they'd disappeared into the forest behind us.

As well as wild ponies, we came across a herd of cattle with shaggy red coats. This time we made sure to stand well back, mindful of the damage they could do with their long horns. We took arty photos on our phones of twisted tree trunks and frosted spider webs. Fin insisted on taking photos of me, but wouldn't let me photograph him in return, so I had to take stealthy pictures while his attention was elsewhere. We laughed and kissed and it was as though we were in this perfect bubble of happiness. Neither of us spoke about everyday things, just content to be in the moment.

'I'm getting hungry,' Fin finally said, yawning. 'Shall we eat?'

I nodded, my stomach grumbling in agreement. We'd brought homemade cheese-salad sandwiches and a flask of tea which Fin carried in a small backpack.

'Let's sit over there.' Fin pointed to a fallen tree in a clearing away from the track, its muddy roots exposed. He led me by the hand and we perched halfway along the trunk. He passed me my sandwich and we sat in silence, enjoying the tranquillity of our surroundings. The air was still with just the odd bird call and occasional rustling from a creature in the undergrowth. 'I could eat that again,' Fin said, popping the last piece of food into his mouth.'

'Here, have the rest of mine.' I passed him the other half of my sandwich.

'You sure?'

'Mm, I've had enough.' Truth was, I could have eaten it, but I'd rather give it to Fin if he was still hungry.

'Thanks. What's the time, anyway?'

I took my phone out of my pocket. 'Wow, it's two o'clock already. We should head back.'

'Let's have some tea first. Warm us up a bit.'

I watched him as he finished off my sandwich, his square jaw moving, dirty-blond hair falling over one eye. I wanted to kiss him again, but felt weirdly shy for some reason. He was the one who usually initiated everything.

Ten minutes later, we packed our lunch things away and I took a couple of steps towards the path, turning to see what was keeping Fin.

'You're going the wrong way,' he said, standing by the fallen tree.

'No, the car park's this way,' I replied. I wasn't in any doubt. I knew because I could see the wood ant nest we passed earlier. It had been built next to a tree stump. And Dad always told us that they build their nests with the shallower slope at the front, facing south. I knew how to navigate my way around a forest – spotting ditches, trees and other markings. As kids, we fished, hunted and did all the other outdoor things that were second nature to our family. 'We'll have to walk fast,' I said. 'Our ticket runs out in less than an hour.'

'Anna, it's this way.' His eyebrows knotted and he shook his head as though I were a child who'd done something wrong.

'There's an ants' nest,' I tried to explain. 'I remember it from before.'

'Yeah, the forest is full of them,' Fin replied. 'Come on, let's go.'

I bit my lip. Fin was stubborn. I knew he wouldn't concede. I'd just have to go along with him and try to get us back on track further along the way. We walked along the trail for about twenty minutes, heading in completely the wrong direction. In my head, I tried out numerous ways to tell him this, but they all sounded like the beginnings of an argument and I didn't want to ruin our perfect day. I knew, though, that if we kept going along this track, we would end up further and further from the car park. I wished one of us had a phone signal.

'You okay?' Fin asked, taking my hand.

'Yep.'

'Cos you seem a bit tense.'

'No, just sad today's almost over. It's been good getting away from work and stuff.'

'Telling me.' He pulled me towards him and we stopped walking for a moment to kiss. When he held me like this, it was as though we were the only two people in the world. Even though we'd been together for almost five years, I still felt like the luckiest girl in the world. 'Shall we stop at a country pub on the way home?' he said. 'Make the day last a bit longer?'

There's nothing I'd have liked more, but I knew we shouldn't. 'We can't really afford it,' I replied. 'How about, we buy a couple of beers to drink at home instead?'

'It's not the same, but yeah, okay, Miss Sensible.' He rolled his eyes, smiling to show he wasn't too upset.

After another fifteen minutes of trudging along the same track, the route veered off in three different directions. I knew we should take either the left or right branch in order to try and get ourselves heading the right way, but of course, Fin took the route which lay straight ahead.

'I have the feeling we might be going the wrong way,' I said.

Fin laughed. 'Your sense of direction is crap, Anna. We'll be at the car park in about half an hour and I promise I won't say I told you so.'

I took a deep breath and let him lead me further into the forest, wishing I could stand my ground, but not desperate enough to provoke an argument.

As the sun sank lower, the cold burrowed its way beneath our clothes, and no amount of brisk walking could warm our hands and feet. The car-park ticket had expired over an hour ago, and our easy chatter had stopped. It would be dark soon.

'Fin…'

He cut me off. 'I think we took a wrong turn at that last fork in the path,' he said. 'Let's turn around. I think I can get us on the right track.'

I heaved a sigh of relief as we finally turned on our heels, heading in the right direction. Without saying anything, Fin let me guide us back to the car park. After a while, dusk faded into darkness with only a quarter moon to light the path. We passed the fallen tree where we'd eaten our lunch – this was the place where it had all gone wrong. I spotted the original path we'd taken from the car park, recognising the wood ant nest, remembering other fallen trees, holly bushes and drainage ditches.

It took us a further hour and a half to reach the car park, our hands numb, our feet ice blocks, our good moods ruined. By that time, it was almost six o'clock and there was only one other vehicle in the car park – a van, its headlights illuminating our car.

'What the hell?' Fin let go of my hand and strode over to our Corsa.

Someone in a high-vis jacket was leaning over the windscreen. Were they trying to break in? I followed Fin, fear replacing tiredness.

'Hey!' Fin called out. 'What are you doing to our car?'

The guy straightened up and pointed to the windscreen.

'You've got to be joking!' Fin removed something from beneath one of our frozen windscreen wipers and started waving it around. It was a plastic packet of some kind.

My shoulders slumped as I realised the man must be a traffic warden. He'd given us a parking ticket. Maybe it wasn't too late, maybe I could appeal to his softer side.

'I'm so sorry,' I said. 'We got lost in the forest. That's why we're late.'

'You should always stick to the trails,' the man said, his voice deep with a rich country accent.

'Come on, man,' Fin said, tilting his head, his voice softening. 'Cut us some slack. We can't afford to get a ticket.'

'Too late,' the man replied with an indifferent shrug. 'It's in the system now, nothing I can do. You can write and appeal if you like.'

'Can't you just take it out of the system?' Fin asked, his arm outstretched, trying to give the man back the small yellow plastic packet on which was written: PENALTY CHARGE NOTICE ENCLOSED.

'No can do.'

'Fuck's sake, man.' Fin squared up to him. He tried to stuff the ticket into the front of the man's coat.

'Fin!' I stepped in and put a hand on his arm. 'Leave it. We'll write to the council. Tell them what happened.'

'Get back, Anna. This is between me and this twat here.' Fin pushed at the man's chest. The guy was shorter than Fin, but older and stockier. If this escalated into a fight, I didn't think Fin would win.

'See that.' The man pointed to a post above the ticket machine. Fin and I turned our heads.

'CCTV camera,' the man said. 'You lay a hand on me one more time and I'll get the cops to rewind the footage. I've taken punters to court before. I can do it again.'

Luckily, Fin backed off. 'Wanker,' he said, walking away. 'Come on, Anna.' He opened the car door, slid into the driver's seat and slammed the door.

'What a bastard,' Fin muttered as I got into the car. 'Bet that CCTV camera doesn't even work.'

My throat tightened as he ripped open the packet.

'Seventy fucking quid,' he hissed. 'You have got to be joking.'

Despair washed over me. There was no way we could afford to pay it. 'I can't believe they have traffic wardens over here on a Sunday evening,' I said.

'Great day this has turned out to be.' Fin tossed the parking ticket onto the back seat, switched off the interior light and started up the engine. 'I should run the bastard over.' We screeched out of the car park, dangerously close to the traffic warden, our back wheels sliding out over the icy surface.

'Careful,' I said, grabbing onto the dashboard.

Fin ignored my warning, careening out into the road, almost driving us into a ditch. I said nothing while he took a breath and righted the car. We drove home in silence, his anger hanging over us, my sense of guilt expanding. I should never have suggested this day out. It was extravagant and stupid. I'd have to make it up to Fin, but not right now. He wasn't in the mood to hear my apologies. I would wait until he'd calmed down.

CHAPTER TEN

2017

The freezing fog has finally cleared, and I gaze out of the kitchen window at the grey, scudding clouds ahead and the murky, roiling ocean below. Normally, I know how to keep myself busy – meeting up with friends, running on the beach, exercise classes, spa days, hair appointments, nail appointments, shopping, reading – but since the text, I can't seem to settle to anything. Will has been out all morning. He wouldn't tell me where he was going. He said it was a secret. I'm not keen on secrets or surprises, which is ironic considering what I'm keeping from my husband. But I'm anxious not to dwell on that. Instead, I'm trying to figure out a plan, now that leaving the country is off the agenda.

I jump as my phone buzzes on the counter top – a call rather than a text. I turn and walk towards it, my palms suddenly clammy, my head swimming with nerves. Will's profile picture stares out from the screen and I instantly relax my shoulders.

'Hey,' I say. 'Where are you? What you up to?'

'I'm outside in the car.'

'Outside the house?' I wrinkle my nose. What's he doing calling me from outside?

'Do me a favour,' he says. 'Go and sit on the sofa in the kitchen.'

'Huh?' Dread taps at my chest. 'What's going on?'

'Can you just do it, Anna?'

'Is everything okay?' I ask, my heart thumping. I'm tempted to go into the lounge and peer out of the front window.

'Everything's fine,' Will says. He doesn't sound worried, or scared. In fact, he sounds... excited.

I hear a squeal. 'What's that noise? Is someone with you? I'm coming out—'

'Anna!' He cuts me off. 'For once in your life, will you just do what I ask?'

'Sorry.' I try to calm down. 'You want me to sit on the sofa? The one in the kitchen?'

'Yes. Please.'

'Oka-y.' I walk over to the sofa and sit on it, crossing my legs, then uncrossing them again. 'I'm sitting.'

'Good. Now close your eyes.'

'Why do I have to—'

'Anna. Please.'

'Okay, okay, eyes are closing. Eyes are closed.'

'Good. I'm ending the call now, and I'm coming in.'

I open my eyes quickly to end the call, place my phone on the coffee table and re-close my eyes, feeling faintly ridiculous. I hear the sound of the front door opening and closing again. Of footsteps getting closer.

'Don't open your eyes yet.' Will's voice. He sounds excited.

I catch a faint malty scent that I can't place.

'Okay,' he says. 'In a second, you can open your eyes, but please don't squeal or make any loud noises, okay?'

'You're scaring me, Will.'

'Open your eyes,' he says.

I do as he asks and have to blink a few times to clear my vision. Will is standing in front of me, holding something. It's moving. I catch my breath.

'Oh wow,' I whisper. 'It's adorable!'

'He's twelve weeks old,' Will says, his eyes shining. 'And he's yours, Anna.'

I'm staring at a tiny puppy with dark eyes and a brown curly coat. He's making little whimpering noises and sniffing at the air. I can barely speak I'm so overcome with emotion. Will sits next to me and places the little bundle on my lap. Its nose goes into overdrive, snuffling me and burrowing into my cable-knit jumper. My fingers grasp him gently, marvelling over his silky soft fur.

'Do you like him?' Will asks, stroking the little guy's head.

'I love him,' I whisper, trying desperately not to let a sob escape. I can feel myself on the verge of breaking down. Of losing it completely. I know these unshed tears are about more than this puppy. I inhale deeply and give myself a shake. 'I can't believe you got me a dog.' I turn to kiss my husband. 'Thank you.' I've wanted a dog my whole life, but with my parents having moved to the UK and then home to Sweden again, they were never in one place long enough for us to make that kind of commitment.

'He's kind of an apology,' Will said. 'For being a prat the other day.'

'What?' I don't know what he's referring to. Will has never been a prat.

'You wanted to go to Sweden,' he explains, 'and I wasn't very nice about it. It's where you're from and I should have been more understanding. Of course you're entitled to want to go back whenever you like without being made to feel guilty.'

Now it's *my* turn to feel guilty. Wanting to visit my homeland has nothing to do with missing the place. It's about running away from my problems. 'Forget about it,' I reply. 'I know you've got commitments. It was unfair of me to ask.'

'We will go, though,' he says. 'Soon as I get the time.'

'No way!' I reply, smiling. 'Not now we have this little cutie. I'm not leaving him.'

Will grins. 'Dad said he'd look after him whenever we want, so there's no problem there.'

'What's his name?' I ask, nuzzling the top of his furry head with my nose.

'He doesn't have one,' Will says. 'I thought *you* could name him.'

'Hm…' I stare down at him and ponder for a moment.

'Any ideas?' Will asks taking the little fella from me and kissing him.

'How about *Bo*?' I ask. 'He kind of looks like a *Bo*, don't you think? And it sounds good in English and in Swedish.'

'Bo.' Will stares down at the puppy on his lap. 'What do you think, Bo? Like your new name?'

Bo gives a little yip, making Will and I laugh.

'Bo it is,' Will says.

Will and Bo are doing a good job of taking my mind off darker things, but fear still boils away beneath the surface, and I know I can't go on like this for too much longer. I've lost my appetite and my stomach is constantly swirling with anxiety. This isn't something that's going to go away on its own, but my mind doesn't want to register what's happening. Even the thought of replying to those texts makes me queasy. I'm burying my head so deep in the sand that I'm in danger of suffocating.

After a lovely day of playing with our new puppy, Will has left to go to the bistro, leaving me and Bo curled up on the lounge sofa. It's only six o'clock, but night is already drawing in, darkness spreading across the sky like ink on blotting paper. Bo snores lightly on a cushion by my side, tired out by the day's events. I already feel protective towards him – his first night without his mum.

I think I might watch a chick flick this evening. I'll see if there's anything On Demand. I stretch and rise to fetch the remote control which has been tidied away next to the TV by our cleaner. While I'm on my feet, I head over to the window to close the curtains. Our front driveway is mainly screened by tall bushes, but the road is still visible through our electric gates. I give a start as I see something out there. Fear crawls over my scalp as I make out the silhouette of a man standing beneath the street lamp. It looks like he's staring this way, right at me, but I can't be sure. I jerk back from the window, bashing my shin against a side table and swearing loudly. Bo wakes and gives a whimper.

Gathering up my courage, I peer around the edge of the curtain, staring hard at the space beyond the gates. But there's no one there. Did I imagine it? Should I go out and check? The thought of leaving the house on my own to go out into the empty darkness is not an appealing prospect. Do I want to know who's out there? No, I do not.

I yank the curtains closed, making sure there's no gap. I glance around for my phone. It's not in here and anyway, who would I call? I can't ring the police. Scooping up Bo in my arms and kissing his head, we make our way back into the kitchen, closing blinds and curtains, and turning on lights as we go. My phone is on the counter top. I set Bo down on the floor before pressing the power button. I see that I have a new message. I tap it.

> *Yes, you guessed right. It was me outside your house just now. You'd better reply. Don't even think about ignoring me.*

I let go of my phone and it clatters onto the counter. From the corner of my eye, I see Bo peeing on the cream rug under the coffee table, but it barely registers. My chest feels tight and I gasp for air. I grip the counter top and try to think.

He's here. He knows where I live. What the hell am I going to do?

CHAPTER ELEVEN

December 2012

I lay curled up on the sofa, under a duvet and two heavy blankets, feeling sorry for myself. I'd had to call in sick to work that week, which I really couldn't afford to do, but stomach flu had me feeling wretched. I could barely eat a thing, my throat was swollen and raw, and my whole body ached. All I wanted to do was sleep, but the flat was so cold I couldn't get comfortable. Our rooms faced north and the single-paned windows rattled in the wind, welcoming in the icy air. We didn't have enough money to leave the heating on all day, so we allowed ourselves one hour in the morning and two hours in the evening. Being at work in the warm, was far more preferable to staying at home.

Fin had been sweet over the past few days – looking after me and telling me to take it easy, telling me my illness was because I'd been doing too much, that my college course had put too much pressure on me and I should consider giving it up. I'd had to reassure him that I'd be fine, that it was just a bug. Trouble was, I didn't feel fine at all. I felt weak and hollow, stretched too thin as though I might snap in two at any moment.

There was no one I could talk to. Sian and I had somehow drifted apart over the past year. Fin didn't get on with Sian's new boyfriend, who worked in banking, and I was either too tired or too busy to see her on my own. I sometimes commented on her social media posts, and we occasionally texted one another, but that was about it. And I wasn't close enough with my college and work friends to discuss anything beyond, well, college and work. I obviously couldn't confide in my parents about how isolated and exhausted I felt as I couldn't bear to hear my mother tell me that she'd been right all along. As far as they were concerned, I needed them to believe that I was the happiest person alive.

Talking to Fin about my true feelings was out of the question. Not because he didn't care, but because if I told him how I truly felt, he would take it personally. He would think I blamed him, which I didn't. Sleep was my only real escape – a way to block out the anxiety in my head and the fear in my gut. Part of me wondered if this bout of sickness was related to my state of mind, rather than from a real virus.

The click of a key in the lock roused me from my half-slumber, and I opened my eyes, peering out from beneath the duvet.

'Hey.' Fin walked in, his eyes scanning the dimly lit room. I looked where he looked, taking in the disarray. The unwashed dishes and general air of cold neglect. Guilt needled me. I'd been here all day, but hadn't lifted a finger.

'Hi.' I croaked, pulling myself up into a sitting position, trying to appear more "with it" than I felt.

'How are you feeling?' he asked.

'A bit better,' I lied, noticing a large carrier bag in his hand. One from work. 'What's that?' I asked. 'A freebie from the shop?'

'I wish,' he replied, sitting on the arm of the sofa. 'No. It's a winter wetsuit. A total bargain – should have been four hundred quid, but it was a faulty return so Damian said I could have it for a hundred.'

My stomach dropped. Was he joking? Did he not realise what a financial mess we were in? That we didn't have one pound spare, let alone a hundred.

'I thought,' he continued, 'I thought, if you don't get me a Christmas present then this can be... you know, my Christmas present.' He grinned, his eyes wide like he'd just come up with a great idea.

I didn't even know what to say. I wanted to yell at him, to scream like a fishwife, but I knew I wouldn't do that. I couldn't cope with any confrontation – not while I felt so ill. I didn't have the mental strength for it. Fin was scary when he got angry. Cold, dark. How could I stay silent, though? He needed to know we couldn't afford it. That our money situation was perilous. I felt the sting of hot tears rolling down my cheeks.

'What?' Fin's brows knitted together. 'What's the matter? Did something happen?'

'We can't afford it, Fin. The wetsuit, I mean. We can barely afford the rent, food, bills. We're beyond skint. I don't think we have enough money for even one more month. We're already in the shit.'

'We'll be okay,' he said. 'It can't be that bad. We're both working.'

'We're both on minimum wage. Do you even know what our outgoings are each month?'

'So, what do you want me to do about it?' He scowled. 'I can't just magic up a better-paid job.'

'We can't afford the wetsuit.' Our eyes locked and I saw heavy disappointment flit across his face. His current suit was ancient, falling apart at the seams. It didn't do anything to keep him warm in the freezing water. I knew he needed a new one, and I sympathised. But we also needed food and heating – a roof over our heads. We had to prioritise.

'Oh for fuck's sake!' He pushed himself up off the sofa arm and tossed the carrier bag across the kitchen floor, turned around and left the flat, slamming the door behind him.

I pushed the duvet off my body and wobbled to my feet, my heart racing. Should I go after him? I wasn't even dressed. I wasn't strong enough. No. I'd give him time to calm down. He'd see sense eventually. There would be no presents for either of us this Christmas. We'd be lucky if we weren't forced to beg Fin's dad to let us live in his garden shed.

I'd tried several times already to tell Fin about our precarious finances, but he'd brushed it off, unwilling to understand our dire situation. He always used his current bank balance to determine how much money he had, never taking into account all the bills that had to be paid at the end of each month. Consequently, we were always going overdrawn and having to work overtime to catch up. I didn't want to be the one to point out our money problems every month, but if I didn't do it, who would? I wished we could rewind to those early carefree days before we had to worry about all this stuff. Those lazy beach days where we couldn't keep our hands off each other, and love was the only thing that consumed our thoughts.

I made a move to clear the breakfast dishes, noticing that this morning's milk had frozen to the inside of the bowls. This was ridiculous. I would have to switch on the heating – just while I cleaned up the place. Once I could crawl back under the duvet, I'd switch it off again. I walked over to the thermostat and pressed the switch. The sound of the boiler firing up lifted my heart momentarily. But it didn't change the fact that Fin was AWOL. Where had he gone? For a walk? To a friend's? Part of me wanted him to come home, but part of me dreaded it. Was it my fault we had no money? Was it selfish of me to want to finish my management course? Maybe I should forget it and work more hours instead, but I knew that would only keep us in this financial mess for longer. What chance did we have of getting married and having a family if we couldn't even take care of ourselves? I dumped all the dishes and cutlery into the washing up bowl and part-boiled the kettle for hot water, placing my palms on the warm plastic jug as it heated up.

It took me around half an hour to get the place looking vaguely tidy. Central heating and a clean room made me feel a little less wretched. At least when Fin came back, he'd walk into a more welcoming atmosphere. I checked my phone, but there were no messages. If he hadn't come home by eight, I would call him. In the meantime, I decided to watch some TV while I waited.

Eight o'clock came and went, and still no sign of Fin. Reluctantly, I had switched off the heating, and the temperature inside was dropping fast. Having crawled back under my nest of covers on the sofa, I sent him a couple of text messages, but they both went unanswered. I finally steeled myself to call him, but his phone went straight to voicemail. Was he mad at me? Did he hate me for asking him to return the wetsuit? I tried to think of a life without him, but I couldn't picture it. I'd built everything around him. Around the two of us. Without Fin, I didn't know what I would do, or where I could go. My head pulsed with anxiety. What should I do?

I slept fitfully on the sofa, the mattress on our bed so cold I couldn't face lying on it without Fin there to warm me up. Still, the icy air penetrated the covers, and my limbs were chilled to the bone, my toes and fingers numb. Every hour, my eyes flew open in a panic, heart sinking each time I realised Fin still hadn't returned home. My throat was on fire, my eyes swollen with tears and exhaustion. I kept checking my phone, but there were no texts. No voice messages. Nothing. Where had he gone?

Finally, at 6.30 a.m., I dragged myself off the sofa, flicked on the boiler switch and called Fin once more. Again it went straight to voicemail and I felt like pitching my phone across the room.

Was this it? Were we over? I should never have asked him to return the wetsuit. We would have managed somehow. It hadn't been worth all this. I realised I would do just about anything to have Fin come home to me. To make things right between us again. Despite everything, I still loved him with the same intensity I did at the start of our relationship.

I crawled back under my covers and stared at the damp patches on the wall which had bubbled the paintwork, at the skin of ice coating the inside of the windows. Through the wall, next door's alarm clock beeped. In the road below, the dustbin lorry growled and screeched. All the everyday noises I'd grown used to, but which meant nothing without Fin. I felt like a stranger in my own home.

And then, finally, the sound I'd been waiting for – footsteps on the landing, a key in the lock. My heart skittered in my chest. I took a breath, preparing myself for whatever came next.

'Christ, it's colder in here than it is outside.' Fin walked into the room, his cheeks red, his hair dishevelled. He didn't look angry or upset. Just dipped his head and gave me a half smile. 'Hi.'

'Hi,' I replied, my heart in my throat.

'Anna, I'm so sorry.'

At his words, all the anxiety and sadness I'd been holding on to evaporated. 'Me too,' I replied. 'Of course you can keep the wetsuit. I was being—'

'No. No, you were right,' he said, 'about everything.' He closed the door behind him and came and sat next to me on the couch, his hands cupping my face, his lips finding mine. Then he leant back and closed his eyes briefly. 'I'm sorry, Anna. I've been a dick. I'm sorry I stormed out. None of this is your fault. It's just… I dunno. I get so angry and frustrated all the time.'

'I know. I know.'

'I see these people come into the shop, dropping five or six hundred quid on a wetsuit, on new surfboards, on clothes and shoes, and I think, how are they doing it? How did they get into the position where their lives are so easy? And why are our lives so hard? I want to look after you. I want us to have an easy, happy life. This shithole, this isn't where I want us to be.'

'It won't be forever,' I said. 'Things will get better.'

'Listen to me, Anna,' he said, his voice more serious. 'If we stay as we are, then nothing's going to change. We're going to keep working our arses off for nothing, just to freeze in a shitty bedsit with no hope of anything else. But I've been thinking… there is a better way… than this.'

I hoped he had come around to my way of thinking. That he'd decided we needed better qualifications if we were ever going to escape our situation. That finally, we were going to do something real. Something that would lift us out of the mire.

'That teacher,' he continued, 'back at school – Dickhead Williams – I don't want him to be right about me. I don't want to be a loser all my life. Do you understand?'

'You're not a loser. Williams was an idiot.'

'I *am* a loser, Anna.' His voice cracked for a moment. He gave a sniff and carried on. 'But I'm not going down easy. I've got some ideas. They're a bit radical, but one of them could work. Every other option I've thought of is either a gamble, or it means years' worth of slogging our guts out. But this way, well, I think we could really turn our lives around.'

For the first time in days, I stopped feeling so wretched. I allowed a glimmer of optimism to creep into my thoughts. I'd never seen Fin so fired up. So determined. 'Okay, so tell me. What are your ideas?'

'Just bear with me while I explain, okay?'

I nodded.

'Neither of us is rich, right? We don't have rich parents, we weren't given any handouts. We just have to carve our lives out of basically nothing.'

'We have each other,' I said with a smile.

'Yeah, sure, but we need more than each other to live. We need a place of our own, clothes, food, warmth.'

'Yeah, I could do with some warmth about now.'

'You're shivering,' he said.

I hadn't even noticed, but he was right. My whole body was shaking.

He took my icy hands and began to warm them in his. 'Better?'

I nodded, even though his hands felt just as cold as mine.

'Anna, those rich kids don't realise how lucky they are. They had a head start. They never played by the rules. You could even say they cheated. They never spent one day of their lives struggling.'

'I suppose. But they're the exception. Most people have to struggle, no different to us. You can drive yourself mad thinking about what other people have got. It's not worth letting your mind go down that path.'

Fin shook his head. 'But why should we struggle when there are other options open to us?'

'Like what?'

'Would you ever consider a change in career, Anna? This is hard to explain. I don't want you to get the wrong idea.'

'Fin. Just say whatever it is you have to say.'

'Okay.' He rose to his feet and went and stood over by the window. Then he turned to face me, his eyes glittering. 'Like I said, I have a few ideas, but this is just one. I'll just come out with it. Tell it to you straight. Anna, do you know how hot you are? Wherever we go, I'm in danger of punching every guy in the room for just looking at you. You could have anyone you wanted.'

His words made my cheeks warm and my skin tingle, but I wasn't sure I believed him. And I wasn't sure where he was going with this, either.

'Well, I was thinking – we don't have great careers, or money, or assets. In fact, right now, we could say that your looks are our only asset.'

'Asset?'

'So, what if... Have you ever thought about becoming an escort?'

'A *what*?' I was pretty sure I knew what he was talking about but I couldn't believe he would even ask me that.

'It's nothing bad. You basically go out with men who are too sad to get their own dates.'

'A prostitute?' Surely he wasn't being serious.

'No! An escort. You just go on dates. You don't sleep with them.'

'Oh, right, okay, and you could be a – what do you call them? – a gigolo.' I gave a short laugh and shook my head. 'Yeah, right. Very funny. That's your plan?'

He nodded.

'Fin!'

'What?' He grinned. 'It's a good plan to get rich.'

'Fin, I am *not* doing that for money, what kind of girl do you think I am?'

'All I want,' he said, 'is to be with you. But I have this dread, that if we go on like this – skint, ill, struggling, arguing – we're going to end up hating each other. My plan is more about love than about money.'

I raised my eyebrows. Fin's plan was definitely more about money. But he had a point. If we carried on as we were, we weren't going to last. I decided to play along for the fun of it. 'So, how much would I charge an hour? A thousand? Two?'

'At least.' He grinned, coming back over to sit with me. 'I'd pay more than that for you if I had the money.'

'Even when I look like this? Hair unwashed, ratty pyjamas, shivering with the flu.'

'Some guys might get turned on by that.'

'Ew, gross.' I shoved Fin, pushing him back against the arm of the sofa. 'Wouldn't it be less icky to just – I dunno – rob a bank?' I laughed.

'Believe me, I've thought about it. But, no. Robbing a bank would be way harder, and we couldn't spend the money here. We'd have to go on the run. This way, we'd have the money legitimately and could get on with our lives without the police coming after us.'

'So, let me get this straight,' I said. 'We go on dates with rich people, earn a ton of money and live happily ever after?'

'Not quite,' he replied. '*You* go on the dates, I run the business side of things.'

'Like a pimp?' I tilted my head to the side. 'Yeah, I can just see you in a long fur coat and gold jewellery. You'd look good. You're such a nutter.' I closed my eyes for a moment. 'Tell you what,' I said, snapping my eyes open with a grin. 'I've got a better idea – you go out and prostitute yourself and *I'll* organise the business side.'

Fin shook his head. 'We'd earn more money my way.'

'Yeah, well, if only there really was such a neat solution to all our problems – one that didn't involve me selling my body and you wearing fur, of course.'

'Yeah.' He sighed. 'If only.'

The sofa moved as Fin shifted up next to me. I leant in towards him feeling much better. Our crazy conversation had cheered me right up.

CHAPTER TWELVE

2017

More than anything, I don't want to be alone this evening. The house feels too big. Too empty. A place of shadows where anyone could lurk. But if I call Will, he's going to wonder why I need him to come home. He's going to ask questions that I can't answer.

I pick up my phone again and begin tapping in a new message:

Hey Sian, what are you up to this evening. Fancy hanging out at mine and watching a trashy movie on TV?

There's barely a ten-second delay before my phone pings:

Yes! What time?

Now?

Give me twenty mins

I send her a smiley-face emoticon blowing a kiss.

While I wait for Sian to arrive, I cross the room to examine the rug that Bo has peed on. It's pretty much ruined – I don't think even the dry-cleaners will be able to save it. It's my own fault. Will said I should take Bo outside every couple of hours, and it's been almost four hours since we were last in the garden.

'Sorry, boy,' I say, crouching down and rubbing behind his ears. 'We're not going out this evening. It's not safe. But you can pee in here.' I grab a kitchen roll from the cupboard and tear off a handful of sheets. Then I lay them down by the back door. 'There. That can be your pee spot for now.' He starts sniffing around the area and promptly squats next to it. I shift his bottom around so that he poos onto the sheet. Then I praise him. At least this little guy is going some way to taking my mind off things.

Finally, Sian arrives. I buzz open the gates and as she drives in I watch from the doorway, making sure there's no one else out there. As soon as her Toyota is through the gates, they close behind her and I release the breath I was holding.

After she's come inside and we've said our hellos, I introduce Sian to Bo and we coo over him for the next half hour. Finally, Bo gives a yawn and flops down in his bed, exhausted.

'So,' I say, pouring us a glass of wine. 'Let's talk weddings. Have you decided on your favourite venues yet?'

I'm obviously not hiding my worries well enough as Sian gives me a look.

'What?' I say, putting the bottle back down and crossing my arms.

'You tell me,' she says.

'Sian. I have no idea what you're—'

'Right, missy,' she says, taking her glass of wine over to the sofa. 'I want you to tell me why you look like someone's just pissed in your Chardonnay.'

'What? I'm fine. I—'

'Save it for someone who believes you.' She runs a hand through her dark blonde hair and gives me a glare that takes me back to our school days. 'How long have we known each other?' she asks.

'Uh, I don't know… ages.'

'Eleven years. You've been my best friend on-and-off for eleven years, Anna. Now tell me what's wrong?'

I join her on the couch, sitting on the opposite corner and pulling my feet up under me. Memories creep in and then spiral away. 'Have you seen Fin recently?' I ask. The question falls heavily from my tongue.

'Fin? Why are you asking about him?' Sian sets her glass down on the coffee table and leans in, trying to catch my eye. But my gaze slides to the floor, to the pee-stained rug.

'Did you hear what happened?' I say.

'Something happened to Fin?'

'His wife,' I say. 'She died.' I look up to gauge her reaction.

'Shit.' She presses her lips together, pauses to digest the information. 'Was she ill?'

'No, not ill,' I reply, the image of her pale, dead body flashing up in my mind. 'She was only twenty-nine.'

'That's terrible. How's Fin doing?'

I shrug. 'I hoped you might still be in touch.'

'Me?' Sian's eyes widen. 'Why would I be in contact with Fin?'

'I don't know. I just wondered.'

She reaches for her glass, takes a sip and leans back. 'So, what happened to her? How did she die?'

'It was on the news.' I can't tell her about the text. 'They were on holiday. She was killed by a speedboat while she was out there swimming.'

Sian inhales sharply. 'That's horrible. Poor Fin. I suppose it would be weird for you to contact him, what with him being your ex and everything.'

I swallow and nod. 'I was wondering… maybe if you got in touch. Sent him a text to see how he's doing?' I figure Sian might be able to meet up with him. Find out his state of mind. See if he mentions me.

'I don't think that's a good idea, Anna. What if he asks for your number? What if he wants to get in contact with you again?

He could screw your life up with Will. It's funny,' she says, tilting her head. 'At one time, I was convinced you and Fin would stay together, get married – you two were inseparable for years. Until... *you know*.'

My stomach tightens as I think back to that terrible time. Anxiety and turbulence compressed into memories.

'And when you went to Sweden,' Sian continues. 'I thought that was the last I'd see of you. Thought I'd lost my best friend forever.' Her eyes narrow. 'You don't still have feelings for Fin? Because if you do, Will would be—'

'No! Of course not.' I shake my head at her suggestion. 'I love my husband. I'm just concerned about Fin after what happened. But I don't want to get in touch with him behind Will's back. It wouldn't be right. That's why I wondered if you would do it.'

She shakes her head. 'I'm sorry, but no. Only because I care about you. It's better to let sleeping dogs lie.' She glances over at Bo in his basket and then gives me a smile.

I nod. 'Okay. You're probably right.'

'I get it,' Sian says. 'He was your first love. He was the passion. The drama. Who wouldn't want to be with him? But Will is so much more than that. He's strong and safe. He's... reliable. Lovely. You know?'

I *do* know. Sian needn't worry about me. Her warnings are not required. But now I have no other option. I know Fin has been sending me the messages so I'm going to have to do something that scares the hell out of me. I'm going to have to contact Fin myself.

CHAPTER THIRTEEN

January 2014

I stepped off the bus onto the wet pavement, waiting until I was clear of the bus shelter before opening my umbrella. A few pedestrians passed me, eyes down, shoulders hunched against the rain. Cars swished by, their headlamps splashing puddles of light onto the dimly lit street. One in front of the other, my feet propelled me forward. Even though I felt like running in the opposite direction.

As I walked past Florence Road, I thought longingly of our studio flat. Granted, it hadn't been ideal when we'd lived there, but at least it had been our own private space. However, we hadn't been able to stump up the rent and so our miserable landlord had kicked us out. We found out recently that we probably could have stayed – that tenants have rights – but it was too late. We were out, and our landlord had changed the locks and re-let the place.

Now, we were living at Fin's dad's, staying in his garden shed, and it was a million times worse than the flat. The shed itself was okay. Being a small space, a single oil-filled heater was enough to heat it up to a decent temperature. We had an air mattress and piles of bedding that doubled up as our sofa. And we'd also bought a second-hand mini fridge and a microwave from Gumtree. It was a bit like camping.

The bad part was Fin's dad, Col. Any time we needed the bathroom, we had to go into his small terraced council house. The lounge sat at the back of the house and was where Col and his mates hung out smoking weed, talking crap and watching movies all day and most of the night. And every time I walked past, they made some sexist or lewd comment. I hated it. So did Fin. But he wouldn't stand up to his dad. Maybe he was scared of him.

That wasn't the only problem. More and more these past few months, Fin had been saying things that unsettled me. Wanting us to come up with plans about how to make money. He wanted a big fix, a big score. He talked about get-rich-quick schemes, going beyond the law and doing things that were… well… crazy.

I went along with his conversations because these were pretty much the only times he seemed happy. But when I sensed he wanted to take things further, to act on his plans, I would laugh it off to let him know I wasn't taking him seriously. Then he would scowl and go in on himself, giving me the silent treatment. I would have to coax him back with fun memories or by asking him about surfing. It was exhausting.

But, as if that wasn't bad enough, I had now discovered something else. Something that would change our lives completely. I had to somehow find the right words to tell Fin. But how would he react? Closer and closer I drew to our new home. If the weather hadn't been so awful, I would have walked around the block a few times. Anything to delay the inevitable. But the sooner I told him, the sooner we could deal with it.

As I turned into our road, the rain grew heavier, slicing through the air at an angle, making my umbrella almost redundant. Moisture-laden air invaded my lungs, making it hard to breathe. Water clung to my eyelashes, stinging my eyes, blurring my vision. A guy riding a push bike headed towards me on the pavement, head down, tyres hissing, no lights. I had to sidestep into the rain-filled gutter to get out of his way. Good job no cars were coming. I should have shouted something rude at him, but I had no stomach for a confrontation with a stranger. I would need all my emotional energy for Fin.

Too soon, I reached the run-down row of terraces which I now called home. The most dilapidated of the lot, the third from the end, was Col's place. Now also *our* place. Reluctantly, I pushed at the rusted side gate and walked down the path which led to the long, narrow back garden, overgrown with weeds and strewn with rubbish. Harsh yellow light glowed from the dirty window of the block-built shed at the far end. Fin was home.

My heart rate sped up as I picked my way along the path. I lowered my umbrella, shook it out and pushed open the door. Moist, warm air hit me. Fin glanced up from his phone and smiled.

'Hey.'

'Hi.' I closed the door behind me, took off my coat and slipped out of my shoes. The rain drummed down onto the felt roof. Even so, the air was calm and still inside. The eye of the storm.

'Good day?' Fin asked.

'Manic. Loads of lessons on at the pool today, and we had a concussion. Little boy slipped on the side.'

'Was he okay?'

'Hard to tell. Hopefully. He wasn't dizzy or vomiting, but he did knock himself out for a few seconds. How about you? Was the shop okay?'

Fin shrugged and pursed his lips.

I came and sat on the bed next to him, winding my arms around him. He pulled me closer and crushed my mouth with his lips. I tasted salt and desperation as he tugged at my clothes and slipped his hands beneath them.

'Wait,' I said, the swirl of an unspoken conversation in my head.

'Anna,' he panted, his mouth moving from my lips to my neck, his fingers tangling in my soaking hair. I twined my legs around him and moulded my body to his. We desperately needed to talk, but maybe we needed this more.

Afterwards, we lay on the bed, warm and wet. Happier than before. But I couldn't delay any longer.

'Fin.'

'Yeah?' He propped himself up on one elbow and turned to face me, his eyes more green than brown today, his surfer's shoulders broad and strong.

I trailed a forefinger over his bicep, then took my hand away, smoothing away an imaginary lock of hair from my face. My voice caught in my throat, but I made myself force the words out. 'I've got something to tell you.' Excitement and fear vied for space in my head. 'I… I'm pregnant.'

The damp air ballooned with silence. Fin's eyes bored into mine, then his gaze slid to the wall.

'Fin?'

He muttered something but I couldn't make out the words. I stared at him trying to work out his reaction, trying to catch his eye again, but his face was a mask, closed off to me. He had always talked about us having a family in the future, but now that it was real, what did he really think?

'Are you okay?' I asked. 'I know it's a shock. I only found out myself today. Can't quite get my head around it. I took a test at work.'

'Fuck, Anna.' His fingers splayed open and he locked his hands behind his head. 'I thought you were on the pill.'

'I am. I am on the pill.'

'So how did this happen? *Fuck!*' He turned, lowered his arms, and his fist shot out. He'd punched the wall.

I gave a yelp, the sound of my heartbeats drowning out the rain.

'This can't be happening,' he muttered, pulling on his jeans and rising to his feet. Blood smeared the grey blockwork and dripped from his knuckles onto the makeshift bed.

'It's okay. It'll be okay,' I said. My voice sounded thin and far away like it was coming from a radio in a distant room.

'How?' Fin sneered. 'How will it be okay? We live in a garden fucking shed. We've got no money. We've got nothing. There's no part of this that is okay.'

'I was thinking… maybe we'll be eligible for something… from the government? Some kind of benefits or something.'

'No!' Fin swung his head from left to right like a cornered animal looking for an escape. 'I won't end up like my loser dad. On benefits, pissing away my life. No.' He turned to me. 'You'll have to get an abortion.'

I felt like I'd been slapped. He didn't even want to talk about this. He didn't even want to consider our options. 'Just like that?' I replied. 'Get an abortion?' I hugged my arms around my body, trying not to cry. 'I'm always so careful to say the right thing to you, to make sure you're okay. I always think about how my words affect you. But *you* – you just tell me to get an abortion. You don't even ask me how I'm feeling.'

He shook his head and looked over at me. 'I'm sorry, Anna. I know I should've asked how you were, how you are, but you've got to realise we can't have a baby. Not the way things are. Here.'

'Maybe we can, maybe we can't, but let's at least talk about it. Do you even care how I'm feeling? I've got a new life growing in my body.' The room was closing in like the walls were about to crush me.

'You can't think of it that way,' he said, his jaw clenching. 'We didn't plan this. We don't have to let it ruin our lives.'

'Screw you, Fin.' I choked out the words and started pulling my clothes back on.

'Where are you going, Anna? We need to decide what we're going to do.'

'Sounds like you've already decided.' I grabbed my coat and bag, slipped on my wet shoes and reached to open the door.

'Anna, wait.'

My hands shook and my chest tightened as I pulled open the door and walked back out into the foul night. I gave a sob as I lurched down the garden path. Briefly, I turned to see if Fin was coming after me, but I could see him through the window, rooted to the spot, his hand pulling at his hair. I hadn't closed the shed door properly, and it banged in the wind, in danger of coming off its hinges.

There was only one place I could go now. One person I could talk to.

I arrived at Sian's parents' house, a dripping, freezing, shaky mess, a blur of emotions numbing my brain. Sian ushered me in, gave me warm towels and a change of clothes, and placed a steaming cup of tea in my hands.

We sat in her room like old times. I curled up at the foot of her bed while Sian leant back against her pale pink velour headboard. She gave off such an aura of calm, I realised this was the first time I'd felt safe for months. Haltingly, I told her about my predicament. About my living accommodation, our lack of funds, and, finally, about my newly acquired pregnancy and Fin's reaction to it.

Once I'd finished, Sian exhaled slowly. 'So, what are you going to do?' Her grey eyes filled with concern.

I blinked and pressed my lips together, desperately trying not to cry.

'Do you still love Fin?' she asked, taking my hand.

I nodded.

'Do you want to have this baby?'

'I… I don't know. I think so. The thought of getting rid of it is so…'

'I know, I know,' she soothed.

'But… how can we have it? We can't even look after ourselves. We've lost our flat, we're always working, we never have any fun. A baby would make things even worse, wouldn't it?'

'Look, Anna, to be honest, I don't know what you should do. But you don't have to decide right away, do you? How far gone are you?'

'I'm not totally sure. Maybe about two or three months.'

Sian picked up her phone and started tapping and scrolling. 'Latest you can have a termination is twenty-four weeks. So don't worry. You've got time to decide.'

'Thank you.' My voice cracked and she laid down her phone and opened her arms. I let her hug me as I cried into her work uniform. 'Sorry.'

'Shut up, you silly moo. There's nothing to apologise for. You're my friend, aren't you?'

I nodded and gave her a last squeeze before breaking away, and sitting crossed legged on the bed.

'Now, are you going to go back to the dreaded shed tonight?' she asked. 'Or do you want me to roll out the camp bed? Midnight feast, anyone?'

I giggled. 'Can I really stay over? Won't your mum and dad mind?'

'Course not. They love you, Anna. You know that.'

'It's just, Fin was so horrible. I can't believe he just told me to get an abortion. Didn't ask me how I was feeling or anything.'

'He's in shock. He's twenty-two and you basically told him he's going to be a dad. Even if you were loaded and living in a lovely place, he'd still be freaking out. Give him time to get his head around it.'

'Do you think he will? Get his head around it, I mean. Because even I haven't got my head around it.'

'Hmm. Fin *is* a bit of a free spirit. But, he loves you, right?'

I nodded. 'Yeah.' Fin always said he wanted us to have kids. I knew the timing was a bit off, but surely he'd come around.

'Don't worry, Anna. He'll stand by you. He'd be mad to let you go.'

Sian's words comforted me and I allowed myself to believe her. I let her soothe and pamper me, too exhausted to consider the alternative.

CHAPTER FOURTEEN

2017

I finally arrive at this out-of-the-way garden centre in North Dorset, and manage to find a parking space at the end of a row. My Land Rover is way too big for most spaces, but it was a present from Will and I do love it. Fin and I have arranged to meet this afternoon in the garden-centre café. I didn't want us to meet in Bournemouth in case we ran into anyone we knew. And I refused to go to his house. This is neutral ground. Plus, I can leave whenever I choose.

I exit the Land Rover, lock it and pull my thin scarf up over my nose. The air is colder here than back home by the coast, the wind is biting and I'm not dressed for it. I walk across the gravel car park towards the entrance. A chalk board outside the main entrance proclaims a two-for-one deal for OAPs in the café on Mondays to Thursdays. Maybe that's why the car park is almost full.

I haven't spoken to Fin for three years. I wonder if he's changed at all. If he'll see differences in me. I push open the glass door, relieved to be out of the stinging cold. I've never been here before. The door swings closed behind me and I find myself standing in a vast shop displaying homewares, plants, garden ornaments and gifts. Normally, it's the kind of place in which I'd enjoy browsing. Not today.

A rumble of chatter and the clattering of plates and cutlery drifts from the café at the other end of the building. I wonder if he's here yet. My heart is in my throat. I shouldn't have come, and yet, did I really have any choice?

I find myself walking into the café, scanning the room. I'm a normal person doing normal things. Except there's nothing normal about this meeting. I blow out a series of short breaths and roll my shoulders to try to dispel my growing unease. But far from easing any anxiety, my insides begin to quiver with nerves.

The café is a self-service place where you queue up with a tray to order your food and drinks. There must be around thirty or forty tables in the place and most are full. It's not the small, quiet café I envisaged. A hand on my shoulder startles me and I turn.

'Anna.'

After all this time, Fin still has the ability to make me catch my breath, and I hate myself for betraying Will like that. Fin looks just the same… although as I take him in, I can see some changes. His cheekbones are more defined and he has a little more stubble on his chin. His hair is shorter and he's dressed more smartly than he ever was when he was with me. Gone are the surfy, casual clothes. In their place are designer jeans, an Aran sweater and a navy, wool military-style coat. But he's still Fin, and all the memories come rushing back, twisting at my heart and making me wish more than ever I'd stayed at home today.

His hand comes up to rest on the arm of my coat and he leans in to kiss me on the mouth. I jerk backwards, the scent of him still so familiar, even after all this time.

'What?' he says, his jawbone tightening.

'I'm married,' I stutter.

Fin's face darkens. 'So was I, remember?'

I'm seized by the urge to run away, but I can't go until we've spoken. Until everything is resolved. I don't want to leave here until I know for sure that I will never have to see Fin Chambers again.

'Shall I get us coffees?' he asks, letting go of my arm.

'Okay. I'll find a table.' I turn away from him abruptly and try to gather up my thoughts, to stop them scattering all over the place. First things first, I need to find an empty table. I pick my way through the diners, barely able to walk, clenching my fists to stop my hands shaking, the smells of lasagne and fish, coffee and warm bread mingling with the scent of old people's talcum-powder and perfume.

'You can sit here, love. We're just leaving.' A woman to my right gets to her feet. Her friend is pulling on her coat.

'Thanks,' I say.

'Is it still cold out?' the woman asks.

'Freezing,' I murmur.

'We've been putting off leaving,' her friend says. 'Been sitting here since eleven thirty, haven't we, Mary.'

'We came for coffee, stayed for lunch, and persuaded ourselves to round off the day with afternoon tea.' They laugh and I force a smile.

'So, I suppose we better go and brave the arctic winds out there.'

Normally, I'd be happy to join in with their friendly chat, but my mind is blank. All I can do is nod and inflict them with my rictus grin. Eventually, they leave and I slide into one of the empty chairs. The table is covered in crumbs, napkins, dirty cups and plates. My gaze drifts over to the queue where Fin still waits to be served. He's not looking my way.

A waitress comes to clear the table with a smile and a few pleasantries; another one comes along with a cloth to clean up the crumbs. They're efficient, friendly. No wonder it's busy in here. I wait, staring ahead through vast windows which look out onto the nursery – rows of plants and saplings waiting to find a home.

'I got you a latte.' Fin has returned. He sits opposite me and puts our drinks on the table.

'Thanks,' I reply. But I know I won't be able to drink anything. His proximity has unleashed emotions I thought I'd buried.

'You look good, Anna. Really good. How are you?'

I stare at my coffee, unsure how to reply. Fearful that Fin will somehow draw me under his spell once more. I can't allow our shared past to ruin my new life. There are things we need to get sorted once and for all, Fin and I. I think of Will. Picture his face to give me courage. Then I think of Fin's poor dead wife. I place the palms of my hands on the damp table and look Fin in the eye, hoping my voice won't betray my nerves.

'I need to get on with my life, Fin. And you should get on with yours. This… all this is screwed up. I don't want anything to do with it… Like I said, I just want to get on with my life.'

'Nothing's changed, Anna.' His voice is soft and works its way through to the core of my body. But these feelings he's stirring up are echoes of another time. They're not real. I can't afford to pay them any attention.

'Everything has changed,' I reply.

'I still love you,' he says rubbing at his cheek. 'And you know you have to do this.'

Is he giving me a choice, or is he threatening me? I can't tell. I take a deep breath. 'You can't still love me – you don't even know who I am any more. I've changed. I'm not the naïve little girl I was back then. We haven't seen each other in years. Haven't even been in contact. We can't just meet up out of the blue and carry on like nothing's changed. It's over. I have a life with—'

'What are you talking about?' Fin leans forward. '*This* was what we agreed – not to see each other. This was our plan. You can't just—'

'No!' I lower my voice and carry on. 'This was what *you* agreed, Fin. This was *your* plan. Never mine. I never thought you would—'

'You can't turn this all onto me, Anna. It was for both of us.' He blinks furiously. 'This can't be happening. Do you realise what I've just done for you?'

'Don't say that. You didn't do it for *me*.' I think about the text and the news report. Bile rises in my throat. 'I can't see you again. I thought, after I left back then, that would be the end of it.'

'The end? It was just the beginning. It was the start of everything.'

I shake my head and try to calm my breathing. 'No. It wasn't. Whatever you've done, Fin. This has to be the end of it.'

'Do you love him?' he asks, pressing his fist against his mouth.

I bow my head, scared to look him in the eye.

'I kept my side of the bargain,' he says. 'We have something incredible. We always have. I can still feel it and I know you do, too. We love each other, Anna. You can't bail on me now. You can't.'

'I'm sorry, Fin. It's over.' I say the words, ignoring the familiar deep pull of attraction. 'Whatever we had... it's been over for a long time. I thought I made that clear.' I grip the edge of the table, scrape my chair back and rise to my feet, desperate to get away from him. From the danger that surrounds him.

Fin rises too, comes around to my side of the table and grabs my upper arm. He's close enough that no one would be able to see anything amiss.

'You're not going,' he hisses. 'Not without promising me that you'll do it. That you'll keep to our agreement.'

'Let go, Fin,' I say through gritted teeth. 'There is no agreement. There never was. And if you did something you shouldn't have, it's nothing to do with me. You're delusional. You need help. Seriously.'

'Bitch,' he mutters, squeezing my arm so hard I give a muffled whimper. But I hold his gaze, glaring at him until he lets go. At this point, I don't know or care if anyone in the noisy café has seen or heard our exchange.

'I mean it, Fin. Leave me alone.' I need to get out of here. I'm barely able to see in front of my face, my eyes are filling with tears and I desperately try to blink them away before they fall. Standing this close to him makes me dizzy. I'm desperate to get away from him. Before I go, I stammer out a final warning. 'Contact me again and I'll call the police. In fact, I should—'

'You're just as much a part of this as I am,' he murmurs. 'You tell anyone and I'll make sure they know you're as involved as me.'

He's not bluffing. I can see it from the look on his face.

'Oh, and Anna...'

I should leave right now, not listen to any more of his crap, but instead, I take a steadying breath and stare at him once more, waiting for him to finish. His eyes have lost their anger, his face suddenly blank. 'If you don't go through with it,' he says quietly, 'then I promise you I'll do it. I'll give you a month. One month.' He gives me a last, piercing look, then turns and walks away.

I can't speak. Can't respond to his outrageous threat. I watch his back as he leaves. I should go after him, tell him to listen to me, to leave me alone. Make him see sense. But I'm not strong enough to speak to him again. Instead, I let him leave. Stupid of me. Stupid. Stupid.

An elderly couple have appeared, hovering at my table. I straighten up, gesture to them to take it and begin making my way towards the exit, threading my way through the tables and chairs, past the happy pensioners drinking tea and eating cake, oblivious to the fact that my life is disintegrating.

A hand taps me on the shoulder, making me jump. I stop in my tracks and swing around to see a young, perfectly made-up woman with shiny hair. She's vaguely familiar. Then it comes to me – she's the receptionist from the tennis club. What's her name again? I can't remember. I really don't want to speak to her. I'm not in any fit state to speak to anyone. I'm on the verge of breaking down. I square my shoulders and fight back the urge to sob.

'I saw you sitting over there,' she says, 'and I *thought* it was you. How are you, Anna? Haven't seen you at the club for a while.'

'No, I've, er, I've been a bit busy.'

'My mum and dad live here. I've brought them out for coffee and cake.'

'Lovely.' I force a smile. Please don't let me cry. I can tell she's waiting for me to tell her what I'm doing here. To tell her about the man I was with. I wonder how much of our exchange she witnessed. Did she see the aborted kiss when we met? The intense conversation? The argument at the end? *Shit.* We should have met somewhere more private. Too late now. I bet she's going to say something – if not to Will, then to someone else. The gossip will fly round the club and everyone will be speculating whether or not I'm having an affair. I'll have to tell Will something before it gets back to him. *Mandy!* That's her name.

'Sorry, Mandy, I'd better dash. I don't want to get caught up in the rush-hour traffic.'

'Sure, of course. Hope to see you and Will at the club soon.'

'Yes, definitely.' I smile again and have uncharitable thoughts about how she must be loving this. But, I don't know that for sure. Maybe she's a sweet girl and gossip is the furthest thing from her mind.

I leave the café and walk back through the gift shop, the bright, piped music jarring with my thoughts. Out through the double doors into the fierce wind, I battle my way across the car park. Fin could be out here, sitting in his car watching me. He's clearly insane. I shiver and keep my gaze focused straight ahead. Finally, I reach my car, open the door and climb into the driver's seat. My whole body trembles. I can't think straight. I want to rest my head on the steering wheel, but if Fin's watching… I can't let him see how much he's unnerved me. I don't want him to see me at all. I shudder. I have to get out of here. I switch on the engine and the lights. I leave the car park and head for home, my mind and body numb.

Driving in a daze, I barely register the route, the traffic, any part of the journey, my mind swimming with this afternoon's events. I can't pretend this isn't happening. I have to do something to stop it. But what? I never imagined I'd ever be lucky enough to meet someone like Will. Someone I feel so comfortable with. Someone who never makes me feel anxious and on edge. I realise now, looking back, that was how Fin used to make me feel – like I was standing on the edge of a precipice, constantly worrying about how he would react to everything. It was a tumultuous attraction, not a healthy relationship. Whereas what I have with Will is real love.

But now… What happens now? This is the life I want to keep. I can't give it all up because of someone else's desires. Someone else's twisted plan.

As I hit the lanes and crossroads of Dorset's small towns and villages, I become hopelessly snarled up in rush-hour traffic. I turn on the radio to try to drown out my thoughts, but nothing can stop the avalanche of fear trying to smother me.

It takes almost two hour to get home. Finally, pulling into our driveway, momentary relief hits as the electric gates whirr shut. Safe. For now.

I stumble in through the front door and tense up as I hear Will's voice in the kitchen. Who's he talking to? I can't cope with visitors. I wonder if Will is going to sense my betrayal. If he'll know I'm keeping secrets. I put my hands to my cheeks, certain the truth is there for all to see. But then, I tell myself, I haven't actually done anything wrong. All I did was meet up with an ex-boyfriend to tell him to leave me alone. I take off my coat and head towards the kitchen. There's no one else here – Will is in front of the bay window, on his hands and knees, playing with Bo.

Bo charges over to me and jumps up, his needle claws sinking into my jeans. I scoop him up and kiss the top of his silky head, trying to keep hold of his tiny, wriggling body, dark thoughts momentarily receding.

'Oh yes, you're a good boy, yes you are, yes you are.'

Will joins us and we both start talking in silly voices to Bo who's lapping it all up, enjoying the attention.

'Have a good afternoon?' Will asks, competing with Bo to try to land a kiss on my lips.

I put Bo down on the floor and kiss my husband properly before stretching my arms above my head, trying to work out the kinks in my neck after such a tense drive home.

'It was okay,' I reply. 'Traffic was terrible though. I went to a garden centre.' I hadn't been planning on telling Will where I'd been, but since I bumped into Mandy, I couldn't take the chance of him finding out.

'I thought you were going shopping, as in *clothes* shopping.' Will raises an eyebrow. 'A garden centre?' He sits opposite me and looks like he's trying not to laugh.

'I know right. Getting all domesticated in my old age. No, I just wanted to get some ideas for some pots out the front. It's a bit sparse out there. Thought it could do with some colour.'

'Ok-ay. So what did you get?'

'Nothing.' I fake a laugh. 'I couldn't decide. There were so many choices. I think I might need some help choosing. Maybe we could go together sometime?'

'Yeah, sure. And then, maybe after that, we could go Zimmer-frame shopping.'

I throw a cushion at his head which he manages to dodge. 'Mock all you like, Blackwell, but flowers are proven to lift spirits and nature is good for the soul.'

'Okay, okay. I'm just teasing.' He raises his hands in surrender.

'Oh, and weirdly, I managed to bump into two people I know.'

'Oh yeah?'

'Mandy from the tennis club.'

'Who?'

'You know... Mandy on reception. The one with all the make-up.'

'Oh. Oh yeah, I know. I wouldn't have put her down as a garden-centre person either.'

'She was with her mum and dad. They live nearby.'

'And who was the other person?'

I bend forward to stroke Bo, trying to hide my flaming cheeks. 'Someone I used to work with at Charwood.'

'The leisure centre, right?'

'Yeah. Haven't seen him in years, so we had a quick cuppa and a catch-up.'

'Anyone I know?'

'Don't think so.'

'Well, I've only got an hour before work. Anything you want to do?'

I release a sigh of relief before crossing the room and snuggling up to him. 'No. Let's just chill for a bit.'

Will pulls me close and I try to slow my beating heart. Hopefully, I've covered my tracks. If Mandy does decide to gossip, at least I've already told Will who I was talking to. But this lie, it's chipping away at what we have together. It's making us less real somehow. Less pure. And I know things aren't about to get any better.

CHAPTER FIFTEEN

January 2014

As my eyes snapped open, the events of yesterday came rushing in, a spring tide of unwelcome thoughts and emotions. I closed my eyes again, wishing sleep would take me back to oblivion, but no such luck. My hands rested on my flat stomach. I couldn't believe there was a little human in there. A mixture of me and Fin. It was… strange. I took a deep breath and sat up. Sian's bed was empty, a scribbled note resting on her crumpled quilt:

> *Had to go to work. Didn't want to wake you. Mum and Dad also at work.*
> *Hope you're okay. Help yourself to breakfast. Spare key on hook. You can stay as long as you need. Text me if you like. See you later.*
> *S x*

I leant down and reached into my bag, pulling out my phone. I checked and saw that Fin had left me numerous messages – all worried and apologetic, telling me he wasn't going in to work today. That he was at home waiting for me. That he wanted to sort things out. Suddenly I could breathe again as yesterday's despair evaporated. As long as Fin was on my side, everything would be okay.

I tapped out a quick text saying I was on my way. My next shift wasn't until this afternoon, thank goodness. So I'd have time to get home and make up with Fin. As I got dressed and put Sian's borrowed pyjamas in her wash basket, my stomach gurgled. But I had no time for breakfast. Fin was waiting at home for me. Hopefully, there would be no more mention of getting rid of our baby. Hopefully, we were about to plan the next stage of our lives together. With hope swelling in my chest, I grabbed my bag and left Sian's without taking up her offer of the spare key. I wouldn't need it now that Fin had apologised.

Fin's place wasn't far from Sian's, and it had stopped raining. Even so, it was a dank, grey morning, the sky dark and heavy, the pavement wet and dirty. I still couldn't get used to calling the shed *our* place. I was hoping another living solution would come along soon. Maybe we could save up and get another flat. Or maybe – like I'd mentioned to Fin yesterday – the fact we were having a baby would mean that the council would help us out until we got on our feet again. I didn't like the idea of benefits any more than Fin, but if we had no choice, then we should at least consider it.

At last, I reached Fin's dad's place, and with an equal measure of fear and anticipation, I pushed open the gate and walked around the house. Before I'd got halfway down the garden path, the shed door opened and Fin stood there in the doorframe, dressed in the same clothes as yesterday, his hair messed up, his face pale.

'I'm sorry,' he said.

'Me too,' I replied, falling into his arms, squeezing him tight, so relieved we weren't mad at one another any longer. I pressed my face into his neck, breathing in his scent. 'I shouldn't have stormed off.'

'Where were you all night?' He detangled himself from my arms and frowned at me. 'I was so worried. You never answered my calls.'

'I'm sorry. My phone was on mute. I was upset. I went to Sian's.'

He stepped back, his face darkening. 'Sian's? You told Sian our private business?'

'No. No of course not.' I couldn't let him know the truth – that I'd told Sian everything. He wouldn't understand.

'So what did you tell her?'

'I just said we'd had an argument, and that we needed some space.'

Fin shook his head. 'I wish you hadn't done that. It makes me look bad.'

'No it doesn't.' I followed him inside and closed the door behind us. 'All couples argue. It's normal.'

'But I don't want us to be like "all couples". We're better than that. What we've got is amazing. We shouldn't argue. Ever.'

I laughed, but his face was serious.

'I mean it,' he said. 'And I'm sorry. I shouldn't have lost my temper. I was freaked out, but it's not your fault. Am I forgiven?' He sat on the bed, his hands clenched, his right foot jiggling up and down.

I sat next to him, my heart filling with relief. 'Of course I forgive you. But there's nothing to forgive. Yesterday we were both in shock. We said things and did things we didn't mean. And… I love you, Fin, okay?'

'I love you, too, Anna.' He smiled. 'More than anything. Which is why this decision to have an abortion is so hard – on both of us.'

'What?' My skin turned cold. Did I understand him correctly? 'You still want me to—'

'There's nothing more I want than to have a family with you. The thought of having a child that's part you and part me, I can't think of anything better. But, not right now. You know this. You know we're not in any position to—'

'You want me to get rid of our child? But you apologised. I thought you had—'

'I've been thinking hard about it. All night.' He took hold of my arms, turning me towards him, his eyes boring into mine. 'We've wasted too much time already. Look, Anna, I've had an idea.' His hands gripped me tighter.

'Idea?' My brain whirred, the room began to spin. 'I hope it's nothing like your last idea, Fin. I'm not going to be an escort, so you can just forget about that.'

'I know. That was a stupid suggestion.'

It was good to hear him say it, but I'd thought about it afterwards, and a part of me had wondered if he'd meant it. A stab of fear crept into my gut. 'Please, Fin, can you let go of my arms?' His grip had intensified. He was holding onto me too tight.

'Listen to me,' he said, giving me a sharp shake. 'A baby will ruin everything.'

'No it won't!'

'Just listen,' he cried. 'Listen to my idea… Time's running out for us. We're already at rock bottom. Already having arguments. We can't afford to wait.'

'Fin! You're hurting me!'

Finally, he let go. 'Sorry, sorry,' he muttered, but his face had a faraway look.

'What idea are you on about?' I asked, rubbing at the sore spots on my arms and hoping his idea would include our child.

'What if we had to split up for a while?' he asked. 'Would you do that?'

My heart twisted. Moments ago, I'd been so happy when I thought we were making up. But was this just his way of letting me down gently? My gaze shifted from his face to our confined surroundings, the stale air damp and cloying. I realised I might be breathing it all in for the last time. Turning back to face him, I felt tears on my cheeks, already mourning the loss of him. 'Are you breaking up with me?'

'No,' Fin replied. 'I would never break up with you. I want to be with you forever, Anna. I want to raise kids with you, grow old with you. I promise.'

I exhaled with relief. 'So why did you say we had to—'

'I'm not talking about splitting up permanently,' he explained. 'Just for a while.'

'For how long? Why?'

'It would have to be for at least a year. Maybe two.'

My mouth fell open. 'You *are* breaking up with me. No one splits up for a year or more on purpose. Just tell me the truth, Fin.'

'I promise you, I am telling the truth. I just… this is so hard to explain. I don't want you to get the wrong idea.'

'Fin. Just say whatever it is you have to say.'

'Okay.' He rose to his feet and went and stood over by the window. Then he turned to face me. His eyes gleamed and his skin had taken on an unnatural sheen. 'Like I said, I have this idea. I'll just come out with it. Tell it to you straight. What if… what if we split up… temporarily? You find a mega-rich boyfriend and I'll find a mega-rich girlfriend, we marry them, then, a year or two later, we get rid of them, have their money, and then you and I get back together again?'

My whole body froze for a moment, my brain trying to absorb what he was saying. 'This is a joke, right?'

'I'm not joking. No.'

I looked into his face for any hint of humour. For a sign that he was winding me up. But all I saw was wild-eyed excitement, his teeth grinding together, his fingers scratching at an angry red patch on the back of his hand.

'Fin, listen to me.' I stood up, took a step towards him. 'We can't do that. It isn't… it's not…' I searched for the right word, '…*moral*.'

'Fuck morals,' he retorted. 'We'll make sure they're not nice people. We'll be like Robin Hood – taking from the rich to give to the poor. Come on, you've got to admit it's a good idea, and it could really work.'

'So, let me get this straight. You want us to marry rich people, divorce them, and then get half their money?'

'Not quite,' he replied. 'We wouldn't want the hassle of divorce. So, we marry them, pretend we're totally in love, then they each have an "accident". A few months later, you and I hook up again and console one another about the deaths of our spouses.'

'Fin?' I stared at him for any hint that he might be joking. But I found none. The look on his face was grim and determined. Desperate. 'Are you serious?' The realisation of what he was actually suggesting made my skin go cold. 'You're not serious. You can't be.'

'I am serious, Anna. It's a bloody good idea. I know it'll work.'

I couldn't believe what I was hearing. My heart battered my ribcage and for the first time in our relationship, I felt something close to terror. 'I… I think I better go.' I turned away from him with shaking limbs.

'Wait!'

I stopped and turned back, hoping he was going to tell me to forget what he had just said. That he was talking rubbish.

'Think about it, Anna,' he said, his eyes glittering. 'Just think about how our lives could be.'

If Fin thought his idea was even remotely okay, then he wasn't the person I thought he was. We'd been together since we were fifteen. He was my first and only love. We'd been through so much together. I thought I knew him. Sure he was a little rebellious, a little "out there". But *murder*?

'Those other ideas we came up with,' he said, 'they were okay, but they weren't ideal. They were too half-hearted. This is so much better. You have to admit that.' He hadn't noticed my horror. He wasn't thinking about me or our baby. 'It'll take a bit of time to set up and a lot of commitment.' His eyes stared off into the distance for a moment as he imagined his perfect plan. 'We'll each have to find someone,' he continued, his eyes focusing on me once more. 'But it'll be easy for you. Then, once you've been married a year or so, you'll have to find a way to get rid of him. For good.'

I couldn't lie to myself any longer. This wasn't a harmless fantasy of his. Fin was intent on this outrageous plan.

'Don't cry,' he said.

I put my fingertips to my face and found my cheeks wet with tears.

'It won't be forever,' he said. 'Two years apart at most. Probably less. But it'll be worth it. And then we can have as many children as you like – four, five, six… more. And we can bring them up in our huge house, far away from here, with no more money worries. We'll never have to work, or have to answer to crappy bosses again.'

I let his torrent of words fade out of my consciousness. He was like a child wishing for Christmas in July. When had he become so deluded? How had I not seen it? Maybe I'd chosen not to see it. The signs had been there for months, but I had clung onto my childish image of him. This perfect god. I snapped myself out of my daze and rose to my feet, thinking about what to take with me. I would need some clothes, my passport…

Words left my lips, but I could barely comprehend what I was saying. 'I don't want to hear any more about your plan. We're finished, Fin. I'm sorry. This is it. We're over.'

'Okay,' he stood up and nodded. I hadn't expected him to take my rejection so calmly. But then: 'Yeah, you're right. We have to act like it's completely over. Like this is the end of us. And then, once we've both done our part—'

'No. Fin, you're not understanding me. Once I leave here, I'm not coming back. Ever.'

'Anna.' He smiled. 'I know what you're doing, but there's no one else listening. You don't have to pretend. Not yet. Let's say two years from now, we'll meet up again. After it's done.'

Shit. He didn't get it. He wasn't hearing me. There was something really wrong with him. Something broken inside. He continued talking about his plans, outlining exactly what we should do next, but I couldn't listen to him anymore. I tried to block out his words. My breathing quickened. I had to get away, but would he hurt me if I tried to leave? This place was sucking the air from my lungs, squeezing the energy from my body. I'd been trapped in this poisonous cycle for far too long. Part of me still loved him – the carefree, blond-haired surfer who everyone adored. But the real Fin was more complicated. Darker. Suffocating. Only, I hadn't wanted to see the truth. I suppose I could have stayed. Could have tried to help him see sense. Get help. But I needed to break free before he broke me.

I kissed his cheek and put a fist to my heart. 'Bye, Fin.'

His face still had that excited, glazed look. The one I'd come to dread because it meant he was thinking up more outlandish plans for our future. Well, he'd just have to make plans without me. I was leaving him for good, and I wasn't coming back.

'I'll get in touch once it's done,' he said. 'You'll need to start planning, Anna. You need to do what we discussed. Go to the doctor, make an appointment for an abortion. Then find a rich guy. And remember, we mustn't have any contact while it's going on.'

'No! Stop talking like that. You're not doing anything to *anyone*, okay.' I stared at him, willing him to understand that I wasn't going to be part of this pact. 'Listen to me, this is not happening. I'm leaving you now. This is not part of any plan, we're finished for good, okay?'

But he carried on speaking. In the end, I gave up. I gathered together my meagre belongings and packed them into the holdall my parents had given me, not bothering to fold my clothes, but stuffing things in as quickly as I could. It was as though I was falling off the edge of a cliff in slow motion, freefalling, grasping out for a safety rope that wasn't there. Tears still rolled down my cheeks, and a hollowness settled in my stomach, which was ironic as my stomach was anything but hollow.

'See you in two years, Anna. I love you.'

I shook my head. 'I'm not doing it Fin.' I turned to look at him one last time, to try to get him to listen. 'Fin, you need help. I'm going now, but will you make an appointment to see a doctor? Talk to them about how you're feeling?'

'I don't need a doctor. Just see the plan through and we can have the life we've always wanted. Don't disappoint me, Anna. You better not.'

Was that a threat? I had to get out of there.

As I bent to pick up my bag, he lunged forward to grab my shoulder. I gave a squeal and twisted out of his grasp, my pulse racing. 'What are you doing?' I cried.

'Promise me, Anna.' His eyes glittered as I staggered backwards, away from him, towards the door, still clutching my holdall. 'Promise me you understand.' He was poised, his body taut as though he was about to fly at me again.

My bones turned to jelly and I prayed my legs would carry me out of there. As Fin darted forward to snatch my bag from me, I turned to make a break for it. Fin lunged at my back calling out my name, but I banged out of the door and fled down the sodden garden, desperate to be far from him. Knowing he could easily catch me if he wanted to. As I stumbled away, I expected, at any moment, to feel his hands on my shoulders, dragging me back. Instead, his voice came harsh and desperate through the driving rain, a last attempt to bind me to him.

'We made a pact, Anna!' he yelled through the driving rain. 'Don't forget!'

Sobbing and gasping, I ran. That person back there, that wasn't the Fin I knew. As I staggered away down the path and out onto the pavement, I realised something else – now that I'd left my life behind, I had nowhere to go. I didn't even have Sian's spare key any more, but anyway, it wasn't fair to lay all this at her door.

I made a decision.

Soaking wet, terrified, my life in pieces, the time had finally come to go home. To put all this behind me and return to Sweden. I would text Sian, tell her Fin and I had split. Then I would call up my parents and ask them to book me a flight. They would help me out in a heartbeat. Maybe I'd even be able to leave today.

At that moment, more than anything, I wanted to see my parents again. To fold myself into Pappa's arms and hear Mamma's no-nonsense advice and comfort. I didn't even care that she would say *I told you so*. I welcomed those words. All I knew was that I had to get out of here. Away from Fin and his terrifying ideas.

CHAPTER SIXTEEN

2017

I've done nothing since I met up with Fin at the garden centre. I have no plan. I have no idea what to do for the best. Fin gave me one month, and that month is almost up. I've wished it away. I only have one day left.

Right now, Will is upstairs in the shower, and I'm sitting on the kitchen sofa, waiting for him. We're eating out at Blackwell's tonight with Sian and Remy. As I wait, I wrack my brains to come up with some way of getting Fin to see sense, of convincing him to leave me alone. But since all this started up my brain has been looping around in circles, never able to settle on a way out. I drain my glass of Chardonnay and set the glass down on the side table with trembling fingers. I pick up the embroidered cushion lying by my side and hug it to my chest.

Problem is, Fin is not a rational person. I know the best thing to do would be to contact the police and tell them everything. Show them the texts and hope they believe I'm telling the truth. But Fin can be extremely convincing. He could make them believe I'm complicit. And the fact I married a rich man doesn't do me any favours. I could probably cope with the police finding me guilty, but the thought of Will thinking that I never loved him, that I married him for his money, that I would want to harm him in any way... I couldn't bear it.

Whichever way I look at things, I'm trapped in a no-win situation. If I tell the police, I risk losing everything. If I do nothing, Fin says he will kill my husband himself. I shiver. If only Will and I could disappear. Run away somewhere where no one can find us. I only have one day left before Fin acts. Why can't I come up with a way out? I'm not stupid. I can work something out. Can't I? But I'm fooling myself. I have no plan. I'm paralysed. Lulled into the sense that it's all been a bad dream. That it will disappear if I ignore it. I gaze down at the cushion in my lap and see that I've managed to unpick one corner of the beautiful embroidery, the strands now frayed and ugly. I've ruined it.

'Can't believe you're ready before me.' Will comes into the room dressed in a suit, his dark hair still damp, the scent of his aftershave so comforting and familiar it makes me want to cry.

'I was ready ages ago,' I say, rising to my feet. I've been too preoccupied to spend hours on my hair, nails and make-up, on deciding what to wear. Instead, I threw on a black dress, boots, a silver necklace, and tied my hair up in a high ponytail. Quick and easy. 'Wait till I tell Sian I got ready in less than twenty minutes. She'll never believe me.' It's a standing joke that we're late for everything as I always take so long to get ready. Will has given up trying to make me go any faster – he's even started telling me we're due places an hour earlier than we really are. That way, we have a chance of getting there at a reasonable time.

Will is shaking his head, laughing, and I join in. I marvel over the fact I can laugh and joke when underneath I feel as though my world is dissolving. Over the past few weeks, my whole life has become an act. Beneath every conversation lies an undercurrent of dread. I've been forcing myself to be light hearted, to make jokes, to laugh and be as loving a wife as I can possibly be. I can't risk Will asking me what's wrong. Because, if he asks the question, I may just tell him the answer.

'I'll drive if you like,' Will says. 'We can always get a taxi back.'

'Okay, thanks.' I'm glad he offered. I don't think I'd be able to keep my mind on the road.

I grab my red wool coat and a patterned scarf, pat my hair and we step outside into the damp and chilly February evening.

We arrive almost on time and find a parking space close to the bistro. It's started sleeting again and we run along the pavement hand in hand, before breathlessly pushing open the door to Blackwell's.

'Didn't you bring an umbrella?' Will's dad holds the door open as we stumble into the warm, dry restaurant, its familiar smells of garlic and burnt sugar making my appetite reappear for the first time in weeks.

'It wasn't raining when we left,' Will replies.

'We're okay, Steve,' I say, kissing his cheek. 'We parked close by.'

'Well, come through and sit down. Sian and Remy are already here. We've all had bets on what time you'd get here. You've managed to surprise us – only ten minutes late. Is that a personal best, Anna?'

'Cheeky,' I say, poking his shoulder.

He chuckles and leads us over to our favourite table near the back, on the small mezzanine area where our friends are already seated.

After more teasing about our unusual punctuality, we sit – me next to Sian and Will next to Remy. Guilt instantly assails me. I promised Sian I would help her choose a wedding venue, but I haven't been in contact with her since our girls' night in together last month.

'How are the plans going?' I ask.

She pulls a face. 'I haven't had time to look at anything yet. Too busy at work. And anyway, the weather's been too crap to look at venues.'

'Let me know when you're ready to look,' I say. 'I can't wait to have a nose around some posh country houses and hotels.'

'Are you sure?' She tilts her head. 'I know you said you'd look with me, but if you're too busy, I don't want—'

'I said I would, and I meant it. Call me with dates, okay?'

She squeezes my arm.

Will pours me a glass of the house white and I take a gulp, hoping more alcohol will ease the tension between my eyes and the racing of my heart. But instead, an acidic burn heats up my throat and dull dread beats a tattoo inside my chest, loosening my limbs and sharpening the sounds around me.

'You look a bit peaky,' Sian says. 'Feeling all right?'

'Just tired,' I say, taking a slow breath, trying to quell the panic in my veins.

Sian's snaps her head up. 'Is that... No, never mind.'

'What?' I follow her line of sight to the bistro window, but I don't see anything.

'Thought I saw someone,' she says, smoothing an eyebrow with her forefinger.

'Who?' I cry. 'Who did you see?' An image of Fin flashes into my mind. The room slants for a moment and then rights itself.

'Everything okay?' Will asks. He and Remy are staring across the table at me like I've got two heads.

I try to relax my shoulders and soften my facial expression. 'Yeah, fine. Sorry. We were just chatting.'

Will raises an eyebrow and I force out a smile. Thankfully, he and Remy go back to their conversation.

'Who did you see?' I hiss at Sian.

'Probably no one,' she says. 'But it looked like... It looked like *Fin*.'

As she says his name, my breath catches in my throat and I'm unable to swallow, unable to speak, unable to think, unable to stay seated here a second longer.

I scrape my chair back, and everyone looks up in surprise.

'Anna?' Will says, rising to his feet.

'Sorry,' I say with a false laugh. 'Bit forceful! Just going to the loo. Order for me, Will. Something fishy – sea bass or sole or something.'

'Sure.' He nods, sitting back down, a glimmer of concern crossing his face. I leave the table, making my way unsteadily to the door at the rear which leads down a narrow flight of stairs to the customer toilets. My heels echo down the stone steps and I press my right hand against the exposed brick wall to steady my descent. I have to pull myself together. I'll splash my face with cold water, do some deep breathing. That should do the trick.

Is Fin really nearby? When I followed her gaze outside a moment ago, I saw nothing but the dark, rainy night. But why would she make something like that up? What if he's lurking somewhere outside the restaurant?

At the bottom of the stairs, I turn right and walk along the brightly lit corridor that's lined with black and white prints of the ocean and other local beauty spots. As I push open the swing door that leads to the ladies' loos, I feel hands snake around my waist from behind. I smile with relief and turn around, thinking my lovely husband must have followed me down here. Instead, I almost have a heart attack as I find myself staring into Fin's hazel eyes.

Before I can let out a scream, one of his hands leaves my waist and comes over my mouth.

'Shh,' he whispers, and releases his hand from my mouth.

'What are you doing here?' I hiss, my heart still hammering. 'You have to leave. Sian thinks she saw you! What if she comes down and finds you here?'

'Don't worry about Sian.'

'This has got to stop,' I reply. 'Just leave me alone, Fin.'

'I'd forgotten how good you look,' he says. 'How good you feel.' His left hand sinks from my lower back to my backside, pulling me closer. 'You smell like—'

I wrench myself away, twisting out of his embrace, trying not to visibly shudder. How could this man – this *murderer* – once have been the boyfriend I adored?

'I haven't heard from you, Anna,' he murmurs, a vindictive look in his eye. 'You only have one more day until your deadline, and I can see that Mr Blackwell is still very much alive and kicking. So when are you going to do it? Do you have a plan yet?'

'Stop this, Fin. It was a stupid, juvenile fantasy.' I clench my fists. 'I didn't for one moment ever think you were actually going to go through with it. So, no, I'm not going to kill my husband. And neither are you.'

His lips tighten. 'Sorry, that doesn't work for me. I told you, I already carried out my side of the deal, so now it's your turn. It's too late to wriggle out of it.'

'Fin, you're a murderer. Do you understand? You've killed someone.' I swallow down bile.

'Yes.' He raises his eyebrows and mimics my tone. 'Yes, Anna. I understand.'

I shake my head. 'You've got your wife's inheritance. I'm sure you have more money than you could ever spend in one lifetime. You don't need Will's money, too. Just please… go and live your life. Leave me alone to enjoy mine. If you ever felt anything for me, then let me go. Just… just try and be happy.' Although I wonder how happy he could ever be, knowing he murdered the person who loved him most.

'Tell me, Anna, why did you marry Will? I'm sure it can't have been for his looks and winning personality. He's not exactly handsome and he looks boring as fuck.'

I push my shoulders back. Will may not be traditionally good-looking, but he's funny and kind, and to me, he's the sexiest man alive. It sets my teeth on edge to hear Fin talk this way about the man I love. 'Will being rich – it's just a coincidence. Despite what you might think, I never married him for his money. I didn't even know how rich he was when we met. He didn't flaunt it. He's not like that.'

'I don't believe you. He's absolutely loaded. As soon as I saw you were marrying him, I knew you must have come fully on board with the plan. Becoming the wife of a multi-millionaire was like sending me a declaration of your love.'

'Just listen to me,' I hiss through my teeth. 'Like I've told you a hundred times before, I need you to forget your "plan" – I make air quotes – 'and get on with the rest of your life… without me. I'm not doing it.' I glare at him.

Fin looks as though he's about to argue, but then he nods silently and walks away, his footsteps echoing along the corridor. I watch as he leaves, as he turns to go up the stairs. My heart is pounding, my palms clammy and I feel as though I'm about to throw up. I can't let Will and my friends see me like this. I need to pull myself together before I go back.

The distant sounds of the restaurant above swell and recede like waves rolling in and out. I push open the bathroom door and head unsteadily towards one of the two cubicles, locking the door and sitting on the toilet seat. Does Fin leaving mean he's accepted my decision? I hope so. But I can't believe it will be that easy. I know Fin. He's stubborn and determined. And now he's also a murderer. Saliva floods my mouth. I stand, lift the toilet seat and throw up my two glasses of wine into the bowl. What the hell am I going to do?

CHAPTER SEVENTEEN

I peer out through the casement doors to the back garden, but the rain lashes down making it difficult to see through the glass.

'Anna!'

There it is again. I'm sure that's Will calling my name. He volunteered to take Bo outside for a pee, but it's blowing a hoolie out there.

'Anna!'

Okay, it's definitely him. As I open the door, the wind catches it, flinging it back against the outside wall. I'm lucky the glass didn't break. Panic grips me. Is Will okay? I can't see him from here. Without pausing for shoes or a coat, I rush outside onto the vast, stone patio which wraps itself around the rear of the house, one-third of it taken up by the swimming pool that's covered over for the winter. The wind snatches my breath away, and I peer down the garden trying to catch a glimpse of my husband, my ears straining to hear his voice.

I move as fast as I can, pushing against the wind, down the sweeping, circular steps onto the emerald lawn, a decent sized garden by Bournemouth standards. The end of the lawn has been sectioned off with a wooden fence, low enough not to obscure the sea view, but secure enough to stop people venturing beyond as the ground isn't stable near the cliff edge, especially after prolonged bouts of wet weather, like now.

As I slip and skid across the grass, all I can think about is Fin's visit to the restaurant last night. And how Will could be in trouble.

In danger. Has Fin engineered something already? I still have a day left. Surely, Fin isn't here. My heart hammers and I choke back a panicked sob. It's my fault. I should have said something. Warned my husband. Please let him be okay, and I promise I'll tell him everything.

Then I see him, a dark shape at the end of the garden. It looks like he's lying by the fence. 'Will!' I scream. 'Will, are you okay?' *No, no, no.*

To my absolute relief, he turns his head and waves at me. 'Get Bo's lead!' he yells. 'And treats!'

Breathless, I dash towards the house, up the steps and into the kitchen where I almost slip onto my arse across the polished limestone floor. I snatch up Bo's lead from the window sill, but I can't spot his box of treats. My mind is whirling. Bo must have slipped through the fence. I hope he's okay. At least Will is fine, I tell myself. That's the main thing. I need the treats to coax Bo back, but I can't think where to find them, so instead, I lurch over to the fridge, open the door and scan its contents, tearing off a chunk of chicken breast from a whole, ready-cooked chicken. Then I dash back outside and half run, half fall down the steps. I squelch across the sodden lawn, in my socks, towards my husband who's now on his feet, calling over the fence to Bo.

'Little monkey got through!' Will cries out to me. 'There's a hole in the fence. I can't believe I never noticed it before.'

I look down to where Will is pointing and see that two of the wooden slats are missing from the bottom, making a gap just large enough for a small dog to wriggle through.

'Bo! Bo!' Will and I call his name, at first in the high-pitched voice our dog trainer uses, but then our voices change to a sterner tone. Nothing works. Bo isn't heeding our cries.

I lean over the fence next to my husband and scan the wild area of lawn.

'There!' I thrust out a finger as I spot a tiny, dark shape in the distance, a subtle movement beneath one of the holly bushes. 'I'll squeeze through and get him. Hopefully, this bit of chicken will lure him back.'

'No, it's not safe.' Will pulls me back. 'The ground's really unstable out there. I'll go. Give me Bo's lead.'

'No way,' I reply, my mind filling with awful scenarios. I realise this has to be something to do with Fin. Fences don't make holes in themselves. I can't let Will go through there. What if Fin's hiding in the undergrowth or behind a tree? What if he's planning to…

But Will has already forced the rusted bolt back on the gate and pushed it open. He snatches the lead from my hand and strides through.

'Stay here,' he orders.

I ignore him, following behind, alert for any other sound or movement – any signs that someone is out here. It's almost impossible to tell, though, as the wind howls and the trees and bushes sway and groan, branches creaking, the surf beyond crashing against the shore.

Will says something, but the wind whips his voice away.

'Can't hear you!' I yell.

'The chicken!' He holds out his hand and I place half of the squashed piece of chicken breast in his palm.

'Bo!' I call 'Here, boy! Treat!' As we draw closer to him, we can see he's chewing and tugging at something gross, ignoring me and Will completely.

'Tread carefully,' Will says. 'I don't know how safe we are here.'

Together, we gingerly step across grass and weeds towards our puppy, calling to him as we go. I wince as something sharp digs into the sole of my foot, but I ignore the pain for now. As we finally reach Bo, I catch sight of the jagged cliff edge ahead and I inhale sharply at the exposed earth and tree roots, at the almost vertical drop. A couple more steps and we would tumble down onto the concrete promenade below. No one could survive a fall like that. I hadn't realised quite how close we were to the edge.

Now we're near him, I can see what Bo is chewing on – a huge great slab of raw meat. How the hell did that get there? My blood turns to ice. I whip my head around, trying to see if I can spot Fin. Has he done this? Or is it just a strange coincidence?

'Bo!' Will calls. 'Here boy!'

I join in, calling to our puppy. But he's intent on his find, ignoring us completely.

'Do as I say this time and stay here,' Will says. 'I don't think the ground is strong enough to hold both of us.'

'Don't go,' I say. 'It's too dangerous. Bo's lighter than you. He'll be fine. He'll come back to us in a minute.'

'But what if he runs the wrong way and goes over the edge?' Will runs a hand through his soaking hair. 'I'll tread carefully.'

'Will, no. Please.' But it's too late. He's already walking over to the edge, and all I can do is watch.

'Be careful!' I cry out, my knuckles in my mouth.

Will wafts the chicken over Bo's nose and our disobedient puppy instantly drops the hunk of bloody meat, snapping at the chicken and wolfing it down in one greedy gulp. Will scoops him up, but as he steps away from the holly bush, I see the bush tilt over.

'Look out!' I scream. 'Run this way!'

Will freezes for a second and then does as I say, sprinting towards me with long strides, Bo in his arms. To my horror, the piece of land where he was standing only seconds ago has crumbled away, sliding down the cliff face. With a roiling stomach, I grab Will's free hand, trying to pull him away, through the gate to safety. But he stops for a split-second and turns back to watch as another metre of land crumbles away.

'Come on,' I yell. 'It's not safe.'

We run together through the gate, across the lawn, up the stone steps and finally into the warmth and safety of the kitchen where

I slam the door closed behind us. My heart batters my ribcage, and the sound of our ragged breathing fills the room.

'Wow,' Will says with a strangled laugh. 'Did I almost die back there?'

I shake my head. 'That was the stupidest thing, Will.' I hit him gently on the shoulder. 'You could've gone over. I could've lost you.'

He breathes out heavily. 'I think I need to sit down.'

'Shall I make you some sweet tea? For the shock.'

'Whisky,' Will says.

I wipe my face, tears mixing with rainwater. 'I thought… I thought I was going to lose you…'

'Shh, shh.' Will pulls me into a bear hug. 'I'm fine. We're fine. Nothing happened, okay?'

I sniff and nod, hugging him, mindful of Bo in between us.

'Is he okay?' I ask, stepping back and examining the shivering little bundle in Will's arms.

Will places Bo down on the kitchen floor whereby he promptly shakes himself spraying yet more water over us. We can't help it, we both laugh, a kind of manic, hysterical, laugh of relief.

'I think he's fine,' Will says, rolling his eyes. 'You're soaked through to your skin, though.'

'So are you.'

'At least I'm wearing a coat. And where are your shoes? Anna, you're bleeding!' His face creases in concern.

'What? Where?' I follow Will's line of sight to the floor where I'm standing in a puddle of rainwater and blood. As I gaze at the red pooling liquid, the pain in my foot returns with a vengeance. 'Ow!' I gasp.

'What did you do?'

'I think I trod on something.' I grit my teeth as pain pulses on the sole of my foot. 'I remember a sharp pain, but then I forgot about it, what with you nearly plunging a hundred foot to your death.'

'Let's have a look.'

I hobble over to the kitchen island, walking on my heel so I don't bleed all over the floor again. Then I hop up onto one of the stools and let Will peel off my sock.

'Looks like you might have trodden on a nail or a sharp stone or something. It's not too deep, just a lot of blood. Is your tetanus jab up to date?'

'How long do they last?'

'Ten years.'

I count backwards on my fingers. 'Yeah, I had a shot about seven or eight years ago, when I was in sixth form.'

'Okay. Let me grab some antiseptic and clean it up. I can't believe you went out with no shoes on.'

'And I can't believe you walked over to the edge of a crumbling cliff in a rainstorm.'

'Yeah, well, let's promise each other to be more sensible in future.'

I try to smile. But none of this can have been an accident. This whole thing was engineered. A hole in the fence? A slab of meat left at the cliff edge? This was Fin's doing. Suddenly anger churns in my stomach, hot as lava, turning just as quickly to ice-cold terror.

I remain seated and let my husband dry and bandage my foot.

'I forgot to get your whisky,' I murmur.

'Let me finish this, then we can both get dry and have a drink, yeah?'

'Thanks.'

Will smiles up at me, rainwater dripping from his hair onto my jeans.

'I wonder how much garden we lost,' I say, picturing that holly bush tilting and sliding away.

'Not too much, I hope. It's all the rain we've been having. Plus my great clod-hoppers trampling near the edge. I'm so stupid. I should've listened to you, Anna.'

'At least you're safe. That's the main thing.'

'We'll have to get someone to come and take a look at the cliffside. It might need serious work to shore it up.' He looks up at me. 'There, all done. Does it hurt?'

'No, it's fine. Thanks, Dr Blackwell.'

'Now, I'll dry off the little hooligan who started all this.' Will straightens up and walks over to the cupboard where we keep Bo's stuff. He takes out a towel and scoops Bo up in it, rubbing at his fur. Bo squirms and growls, thinking it's a game, biting at the edges of the towel. After a minute or so, Will deposits him into his furry bed, and he flops down with a contented sigh, his nose buried under his tail.

'I think we need to dry off, too,' I say with a shiver, sliding off the stool and testing my weight on my injured foot. To my relief, it feels fine, just a little sore.

'That was weird, though, wasn't it?' Will says, staring out of the kitchen window. 'That hole in the fence – I've never noticed it before. And that meat on the cliff edge… What the hell was that doing there?'

This is the moment to tell Will what's really going on, but I'm too shaken up to know where to start, I need some time alone to think about how to broach it. I don't want it to come out the wrong way. 'We've never had a tiny puppy before,' I say. 'I guess a hole in the fence isn't something we'd necessarily pay attention to if we didn't need to.'

'I suppose.' He turns back to look at me, his expression thoughtful. 'But it's still a bit odd, don't you think?'

I shrug, faking nonchalance. 'We'll have to get a new fence panel.'

'Yeah, looks like we'll have to take a trip to a garden centre after all,' Will says, raising his eyebrows and smirking.

'Ha ha,' I reply. But inside, my gut clenches and my throat tightens. Was Fin out there earlier, watching us? Is he out there now? Dark spots appear at the edge of my vision. I lean on the island and breathe in slowly. And out again. In. And out. My perfect life is being taken apart. Soon it will be completely destroyed… if I don't do something to stop it. To stop *him*.

CHAPTER EIGHTEEN

'Anna. Anna!'

'Huh?' His sharp tone jolts me out of my mini-panic attack.

'I think Bo's about to throw up!' Will strides across the kitchen to where Bo's body is heaving, his head thrusting forward as he retches and gulps.

I grab the weekend newspapers off the coffee table just in time to shove them in front of Bo as he pukes all over the sports section. Chunks of undigested chicken breast and raw meat froth into the newsprint.

'Bo!' I cry.

'It's the meat. Probably disagreed with him.' Will bends down to soothe and stroke Bo as he continues retching. 'Do you think he's going to be okay?'

'He doesn't look okay,' I say. 'Will… that meat… I think he might have been poisoned.' Would Fin really do something so evil? Bo is panting and heaving again. 'We need to get him to the vet's.'

Will stares up at me, eyes wide, still stroking Bo. 'You're right. You call them while I clean him up.'

We've already registered him with a local veterinary clinic, so I grab my phone and call the number.

'Vet's on the Corner, can I help you?' The receptionist's voice over the phone is calm and efficient.

'Our puppy's only four months old and he's vomiting and panting,' I say, my voice breathless and wobbly.

'Are you registered with us?'

'Yes. Our dog's called Bo. Bo Blackwell.'

'Bring him in now,' she says, still calm, still efficient. 'Mark will see him straightaway.'

'Thank you so much.' I give Will a nod and we pull dry coats over our soaking wet clothes, slip on our shoes and leave the house, oblivious to the wind and torrential rain. 'You drive the Land Rover,' I say to Will. 'I'll take Bo.'

Once we're in, Will pulls out of the driveway. Bo is lying on my lap, whining, his eyes half-closed.

'Hurry, Will. He's in a really bad way.' I stroke his tiny, damp body, praying the vet will be able to do something. 'It's okay, little one. It's okay,' I croon. 'You'll be fine.' But I'm not at all sure that he will be.

Will screeches into the vet's car park, parking across three spaces, and now we're rushing as fast as we can into the practice, crossing the waiting room to the curved reception area.

'Bo Blackwell,' Will says to the receptionist in a loud voice. 'We just called.'

She nods and picks up the phone. 'The Blackwell puppy's here.' She replaces the phone and gives us a sympathetic smile. 'Mark's coming.'

We turn towards the door on our right, not bothering to sit down. Seconds later, the door swings open and a thirty-ish-year-old man in a white coat pops his head through the door, sees us standing there and beckons us to follow him.

'Bo?' he asks, as we walk down a corridor which smells of fur and antiseptic.

'Yes,' Will replies. 'He's been throwing up.'

'But now he's gone really still,' I add, my voice wobbling. 'He ate some raw meat that he found.'

We follow the vet through to a small room with a high steel counter. I relinquish Bo, laying him carefully on the counter. He is barely moving; his eyes are half-lidded.

The vet takes his stethoscope and places it on Bo's chest. I hold my breath. Will takes my hand and squeezes.

'Is he going to be okay?' Will asks. 'He ate some raw meat that he found outside. He was fine one minute, and then suddenly he threw up, and then he just lay there panting.'

The vet holds up a finger to tell us to give him a minute. Unsmiling, he removes his stethoscope, letting it hang around his neck, then he rests his hand lightly on Bo's ribs. Next, he places two fingers on the inside of Bo's back thigh. Finally, after what seems like an age of waiting, he looks up at us. 'Okay, it's a good thing you brought him in when you did.'

'Will he be okay?' Will asks.

'Do you have any of the raw meat with you?' the vet asks. 'I need to test it.'

Will explains about the landslide at the end of the garden, and how the meat has gone down the cliffside along with several feet of our garden.

'Sorry, to hear about that,' the vet says. 'You should check that the meat didn't end up on the promenade below. It could end up poisoning someone else's dog.'

'But will Bo be okay?' I ask, my voice unnaturally high.

'There's every chance he'll be fine,' the vet says. 'I'll put him on some intravenous fluids to dilute anything untoward. And I really do advise trying to get hold of the rest of that meat. If someone's going around poisoning dogs, we need to warn people to be on the lookout.'

'Okay,' Will replies.' We'll try to find it.'

I know very well that the dodgy meat was meant for our dog alone, and a burning rage begins to swell in my belly. This is like a waking nightmare, like I've entered some alternate reality where nothing is as it should be.

'Leave Bo here,' the vet says. 'I'll do everything I can to get those toxins out of his body. I'll give you a call in a couple of hours to let you know how the little fella's doing. But in any case, I'd like to keep him in overnight, maybe longer, until we're sure he's back to full health.'

I bend down and place a kiss on Bo's silky head, stroking his warm body and telling him he's going to be fine. Will does the same before we leave him in the care of the vet. We've only had Bo a short time, but he's already part of our family. I love him so much, it's like a physical pain to leave him behind.

In a daze, I walk with Will out of the building and back to the car. As I click my seatbelt on, my phone buzzes, announcing a text message. I reach into my bag and pull it out. I can already guess who it's from. Dread and anger vie for space in my chest. I stare at the screen with glazed eyes:

I set it all up for you, and you wasted the opportunity. All you had to do was nudge him over the edge. No more second chances. I'm going to do it myself.

I can't put this off any longer. I can't not act. It's time to tell Will what's going on. Fin has tried to kill our dog and Will is next on his list. I toy with the idea of limiting the truth. Of telling Will that Fin is simply a deranged ex-boyfriend trying to split us up. But I can't do that. My husband deserves to know what he's up against. I need to tell Will that Fin has killed before. If I am to keep him safe, I must tell him the absolute truth. And I must tell him tonight.

The thought of Will not believing me, the thought of him no longer loving me hurts so much. But the thought of Fin hurting him scares me more.

After a silent drive home, Will pulls into the driveway and turns off the engine. As dusk blooms around us, we sit in the car next to one another. I'm so worried for Bo, but I can't allow myself to cry. I have to tell Will that he will be targeted next. If it wasn't so bloody terrifying, I would laugh at the absurdity of it all. Am I losing my mind? It certainly feels that way.

'Anna?' Will is already out of the Land Rover. He has opened the passenger door and is waiting for me to get out, too. I slide out, closing the door behind me. We stare at one another for a moment, our eyes glistening. Will clears his throat and I turn away, head towards the front door and slot my key into the lock. The wooden door is stiff, swollen with rainwater. I give it shove and it finally scrapes open. Bo doesn't come rushing into the hall to greet us. The house is silent and dim.

Will heads straight through the hallway while I disable the alarm. I straighten up and press my palms against the wall, leaning there for a moment, taking a breath until I finally gather enough energy to follow Will through to the kitchen.

'Who would have done this?' Anger twists his voice. 'It can't have been deliberate, can it?'

I stand there, my brain working, trying to figure out exactly how I should tell my husband about my ex-boyfriend.

CHAPTER NINETEEN

Will has fired up the log burner in the lounge. We've showered and changed and I've poured us each a glass of wine. My body has warmed up, but a coldness has settled inside me, a dark chill spreading outwards.

'Here's to Bo getting better quickly.' Will raises his glass.

'To Bo,' I murmur, hardly able to get the words out. My throat is tight, my chest constricted. I sit next to Will on the sofa watching the yellow flames dance inside the burner. 'Will,' I begin, but then trail off.

'What is it?' he prompts.

'I know what happened… to Bo. The poison. It was deliberate.' I gaze across at my husband to register his expression. But he just gives me a sad smile.

'He might not have been poisoned,' Will says. 'It might have been something—'

'No.' I cut him off. 'I mean I actually know what happened…' My heart begins beating inside my ears and I'm trying desperately not to cry. I have to get this out. He needs to know what's going on.

'Anna, what is it?'

'You know I had a boyfriend at school – Fin.'

'Yeah. You told me about him when we first started going out. A surfer, right?'

I nod.

Will is frowning now, staring hard at me. I've started this, so I must push on and tell him the rest. 'The thing is, Will…'

'You don't still love him, do you?'

'No!' I cry. 'Absolutely not.'

'Okay.' Will exhales. 'I thought, for a minute you were going to say…' He takes my hand and kisses my knuckles.

'It's nothing like that,' I say, wondering if he'll think what I'm about to tell him is better or worse than what he thought. 'Just please let me finish explaining.'

'Of course.' He lowers my hand back onto my lap and takes another sip of his wine. I take a large gulp of mine. The wood burner roars and my cheeks grow hotter with every passing second. I place my glass on the arm of the sofa and shift my position.

'Fin has issues,' I say. 'Serious issues. The reason we broke up is because he was becoming delusional, bordering on insane. When we were together we were dirt poor. We lived in his dad's shed. It was a pretty desperate situation.' I glance up at Will and he's looking at me, nodding, sympathetic. I swallow and continue. 'Fin used to come up with these mad ideas for us to make some money. I always thought he was joking. But towards the end of our relationship, I realised these ideas of his, they weren't jokes. They weren't hypothetical. They were real plans that he wanted us to go through with.'

'What kind of plans?' Will asks.

'Dangerous ones,' I reply.

'Anna. Just tell me.'

'He…' I inhale deeply and stare up at the ceiling, tapping at my cheek with my forefinger. 'Before I tell you this, I need you to know that I did not go along with his schemes. And when he told me about it, I finished with him immediately. And I never saw him after that. I honestly thought that was the end of it.'

'You're scaring me, Anna. Did he have something to do with what's happened to Bo?'

'Yes.' I put my fists up to my face, pressing them against my mouth, trying desperately not to cry. I need to finish telling him the rest without losing it.

Will rises to his feet and holds his hands up, his fingers splayed. 'Your ex-boyfriend tried kill our dog? Why? Why would he do that? If he did it, we need to call the police. Now.' He glances around, presumably for his phone.

'Wait,' I say. 'It's worse than that. There's more. Please, sit down.'

Will shakes his head. 'I can't sit down. Just tell me the rest.'

'Please, Will. Sit down. I can't talk to you while you're—'

'Fine,' he snaps, sitting back on the sofa. Then his face softens. 'Sorry, I didn't mean—'

'It's okay.' I take a breath. 'Fin had this crazy idea. When we were together, he wanted us to split up temporarily. He wanted us to find wealthy partners to marry.'

Will presses his lips together and frowns.

'At first, I thought he wanted us to marry them, divorce them and keep half the money – which, by the way, I would never have done. But it was so much worse than that. He wanted us to marry and then arrange for our rich partners to have an "accident".' As I try to explain, sweat forms on my upper lip, on my scalp, under my armpits.

'Murder,' Will says, shaking his head.

I nod.

'You're supposed to murder me?'

'No! I told you, I never agreed to anything. I finished with him the minute I knew he was serious, long before I even met you.'

'But you married me. And I'm… rich.' He gives a bitter laugh.

'Oh, Will. This isn't coming out the way I wanted it to.' Now it's my turn to get to my feet. My brain is racing, and I can't think of the right words to explain what's going on. I walk towards the fireplace and then back again.

'Sit down, Anna, and tell me the rest.' His voice is hard. Harsh, even. But I can't blame him. This is a lot for him to take in. A shock.

I do as he asks and sit on the edge of the sofa, my fingers knotted together. I try to get my thoughts in order so I can explain the rest.

'When I left Fin, I put him out of my mind. We never had any contact and I never thought anymore about his suggestion. Not for a moment. We broke up over a year before I even met you.'

'At the tennis club,' Will says. 'We met at the club.'

'Yes. I was living with Sian at the time. I was miserable, depressed.'

'Because of Fin? You missed him?'

'No. I was glad to be away from him. I was depressed because I had nothing in my life. No qualifications, no proper career, no relationship. Sian made me join the tennis club to try to cheer me up.'

Will's eyes narrow and he shakes his head.

'What?' I say. 'Don't you believe me?'

'I never thought of you as a gold digger,' he says.

Those two words wound me. They slice at my heart.

He continues, 'I purposely never tell people I'm wealthy to avoid them treating me differently. But maybe you'd already done your homework.'

'Will! No! I promise you!' A hard lump has formed in my throat. My whole life is disintegrating around me like ash.

'Anna, you're telling me about Fin's plan and saying you never went along with it, but then you just so happen to bump into a multi-millionaire at the tennis club. I don't understand. I mean, look at you – you're movie-star beautiful, and I'm not exactly Leonardo Di Caprio.'

'I never knew you were rich. I fell for *you*, Will. I love you. You *know* that.'

'I only know what you chose to tell me. Is Sian in on the deal, too?'

'Sian?' I blink and try to refocus. 'What! There is no deal– not as far as I'm concerned! Please, Will. I love you. I adore you. You're the best thing that's ever happened to me.'

'And Bo?' He shakes his head rapidly as though trying to rid himself of something. 'Our sweet puppy? Fin poisoned him? Or was it you?'

I jerk back as though punched. 'Will! No! I would never… I love Bo. I don't know how you can ask me that.'

'You're my wife and… I don't even know you.' His voice breaks, but then he sniffs and sets his face into a hard mask.

'You do know me.' I say, trying to catch his eye, trying to make him see I'm telling the truth. 'I am exactly who I've always been, Will.'

'That's what scares me,' he says. Then he takes a breath and lowers his voice to almost a whisper. '*You* scare me, Anna. The things you're saying…'

'I know. I know.' I press my palms together and bring them up to my face in mock prayer, my thumb pads under my chin. 'It's a massive shock. Look. Whatever else you believe, please believe me when I tell you you're in danger. Fin is completely deranged. He's killed his wife and now he wants to kill you.'

'He's *killed* his wife?' Will rubs at his mouth with the flat of his hand. 'He's actually killed her?'

'He…' I stammer out the words. 'He made it look like an accident while they were on holiday.'

'So, you're in contact with this psycho? He keeps you informed of his progress?'

'No!' I cry, willing him to see into my heart. To realise that I would never conspire against him. 'Fin sent me a text last month, and that was the first I'd heard from him since we split up. He sent me a picture of his dead wife. It was sick. He told me it was my turn next, that I had to kill you and that if I didn't do it, then *he* would. I think he poisoned Bo as a warning to me. As a threat.'

'Fuck!'

Will never swears. I clutch at his arms, trying to get him to look at me, but he shakes me off, lurches abruptly to his feet and strides across the lounge and out into the hall.

'Will! Where are you going?' I get up to follow him, but he's out the front door too fast, slamming it behind him. I wrench it open.

'Will!' I call. 'It's not safe!' But he's already in his Merc. The gates are swinging open and he drives away, foot hard on the throttle.

I stand in the doorway, my heart hammering, my body shaking. How did that all go so wrong?

My bag sits on the hall table, I fumble inside for my phone, pull it out and clumsily call his number. But his ringtone sounds from the kitchen. *Damn.*

I grab my car keys from the hall table, slip on a pair of trainers, set the alarm and step outside, pulling the front door closed behind me. It seems like weeks since Will and I were in my Land Rover coming back from the vet's. I can't believe it was only a couple of hours ago. I climb into the driver's seat and screech out of the driveway, turning right, hoping to catch a glimpse of tail lights, but the road is empty. I drive to the end of our road and bring the car to a stop, glancing left and right, head spinning. I'm panting as though I've run a marathon. Where could he have gone?

Is this it? Are we over? What do I do now? And how do I keep him safe?

CHAPTER TWENTY

I remember a night, years ago, waiting for another man to come back to me after an argument. But this is so different. I love Will with every part of my being. He's kind, funny, gentle. I would trust him with my life. And I went and shattered that trust this evening. As soon as I received that first text, I should have told my husband. We could have worked it out together.

From my car, I call Sian, call Remy, call his dad, asking if Will is with them, saying he's left his phone at home, trying to keep my voice light so they don't realise anything is amiss. But no one has seen him.

I search all our usual haunts – the bars and the restaurants – not really believing he'll be in any of them. I even scour our local beach in the dark. But he doesn't seem to be anywhere. I drive home, hoping he'll be there, waiting, willing to forgive my secrecy, to believe I've always loved him. But the house is empty so I scribble him a note and leave it by his phone, telling him to call me as soon as he gets in.

I drive around some more, cruising the quiet streets of Westbourne, the beach roads and chines. But I don't see him anywhere. Now I'm parked up on the clifftop, my phone in my hand, willing him to call me. He can't stay away forever. He'll have to come home eventually. Did he not hear me say that he's in danger? Fin is out there somewhere with evil intentions. Will isn't safe. Not at all.

And then it hits me. I think I might know where Will has gone.

I tap the location into my GPS and follow the disembodied woman's voice to where I hope my husband will be. I barely pay attention to the road, my mind awash with guilt and fear. Wishing I could turn back the clock. My route takes me through Canford Cliffs village, down the hill towards the harbour, and then up along Shore Road and into Sandbanks Road. The streetlights reflect off the water and off the wet tarmac of deserted pavements. I make a right into Elgin Road and drive a short way along the residential street until I see it – Will's Mercedes, parked up on the left by a neatly clipped hedge.

I pull over at an untidy angle behind his car and unclench my fists from the steering wheel. Sadness slows my racing pulse. I was right. Will has come to the cemetery. To see his mum.

As I get out of the car, the wind hits me, making my eyes water. I turn left onto the pathway that leads to the graves. There are no locked gates to climb over, but there are also no lights. The way is dark and silent apart from the gusting wind, the rustling leaves, and my sneakered footsteps on the concrete path. I know where Helen Blackwell's grave is – we visit her quite often. She was one of the last people to be buried here before the cemetery was deemed full.

Will used to come here a lot before he met me. He said whenever he had a problem or felt low, it always helped to talk things through with her. I guess sometimes it's easier to talk to a dead person than a living one. Now he says he has me to talk to, and although he still comes here, it's more to do with memories and comfort, than with sadness.

The cemetery pathway is laid out like a back-to-front letter D with a cross in the middle. I need to turn left into the cross to reach her grave. Pitch black, the moon obscured by clouds, I can barely see a thing. But I'm too worried about Will to be spooked by my gothic surroundings.

Will first brought me to his mother's grave after asking me to marry him. I remember trying not to cry as he chatted away to her, telling her how he wished she could have met me. I wonder if he still feels that way now. I rub at my platinum wedding band with the pad of my thumb, thinking back to the day when Will slid it onto my finger with so much love in his eyes. Will he ever look at me like that again?

I stop. A light over to my left illuminates one of the gravestones. Then it shifts, blinding me. I raise my arm to shield my eyes. The light wavers, getting brighter. It must be Will with a torch. But what if it's not? I hope it's not some nutter. Not Fin. I take a step backwards. And another. I want to run, but I don't. Instead, I call out in a wavering voice:

'Will?'

'Anna?'

It *is* Will. I exhale and walk towards the light.

'What are you doing here?' His voice is harsh, accusatory. He lowers his torch and I'm able to see his face, pale and taut.

'Will, thank goodness I found you.' The words tumble out. 'I was so worried. I've been looking everywhere. I came to sort things out.'

He doesn't speak.

'Will. I love you. I don't care about your money. You can write me out of your will if you want. Leave everything to charity. I don't care. Please. You have to believe me.' My voice is trembling, breaking. Tears spill down my cheeks. 'Fin's unhinged, mad. His plans are nothing to do with me. I'm scared, Will. He wants to kill you. We should go to the police.'

I realise the only way to truly convince Will of my feelings is to show him I have nothing to hide. If I go to the authorities, tell them everything, then surely he'll know I'm not in league with Fin. 'We can go to the police station now if you like.' I want to keep talking, to explain further, to make him believe me. But I force myself to stop, waiting to see if he's forgiven me at all.

Will's torch points downwards, illuminating a circle of wet grass. For a while, there's silence. Even the wind seems to have paused for a moment. And then Will finally speaks, his voice soft. 'A few days after you and I first met, I came here to see my mum. I told her I wanted to marry you. I told her I wanted to propose to you straightaway. Because I knew you were the one.' He pauses. I'm not sure if he's waiting for me to reply. I open my mouth to speak, but before I can say anything, he continues: 'I wanted to marry you but I got the sense that Mum wanted me to wait a while. That it probably wasn't wise to marry someone I'd only just met. So I heeded her advice from the grave and I waited a few months. It was probably more to do with the fact that I didn't want to scare you off by proposing too soon.'

'I felt the same way,' I say. 'I remember telling Sian that you were "the one". My soulmate.'

Will ignores my interruption and continues: 'From the day I met you, right up until tonight, I have never had any doubts about us, Anna. I've been the happiest I've ever been in my life. So, when you told me all that stuff tonight about Fin wanting you to marry someone for money, it made me feel like the past few years have been a lie. Like my happiness was an illusion you created for me. Like everything from now on will be dark and sad. Like, you may as well kill me and take my money because without you nothing is worth anything. But do *you* even exist? Are you real, Anna? Are you *my* Anna, or are you Fin's?'

'Of course I'm yours, Will. I'm here. I'm no one else's.' I take his hand and bring it to my tear-streaked face. 'I promise I will do anything to prove it to you. And I'm so, so sorry I didn't tell you what was going on sooner. I just… I didn't know how.'

'You swear it,' he says. 'You swear you're telling me the truth. Because—'

'I swear it, on my life. Will, you mean everything to me. You always have and you always will.'

'No more secrets, Anna.' He takes his hand away from mine. 'If there's something troubling you, you have to trust me.'

My heart lurches at his words. At the secret I have yet to tell him. But now is not the time. Now, the most important thing is to keep my husband safe. Everything else can wait. 'I'm sorry,' I say, the words sounding inadequate, defensive. 'I was scared, that's all. I thought if you knew about Fin's insane plan you'd think I had something to do with it.'

He rubs the bridge of his nose with his forefinger. 'I wish you'd told me the truth right from the start, Anna. I would have believed you. I love you. You're my wife. But trust is everything.'

'I know. You're right. I'm sorry. As long as you believe me now…'

'I think if you were going to bump me off you would have just done it. You wouldn't have told me about it.'

'Just thinking about it makes me ill. I would never hurt you, Will. You have to believe me.'

'I don't like the fact that you kept all this from me. But yes, I do believe you, Anna.'

My relief is overwhelming, but I don't have time for the luxury of emotion. I need to keep my husband safe. 'We have to get out of here.' I take his hand again. 'I meant what I said about going to the police, Will. I'll go now and tell them about Fin. He can't get away with killing an innocent woman. He's dangerous. I'm scared for you. For us.'

'Let's go home first,' Will says, as we walk back towards the main path.

'But what about Fin? He might be—'

'We'll be fine at home for now. I can take care of myself. I can take care of both of us.'

'But you don't know him. He's not right in the head.'

'At this precise moment, I don't exactly feel right in the head either.' He's walking so fast that I have to almost jog to keep up.

I bite my lip and then reply. 'He's already killed once.'

'Yes, and the bastard poisoned our dog. Look, Anna, if we go to the police and you tell them what you just told me, they might not believe you're innocent. Hell, I'm your husband, I love you and even *I* wasn't sure you were telling me the truth. What do you think will happen when they arrest Fin? He'll tell them you agreed to the plan. From the sounds of it, he already thinks you did agree to it. You could be arrested, too.'

'But I didn't do anything. He did.'

'Even if they believe you and eventually let you go, it'll be a bloody nightmare. His wife's dead so it'll be a murder investigation. Our lives will be torn apart, shredded. Think of what we'll have to go through. What about my dad? I can't put him through something like that. Think of the strain on all our lives. On our marriage.'

'I know what you're saying, but our lives are in danger while Fin's still out there. I really think reporting it is our best option.'

'No,' Will says, suddenly coming to a halt and turning to face me. 'No, I don't want you to go to the police, Anna. Didn't you hear what I said? What if they find you guilty?'

'But I'm not guilty. Please, Will.' But I know he's right. Fin could easily twist the truth to implicate me. It would be my word against his, and that scenario never turns out well. It's enough that my husband finally believes me.

'No,' Will says once more. 'We'll think of something else. There has to be another way to stop him.'

CHAPTER TWENTY-ONE

Back home, Will and I go from room to room together checking all the doors and windows are locked. We've checked downstairs, and now we're making our way up to the bedrooms.

'What if he's already in the house?' I whisper.

'You set the alarm. So unless he knows the code…'

'You're right. I'm just being paranoid.' Even so, as we step into each bedroom and bathroom I find myself holding my breath until we've secured every window and checked under every bed and in every wardrobe, my heart hammering.

Downstairs, we go into the lounge, make sure the curtains are tightly drawn as if these swathes of flimsy material will protect us from a lunatic. Will sits on one sofa, I sit on another.

'You hungry?' I ask.

Will shakes his head.

'Me neither.'

The silence in the room swells, the air heavy with unspoken words. Normally, this is a cosy room, a room to snuggle up in, to watch a flickering fire or an escapist movie. A room where we light the table lamps for their warm glow, not the harsh overhead chandelier which now highlights our pale, drawn faces and casts unfamiliar shadows.

'Will,' I blurt out. 'I really am truly sorry about everything. I should have told you what was happening from the start, but I couldn't think straight. I didn't know what to do.'

'Yeah,' he says. 'Well, let's not worry about that now. We need to work out what we're going to do next.' Although Will has already reassured me he still wants to be with me, his body language says differently. His manner has become abrupt, his expression tight-lipped. I guess I'd be the same if I were in his position, but it doesn't stop my head swimming with anxiousness that our marriage might not make it through all of this.

'Right,' he says, slapping his knees. 'There's only one thing we can do to be safe – we need to get out of the country.'

I exhale, relieved. This is what I wanted for us all along. It's the only way. Something else occurs to me: 'I think we might have to take your dad with us.'

'My dad?'

'Just as a precaution. Just in case Fin tries to use him… to get to us.'

He rubs his temple. 'This is a bloody nightmare.'

'I'm so sorry, Will.' My voice cracks. All I seem to be able to do is apologise.

'No. You're right. My dad's not safe. It's not your fault Fin's a lunatic. Glad your taste in men has improved since then.' He gives a grim smile and exhales.

I lean over and touch his arm, my heart swelling with love for this man who's so ready to believe me, to take my side after I've brought all this trouble to his door. 'What will you tell him? Your dad, I mean.'

He shrugs and throws up his hands. 'I'll say we're taking him on a family holiday. He won't be pleased to leave Blackwell's, though. You know what he's like.'

'Shall I go online? Book the flights now?'

'Yeah, I guess. Where do you think we should go?'

There's only one place I can think of. I just hope Will agrees. 'We could always go to Sweden,' I say. 'It'll be easy. I know the place. My parents are there if we need any help. And…' I pause.

I can't tell him the rest. Not yet. Maybe later. When we're on our way. '…No. Yeah. That's it, really. That's my suggestion.'

'Yeah, okay. Do it. Book the tickets. I'll go and get Dad. I'll text you his passport details.'

'Will, please be careful. Fin is probably out there watching us, you know that, right?'

'I'll be fine. He can't just go ahead and kill me. Not if he wants to make it look like an accident. He'll have to plan something convincing. That takes time, surely.'

'Take the Land Rover,' I say. 'He'll have a hard job trying to run you off the road in that beast.'

'Good idea.' Will rises to his feet.

I want to throw my arms around him, but I'm not sure if he'll hug me back, so I stay standing where I am, wrapping my arms around myself instead.

'Okay,' he says, scratching at the side of his chin. 'You start packing and closing up the house, I'll go and break the news to Dad that we're taking him on a little holiday. No idea what he's going to say to that.'

'I won't pack much,' I say. 'Just carry-on stuff. We can buy anything else we need when we get there, yeah?'

'Okay. Whatever you think.'

We face one another like strangers. Awkward. Unsure. He leans across and gives me a peck on the lips. It's not enough, but I make do.

Once he's gone, the house becomes even more alien. A cavernous space with too many windows and too many doors. Thankfully, I've got lots to keep me occupied. I'll book the flights first, then pack.

I go into the lounge and sit cross-legged on the sofa with my iPad. After ten minutes or so of searching, I finally find three flights from London Heathrow to Stockholm's Arlanda Airport, flying Business Class with Scandinavian Airlines at 6.40 a.m. tomorrow. I'd hoped for something sooner, but it will have to do.

I book the flights and fill in mine and Will's details. All I need now are Steve's, and we'll be good to go. I won't be able to relax until we're all on the plane.

Now, I have to pack. Still holding my iPad, I'm about to get up off the sofa when the gate bell rings. Its chime echoes through my body. I stay seated, unable to move. It rings once more, sounding louder to me this time, discordant, setting my teeth on edge. I'll ignore it. If it isn't Will or Steve, then it isn't anyone I want to talk to. At least whoever it is isn't right outside the front door – they're beyond the electric gates. They can't get in. Anyway, it can't be Fin. He wouldn't ring the bell, would he?

My phone buzzes in my handbag. Probably Will with Steve's passport details. I reach into my bag and pull out my mobile. Sian's face flashes up on my phone screen. I really don't have time to talk to her and the gate bell is ringing again. I almost ignore Sian's call, but maybe I need to hear a friendly voice to quell the total panic that's threatening to overwhelm me.

I slide my finger across the screen and hold the phone to my ear. 'Sian, hi.'

'Hey. Where are you?' she asks.

'Erm, I'm at home, but look, it's not a good time at the moment.'

'I'm outside.'

'What, here?'

'Yeah. Parked outside your gate like a loser. Been pressing the buzzer for ages. What you doing in there?'

My pulse slows and I let out a breath. 'Hang on.' Even though I don't really have time for her visit, I have to admit I'm relieved she's here. I get up and go into the hall, press the gate remote and open the front door. The gates swing open and Sian grins and waves as she drives in. She gets out of her car and totters over towards me in crazy high heels. She looks even prettier than usual, like she's ready for a night on the town.

We kiss on the cheek and she follows me in.

'Nice footwear,' I say. 'You look gorgeous.'

'I treated myself this afternoon,' she says. 'Me and Remy have been saving so hard for the wedding, I couldn't stand it any longer – went crazy in Westbourne with our joint-account visa card. He's going to kill me.'

'Remy won't mind. He loves you. And he'll love you even more when he sees you in those.'

'Ha-ha. Thanks, lovely. Is it wine o'clock yet?' she asks as we head into the kitchen.

'Sian, of course it is. It's after ten!'

'Really? Sorry. Didn't realise it was so late.'

'Anyway, look, I have to go out in a minute.'

She pulls a face. 'I really need to talk to you.'

I don't like turning her away when she's been such a good friend, but I don't have a choice. 'Sorry, but I have to go to Blackwell's – staff crisis.'

'Just half a glass of wine? A quarter of a glass? A fifth? Five minutes of your time? Ple-e-ease.'

'Okay. Come on then,' I say, striding through to the kitchen.

'Where's your gorgeous doggie?' she asks.

Her words are like a punch to my heart, but I don't have time to explain. 'Er, he's out with Will.'

'At the bistro?' She raises her eyebrows. 'Wouldn't have thought he'd be allowed in there – health and safety and all that.'

I go to the fridge, lift out a half-empty bottle of Pinot Grigio, reach for a glass and fill it half full. It's stingy of me, not giving her a full glass but I really should be packing right now.

'Thanks,' she says, taking her wine and sipping. 'Mm, that's good.'

I envy her. I would love a glass myself, but I need to keep a clear head. 'What did you want to talk about?' I ask.

'Shall we sit in the comfy chairs?' Sian walks over to the kitchen sofa, kicks her heels off and sprawls out, putting her feet up.

I don't think she's grasped how quickly I need her to leave.

'That's better,' she says. 'Love my new shoes, but I haven't worn them in yet. Feet are killing me.'

I hover by her side.

'Sit down,' she says with a grin. 'You're making me nervous standing over me like that.'

I do as she asks, sitting down on the edge of the sofa, but I decide to be blunt. 'Sian, you know I love you, but I really need to—'

'Yep, yep, sorry. I'll get to the point and leave you to your evening.'

'Is it the wedding?' I ask. 'Is everything okay with Remy?'

'Yeah, that's all fine. No, I wanted to talk to you about Fin's wife.'

It takes a few seconds for her words to sink in. Once they do, my pulse quickens and my cheeks heat up. 'His wife? You mean the accident?' *What can she possibly know about it?*

She nods, her eyes bright. 'I know who did it.'

The air goes out of my body. Sian knows about Fin. But maybe she doesn't. Maybe she's just guessing. I take a breath. 'What? How?' My voice sounds wooden. Fake. 'You know who killed her?'

She nods and takes another sip of her wine. 'Yup.' A smile forms on her lips. 'It was me,' she says, her gaze unwavering.

I stare back at her, not quite understanding what she's saying.

'Are the pieces falling into place yet?' she asks.

'Is this a wind-up, Sian? Because, it's not very funny.' And then something occurs to me. 'Has Fin put you up to this?' I lower my voice. 'Are you in danger?' I get to my feet and glance around the kitchen, checking to see if he's somehow managed to get in.

'The look on your face, Anna. It's priceless,' she says, standing up and downing the last of her wine. 'No, it's not a joke. It's true.' She places her empty glass on the arm of the sofa. 'I took the side of Katie's head off with a speedboat. It was very satisfying. Made a loud crunching sound. Lots of blood.'

'You?' Bile rises up into my throat and I try to swallow it back down, the acid burning a path to my heart.

'Yeah, me. Me and Fin, we're kind of together. Actually, not "kind of". We *are* together. As in "in love".'

My legs suddenly feel unsteady. I back away from Sian and lean against the kitchen island. This is too much to take in.

Sian is my best friend.

She can't have done this.

She can't.

CHAPTER TWENTY-TWO

'Sian. No.' It's like I've entered another dimension. 'What have you done?'

'Haven't you been listening?' She drops the smile and shakes her head. 'Fin and I are together. And I have to say, I'm a much better girlfriend than you ever were. You never supported him. Never understood him.'

I run a hand over the top of my head and try to force some air into my lungs. 'You're saying you and Fin are together? That you killed his wife?'

She tilts her head and looks at me, her lips pursed for a moment. 'After you broke up with Fin and ran home to your parents, I went round to see him, to find out what had happened.'

'I told you what happened. He wanted me to get rid of the baby.'

'Okay, well, I'll be honest. I went to see Fin because I knew that with you finally out of the picture, I might actually have a chance with him.'

I flinch at her bluntness. She may as well have punched me in the face. 'You liked Fin even back then? When we were together? For how long?' Who is this woman? How did she morph so suddenly from my lovely friend into this bitter stranger standing before me? Did she really kill Fin's wife? Is she a murderer?

'Course I liked him,' Sian sneers. 'Every girl in the whole damn town liked him. Only you were too stupid to know what you had. And after you finally left, we grew close. But our relationship was always a secret. It had to be, because he told me about your genius idea.'

'He told you *what* exactly?' I glare at her, noticing harsh new angles and expressions in her face – ones I'd never been aware of before.

'You know what he told me - he told me about your pact. I never would have thought you had it in you, Anna. It really didn't sound like the sort of thing you'd go for.'

'It wasn't. It was his idea, never mine! That crazy plan was the reason I eventually left him. He was delusional. Still is.'

Her eyes narrow. 'You really think so?'

'Of course! Do you actually think I'd marry someone for money? Let alone kill them.'

'Yeah, well,' she takes a step towards me and her gaze intensifies, 'that's why I took you to the tennis club with me when you came back from Sweden. I made out I was taking you there to cheer you up, take your mind off things. But there was another reason.'

My skin goes cold at her words and my whole body begins to tremble. Please don't let her say what I think she's about to say. I grip the counter top to steady myself. Grip it so hard, my knuckles go white. I want her to stop talking. I don't want to hear her say it.

'Fin realised you might not have the balls to go through with the plan, so I told him I'd give you a helping hand. Fin and I handpicked William Blackwell for you. Thought he would be a prime candidate with all his lovely millions. And he's not flashy with it. He's boring and subtle. Like you. So, I'm afraid it wasn't fate that you met Will at the tennis club one sunny afternoon. It was me.'

'No.' My voice is small, barely audible.

'Yeah. 'Fraid so.' Her eyes sparkle and a smile creeps back onto her face.

The weight of her admission slams into me like I'm being run over by a freight train. Each of her words a metal wheel to crush my heart, my body, my whole life. Sian is enjoying my horror. My revulsion. She's loving this. All I can think of is that my marriage is a sham. A device for someone else's greed and depravity. How can I tell Will that our relationship was engineered by my ex-boyfriend? It will break him. Break *us*.

'And what about Remy?' I ask, my voice quavering.

'Ah, Remy. He's sweet enough. He's easy to fake it with.'

'So, the wedding plans? I take it you're not going to marry him, then.'

'He's not rich enough to bother with. Remy was just my cover story. You know – two girls at the tennis club meet two guys, become an inseparable foursome. It's all puke-worthy and perfect. Plus, I get to keep an eye on you, and Remy tells me all the stuff going on with Will. It's funny, I heard about all your life-changing decisions before you ever did – I knew when Will was going to propose, that he was going to give you his mum's engagement ring, that once you got married Steve was giving you the house and two-thirds of Will's inheritance. Will and Remy tell each other everything. And I mean *everything*.' She smirks, and my hurt and shock and betrayal and fear are replaced with a flash of rage. How dare she manipulate my life like that. How bloody dare she.

'You...' There isn't a word in the English language bad enough to describe what I think about Sian right now.

'Yeah, yeah. I'm a bitch. I know. But *you*... you're such an annoying cow, Anna. Being your friend was like signing up to a life in the shadows. I'm attractive enough. I can get a guy if I want. But you were always more beautiful, more exotic, more likeable, more intelligent.'

'That's total crap.'

'Is it?' Sian gives a dry laugh. 'Anna, everything has always been about you. About your life, your boyfriend, your drama.'

I shake my head and loosen my grip on the counter top, unable to process everything she's telling me. I thought she was my friend, on my side. When did she start hating me? 'So,' I say, trying to keep the tremble out of my voice, 'you and Fin are what? Lovers?'

'Fin and I are more than that. We're soulmates. We should have been together from the start. He admits you were a mistake. You were too weak and pathetic to be with someone like him.'

'A psycho, you mean. Because that's what he is. And by the sounds of it, that's what you are, too.'

'No, Anna. We're just not tied to convention, that's all – what's *wrong*, what's *right*. Society has told us all this stuff we can and can't do, but society is hypocritical. Look at all the people in power who do this stuff. But they do it sneakily – fraud, embezzlement, theft. Bankers and directors taking massive bonuses, politicians taking backhanders and fiddling their expenses. Everyone does it. They just don't admit it.'

'I don't do it. Nor does Will. And murder is a little different to fiddling expenses.'

'Yeah, well, that's because you're both multi-millionaires. It's easy to be good when you've been handed everything on a plate. You don't *need* to take the low road.'

'I *was* on the low road, remember? I had nothing, but I didn't go around killing for money, deceiving the people who loved me. I don't care about Will's money, anyway. We could be penniless and I'd still want to be with him.'

'Bollocks. How long did you and Fin last when you were living in a shed with fuck all?'

I catch my breath for a second. Does she have a point? Did Fin and I fall apart because we were poor? Sure, that didn't help, but our problems went much, much deeper than that. 'No,' I say, shaking my head. 'No, Sian. You're wrong. Our break up was nothing to do with money. It was about something else entirely.'

'Yes,' she replies. 'It was about getting pregnant. And do you think you'd have been talking about an abortion if you'd had the money to raise a kid?'

'Like I said, it was nothing to do with being poor. It was about Fin's state of mind. His crazy ideas.'

'Believe what you want, Anna. But at the end of the day, it all comes down to money.'

'But that's what I don't understand. Fin's already wealthy. He killed his wife, he must have inherited her fortune, surely.'

'You'd think so. But it was all in trust. Katie's parents still own it. Fin got the house and a few hundred thousand, but not enough to retire on. He wasn't savvy enough to realise it back then when he married her. He's wiser now.'

Something doesn't add up about their plan for me to marry Will. It's bugging me. 'Why didn't you just take Will for yourself? Surely it would've been easier. You marry him, you kill him, you inherit.' I spit the words out at her.

'Well,' she pauses. 'It was less suspicious this way.'

'Less suspicious? No it's not.'

Sian sticks her chin out and crosses her arms. She suddenly looks defensive.

Something occurs to me. My mouth drops open. 'That was what you meant to do, wasn't it?'

'What are you on about?' She starts chewing the inside of her lip.

'I'm right, aren't I? Will was supposed to fall for *you*!'

Sian's cheeks flame and her nostrils flare.

Despite the horror of the situation, I give an incredulous smile. This means they didn't force mine and Will's relationship. It means we really did find each other. Sian wanted him for herself – to kill him and take his money. But instead, he fell for me, and I fell for him. 'You must have been so pissed off,' I say. 'We ruined your schemes.'

'Yes, well it doesn't matter,' Sian snaps. 'What matters is where we are now. Fin and I are in love and as soon as we get Will's money we're out of here.'

'And how do you think you're getting hold of Will's money? You can't inherit it. And you're not getting a penny from me.'

But I don't like the smug expression on Sian's face. She's still not telling me everything.

'Once I realised that you and Will were going to be an item,' she says, 'Fin wanted us to leave you alone, to find some other rich guy for me to marry, but I persuaded him that this was better. That this would be a perfect opportunity.'

'I don't see how. Sounds like you just wanted to make my life hell.'

'That's a bonus, I'll admit it,' she says. 'But no. Like Fin already told you, Will is going to meet with an accident and you're going to inherit his money. Only now there's a slight change of plans. I'm afraid both Will and his dad will have to die in an accident so that you can inherit everything.'

My mouth falls open as she relays their outrageous plan.

'Then,' she continues, 'instead of marrying Fin, you'll transfer the bulk of the money into an offshore account that Fin and I have set up. We'll leave you with just enough to carry on with your lifestyle so people don't become suspicious.'

'I think you've been watching too many movies, Sian. You're crazy if you think you can harm Will or Steve without anyone finding out. And anyway, how can you even think about doing something like this? You know Will. You know his dad. They love you like family. Why would you—'

'Oh, shut up, Anna. You're so predictable. So irritating.'

Up until this point, I've been in shock, my brain rebelling against Sian's revelations. But now, suddenly, that earlier flash of fury is back, my blood heating, joints locking, fists clenching. 'Don't you dare touch Will or Steve. I can tell you now, whatever you do, you'll never get your hands on their money.'

'Yes, I will, Anna.' Sian walks towards me, now, coming around the central island to face me, only a few feet left between us. She reaches into the pocket of her wool coat and I take a step backwards, convinced she's about to pull out some kind of weapon. I glance about me looking for something, anything, to defend myself, but the kitchen knife block is behind her. All I can see is the quarter-full bottle of Pinot Grigio on the counter next to me. I'm about to reach for it when I realise she's not holding a gun or a knife, but a phone. It's a cheap, plastic smartphone, not her usual rose-gold iPhone.

'Watch,' Sian says swiping at the screen a few times, then pointing it towards me, her eyes bright, a triumphant smile on her face.

I cast my gaze from her face to the phone, praying they haven't hurt Will or Steve. Will should never have gone out on his own. A video plays. I step closer. It's Fin. He's filming himself in a dimly lit room – a wooden hut of some kind. Everything shrinks down to what's on the screen. I can barely breathe.

'Hi Anna,' he says cheerfully, his voice tinny and faraway sounding. 'Look who I've just met.' Fin switches his phone so he's now videoing the corner of the room, and as he does so, my insides turn to liquid.

My hands fly to my mouth. 'No,' I gasp.

'Yes,' Sian replies.

CHAPTER TWENTY-THREE

Fin knows. I stare transfixed by the video. In the corner of an unknown room, my two-year-old daughter Olivia is playing with a doll, chattering away to it, seemingly unworried that she's with a complete stranger – her father who she's never met before now. How can he have found out that I never had the abortion? I never told him or Sian that I had the baby. I was so careful to hide her. To keep her safe.

I never wanted to be an absent parent, but after Olivia's birth, I was in no state to look after her. Diagnosed with post-natal depression, my parents offered to help me out until I got better. But I just got worse and worse, barely able to drag myself out of bed each day, dark feelings of despair washing over me, the fog in my brain refusing to clear. In the end, Pappa suggested I go and have a holiday in England, go and stay with Sian, have some fun. I didn't want to go. I didn't want to leave my little girl. But they bought me a ticket and practically pushed me onto the plane. They were desperate. Hoping a change of scenery with my best friend would help me. Hoping I would come back as the happy daughter they remembered.

It worked.

After a few weeks of moping around in England, I met Will. And sunshine returned to my life. I wanted to tell people I had a daughter, but I needed to keep the news from Fin. So, I hid my child away with my parents, terrified of what Fin might do if he found out I hadn't gone through with the abortion, terrified that he might hurt her. And when Sian asked me about the termination, I told her I didn't feel up to talking about it.

I flew home every few weeks, ostensibly to see my parents, but in reality, it was to be with Olivia. To reconnect with her. As I was falling in love with Will in England, I was also falling in love with my daughter in Sweden. Getting to know her. Taking her to the park, making her meals, reading her bedtime stories. The dark clouds of depression had lifted and joy filled my heart. The only downside was that I still hadn't told Will.

And then he proposed.

I accepted straightaway, telling myself I would introduce him to Olivia that week. But that week became the next week and the next month. It was my idea for us to have a small UK wedding – no fuss, no family, apart from Steve and a couple of witnesses. Before long, it was clear to me that if I told Will, after all this time, he would be horrified at my deception. And I still reasoned that it would be safer for Olivia to remain out of the country. Then, just before Will's thirtieth, a sense of calm came over me. It had been three years since I'd last seen Fin, way past his original deadline for us to meet up again. I was convinced everything would be ok. I loved Will and he loved me – I would confide in him about Olivia.

I was on the brink of telling him, when I received Fin's text with the photo of his murdered wife, and this nightmarish horror began. How could I tell Will about Olivia now, with all this going on? And how could I place my child in danger by making her existence common knowledge?

'Where are they?' I cry, leaning forward, attempting to swipe the phone from Sian's hand. But she's too quick and whips it out of my reach. 'How did you find out about my daughter?'

'Just a hunch,' she says. 'I've got a good sixth sense about these things.'

'A hunch?' I raise an eyebrow. 'I don't believe you. I never said anything to you about her. Never gave you any reason to suspect.'

'Okay,' she says, rolling her eyes. 'Busted – I snooped on you. Sneaked a peek at your phone and saw the photos of Olivia your parents sent. I read your texts and worked out you had a child. I was hurt you never told me about her, Anna. Thought I was supposed to be your friend.' She laughs and I want to grab her by the throat.

'Why is Fin with Olivia?' I ask. 'What does he want? To be her father? They'll never let him take her out of the country.'

'Take her out of the country?' Sian sneers. 'He doesn't want to take her anywhere.'

'So what's he doing with her?' My voice rises to a screech and I exhale slowly through my mouth, trying to calm myself down.

'Once Will and Steve have met with their accident and you inherit their millions, you can transfer it to our bank account, and we'll let you have your daughter back. And if you don't, well, you can just imagine what Fin's going to do.'

Her words hang in the air like daggers. The room is closing in, shrinking down to me, Sian, and her phone. My whole family is in danger because of this evil woman standing before me. How did I never see it? How did I ever trust her? I reach out beside me and my fist closes around the neck of the wine bottle, the glass cold against my fingers. Raising it high above my head, I charge at Sian, spitting rage.

Her smug expression falters and she staggers back. But I am pure animal fury. This woman is threatening my child. I'm going to smash her face in. As I bring the bottle down, she raises her arm to protect her face and the heavy base connects with her wrist, rather than her head. The glass doesn't break so I raise it again and bring it down once more. My aim is true this time, connecting with her temple. Still, the bottle remains intact.

'Anna!' she yells. 'Get off me you crazy bitch!' She drops her phone and grabs the front of my jumper. Tries to push me away.

I stamp my trainer down on her bare foot and she howls in pain – pity I'm not wearing stilettos. Next, I swing the bottle out to the side and sweep it forwards, whacking it against the side of her head. A satisfying crack rings out as the bottle breaks against her cheekbone, drawing blood. Sian screams and brings her hands to her face. I drop the shattered bottle and lunge forward. Grab the knife block which sits on the counter behind her. I raise it up high and bring the whole thing down on top of her head. All the knives jolt out of their slots, flying through the air. I don't pay them any attention. I don't care where they land. Whether they cut me or her.

My breathing is ragged as I watch rivulets of blood stream down Sian's face – whether from her cracked cheekbone or from the knife block, I can't tell. Her eyes roll up into her head and she crumples down over the stainless-steel range cooker, then slides to the floor, unconscious.

I'm panting like a demented creature. Triumphant yet terrified. What have I done? Is she dead? What's going to happen now? What about Olivia? I need to find her. I set the empty knife block on the counter and cast my eyes downwards, scanning the glass-strewn floor for Sian's phone, praying it isn't broken.

It's there! I spot it underneath one of the kitchen stools and bend to retrieve it. A noise startles me, makes me aware of my clattering heart.

'Anna?'

It's Will. I grab the phone and straighten up, turn around to see my husband standing by the entrance to the kitchen.

'What the hell? Your face is bleeding. Are you okay?' I realise Sian is obscured behind the huge kitchen island. Will can't see her.

'Will…' I begin, but I don't know what to say. My mind is still focused on Olivia. 'I need to… Just stay there, hang on a minute.' I swipe at Sian's phone, desperate to see the video of my daughter. To see if I can work out where Fin is keeping her. While I'm swiping the screen, Will makes his way over to me.

'What's going on? There's glass everywh— is that Sian? Anna, talk to me.' He's pulling at my arm, but I shrug him off as I tap the video and it starts to play. 'What's happened to Sian?' Will brushes past me and kneels down in front of her. 'It's okay. She still has a pulse. Was it Fin? Was he here?' He gets to his feet again and grabs me by the shoulders, giving me a gentle shake. 'Anna! Talk to me!'

I drag my eyes away from Fin's face on the screen and stare at my husband as though he's a stranger. The scent of night air clings to him and his eyes are wild with confusion.

'I'll call an ambulance,' he says, pulling out his phone. 'Or have you already called them?'

I snap out of my trance and snatch his phone away with my free hand. 'No!' I say. 'No ambulance.'

'But what about Sian? She's—'

'I said *no*. Please, Will. Just trust me. Everything's changed now. I… I need to tell you everything.' I take a breath. 'Will, I really need your help.'

CHAPTER TWENTY-FOUR

'Anna, you better tell me what the hell's going on here. I was worried *before*, but now you're really starting to scare me.' He crosses his arms over his chest and narrows his eyes.

'I know, I know. I'm sorry. It's all gone wrong. I thought it was just Fin doing this, but Sian's in on it, too, and now they've kidnapped Olivia. Will, I don't know what I'm going to do!'

'You're not making any sense.' He glances wildly from me, to Sian on the kitchen floor, and back to me again. 'We need to call an ambulance. She was breathing a second ago, but I can't tell how serious her injuries are. Give me my phone.'

'No! Will, please, just forget about Sian for one minute.' My voice veers towards a scream and I run my hands through my hair, gripping my scalp as if that will slow my racing brain.

'Anna,' Will says. 'Why aren't you helping Sian? Calm down and tell me what's happened. Who's Olivia?'

'I'm so sorry, Will. I should have told you before, but I was scared that Fin would get to her – take her away from me, or worse. And now… and now it's happening anyway.'

'Take who away? Sian?'

'No. Will…' I place my hand on the sleeve of his coat. 'Will, I have a daughter.'

He stares at me, eyes wide, mouth hanging open.

'I'm so sorry. I know I should have told you.'

'Jesus Christ, Anna. Do I know you at all?' He turns away and walks over towards the dark bay window in front of the sofa, stops and stares out at the blackness. 'More secrets,' he mutters. 'Lies and secrets.' Then he spins around to face me. 'How many more skeletons are there? Do you have an evil twin I don't know about? Bodies in the basement? This is starting to get way too crazy.'

'I promise there's nothing else. I was going to tell you last month, but then I got that awful text and—'

'Last month? Last *month*?' He shakes his head rapidly, then locks his fingers behind his head. 'What about telling me two years ago when we first met? That would probably have been the ideal time to let me know you have a secret child. I suppose she's Fin's daughter, right?'

I nod, pulling at my hair. 'But he never knew she existed. When I got pregnant, he wanted me to get rid of it – of her – but I just couldn't do it.'

'So, you lied to him, too? You lied to Fin about his child.' He exhales.

'Yes, but only to keep her safe. I thought he'd be a danger to her. And I was right. He's got her, Will. He's got my baby.' Tears are dripping down my cheeks, salt water stinging my dry lips, but I wipe them angrily away. I can't afford to fall apart now. Not when I have so much to do. Not when I have to rescue my daughter from a madman.

'And Sian?' Will says. 'Is there an explanation as to why your best friend's lying unconscious on our kitchen floor? And why you don't want to help her?'

I cross the room to get closer to Will. But his expression is thunderous so I stop once I reach the sofa, unbalanced by his glare. 'I just found out Sian's part of it.'

'What? What do you mean?'

'Apparently, she's been with Fin since before I met you. I never suspected. She just admitted that she…' I take a breath.

'That she what?'

I squirm beneath his gaze.

'Anna.' His jaw tightens.

'She was the one who was supposed to marry you.'

'What?' His gaze slides over towards the kitchen where my ex-best friend lies on the floor.

'I only just found out myself,' I say. 'She told me that when you and I met at the tennis club that first time, it was supposed to be *Sian* you fell for, not me. She wanted to marry you for your money. Instead, we ruined their plans because you and I fell in love.' The words tumble out of my mouth, and I'm willing him to understand what's going on. To realise that it's not just Will being taken for a fool. It's both of us.

Will's jaw slowly drops down. He doesn't reply.

I keep going. Spilling all the gory details. Getting everything out in one painful splurge. 'She also told me that she's the one who killed Fin's wife. They planned it between them.'

'I don't believe this,' Will murmurs.

I shake my head. 'It gets worse. They want you and your dad to have a fatal accident and then they want me to transfer your money over to them. Otherwise, they're going to do something terrible to my daughter.'

'This is insane.'

'Looks like Sian is worse than Fin,' I say. 'If it wasn't for her, I don't think any of this would have happened. Fin would have left me alone.'

'Shit.' Will runs both hands across the top of his head and clenches his jaw. 'Shit!' he cries, louder this time. 'And Remy?'

I shake my head. 'She doesn't love him. Being with him was her way of keeping an eye on both of us. But, Will, listen… Fin has my little girl. And Sian said…' my voice trembles and I take a breath. 'Sian said that if I didn't kill you and transfer your money over to them, that Fin would hurt Olivia. That I'll never see her again. So that's when I bashed Sian over the head with a wine bottle.'

Will exhales. 'Okay. Okay, I can see how you would have wanted to do that. But at least you didn't kill her. We can let the police deal with her now. Where's Fin?'

'I don't know. I'm pretty sure he must be somewhere in Sweden. Looks like he's in a wooden cabin of some kind. He wouldn't be able to take Livi out of the country. She doesn't know him. She must be so scared. Sian showed me a video as proof that Fin has her.' I wave the phone at Will.

'Is that Sian's phone?' Will says.

'Yeah. It's not her regular phone though.'

'Let's see the video,' he says.

As I sink onto the sofa, Will comes over to join me. I soak up his proximity, wondering if this will be the last time we're this close, certain he'll leave me after this is over. I wouldn't blame him.

I show him the short film, trying not to sob as the camera pans over to my daughter, her tiny blonde head bent over as she talks to her doll. I glance at Will, trying to gauge his reaction, but his face is blank.

'They're in some kind of wooden summer house or cabin,' I say. 'I'll never be able to find them. If only I knew where they were, at least I'd have some chance of—'

'So, let's have a look,' Will says. 'See if there are any texts from Fin telling Sian where they're holed up.'

'Yes, you're right!' A flicker of hope stirs in my chest. I stop the video and go to Sian's messages. There's only one other number listed, no name attached to it. It must be Fin's.

The latest text was sent from Sian. It looks like she messaged him just before coming here tonight:

Going in. I'll text you after xx

I scroll back so that we can read them all in order. The first text is from Fin and reading it makes the hairs on my neck prickle, makes me feel grubby and nauseous. They were watching me, both of them, discussing me like I was some kind of science project. I'm guessing this first text relates to the message he sent me during Will's thirtieth:

Just about to send the text. Watch her face, see what she does.

Sent :)

She didn't read it. She put her phone in her bag.

Damn. Let me know when she does.

Ok xx

She got him a Mustang for his bday – Remy said it's worth over $300k

Fuck

Ikr, that should be ours

Too right. Not long now.

Gtg text you later xx

Omg, she's read the text and now she's puking her guts up outside

Fucking yes. This will be easy. Can't wait to see what she texts back.

Anything yet?

Nope

Let me know when she replies

Yeah, of course

Did she reply last night?

Nah

Send her another one. Tell her she needs to reply.

Done

Anything?

Nope.

You'll have to do something to make her reply.

I'm outside their place. He's gone out. Shall I stand outside her gate and freak her out?

Yeah, Do it

I did it, then sent her a text. It was fucking awesome. She must be wetting her knickers right now.

Perfect! Xx

As I scroll through the conversations, each event comes back to me with sickening clarity, only this time I can see it through Fin and Sian's eyes. How they were manipulating me. Laughing at me. I turn to Will and see disbelief and horror on his face. I want to hurl the phone at the wall then stamp on it until it's nothing but crushed glass, metal and plastic. But I can't destroy it. It's evidence.

'They're absolute scumbags,' Will says through gritted teeth. 'How dare they. Look, Anna, are you okay to read this?' Through the pain of their betrayal, I realise that Will truly does believe me now. He knows I was telling him the truth, and he wants to help me. His voice softens. 'This can't be easy for you. I can scroll through the rest if you like – see if there's an address.'

'Thanks, but no. I need to see this.' I take a breath and we continue reading:

> *Stupid cow has asked me to go over. You must have really shit her up. Can't believe she still thinks I'm her friend. Wonder if she'll tell me about you…*

Careful

Of course

Well????

She told me about the speedboat accident. I faked concern, lol. She wanted me to get in touch with you to "see how you are". Yeah right. I told her to stay away, to forget about you.

Was that a good idea?

Trust me. Bet she gets in touch with you now.

We'll see.

Oh, btw, they have a new puppy

You were right, she texted. We're meeting later today at some weird garden centre!

Yesss! Good luck x

Cheers

I convinced her that I'm still in love with her but she still didn't go for the plan :(

I told her if she doesn't do it, I will.

Told you she wouldn't do it. Pathetic bitch.

Guess you were right, smart ass

:)

We'll have to think of something else.

Wish I could see you

When can you next get away?

Thursday. Usual time and place.

Can't fucking wait.

...

I did it. Followed her to the bathroom at the restaurant, told her I'm still in love with her. But she didn't want to know. There's no way she'll go through with it. I think we should forget the whole thing.

No way. We're doing this. I'll think of something.

Like what?

Not sure yet

Could poison her dog...

Not a bad idea xx

I meant it as a joke, but yeah, why not.

Could combine it with a test to see if she's willing to do the rest. Am getting a really good idea. Will get back to you soon. Need to talk properly.

Just landed

Good. But miss you already xx

...

She didn't push him over the cliff. You need to send her a text to say you're going to finish the job yourself.

I knew she wouldn't do it. No balls.

Unlike you xx

<3

Okay, have sent text. Am outside her parents flat. Will get the kid after they put her to bed

Good luck.

...

Pretty sure the dog's screwed. Pity its owner didn't chow down on that raw steak, too. Would've saved us some hassle.

LMFAO Will text you when I have her

Don't forget to send me a video

On it

Love you xxxxxxxxxx

You too xx

Soon be over. Dying to be w/you 24/7

Not long now :)

...

Got the kid. Sending video.

Am outside A's house. Can't wait to see her face when I tell her about us.

Be careful. Good luck xx

Going in. I'll text you after xx

Will and I sit side by side on the sofa in silence for a moment. I put the phone on the coffee table and wipe my palms on my jeans, feeling contaminated by those toxic words. All that hatred directed at me. Do I deserve any of it? I don't think so.

'I wish Fin was here,' Will says, 'so I could smash a wine bottle over his head, too.'

His words set something off in me and I drop my head and push the heels of my hands into my eye sockets, trying to stem the flow of tears. I feel Will's arm come around me. He kisses the top of my head. Despite my betrayal of his trust, he's still on my side.

'They're evil,' he says. 'Anna, listen to me. Don't let them get to you. There's something wrong with both of them. They've been playing us, but now we know, okay? Now we have proof, we can go to the police.'

'But he has Olivia,' I sob, turning to him. 'And there's nothing on the texts to let us know where he is.'

'The police will be able to track them—'

'But what if they screw it up? Fin will hurt Livi.' My terror and helplessness at the situation hits me all over again.

'He won't hurt her. She's his daughter.'

'I can't take the risk. And even if he doesn't harm her, he could easily take her away from me, out of spite for hurting Sian.'

'How will he know?' Will's expression suddenly changes from worried to something else, his eyes brightening. 'We can pretend to be Sian! We have her phone. Why don't you text Fin. Tell him you're coming to Sweden. Tell him to give you the address.'

'Will. You're a genius!' I sniff and swipe a hand across my eyes, my tears forgotten for the moment. I snatch up Sian's phone from the coffee table and press the power button, bringing up the stream of vile messages. Then I start tapping out a text:

> *Anna has agreed to do it! She'll do anything to keep her daughter safe. I'm going to come and join you. Text me where you are x*

I show the text to Will to get his opinion before I send it.

'Good,' he says, 'but change the word "daughter" to "kid". Sounds more heartless.'

'Okay. Good idea.' But it kills me to change the word. To talk about Olivia as though she's just some random stranger's child:
Anna has agreed to do it! She'll do anything to keep her kid safe. I'm going to come and join you. Text me where you are x

We don't have to wait long for a reply:

That's good news. But I thought you were going to stay there to keep an eye on things

I text him back:

Changed my mind. Nothing left for me to do here now. Plus it'll be easier with two of us there. We just need to wait for A to do what she promised xx

Will nods and I hit send.

A few seconds later I almost drop the phone when it starts vibrating in my hand. A call is coming in… from Fin.

'Shit, shit, what shall I do?'

'Don't answer it,' Will replies. 'You can make up some excuse why you couldn't get to it.'

As we wait for the phone to stop buzzing, I pass the phone to Will and get up off the sofa. I'd almost forgotten that Sian is still here, unconscious. But I guess she could wake up at any moment.

'Have we got any rope?' I ask. 'We need to tie her up.'

'Duct tape would be better,' Will says, rising to his feet and passing me the phone which has thankfully stopped vibrating. 'I'll go and get some from the garage.'

'What shall I text Fin?' I ask.

'Say you're on your way to the airport. Then, hopefully, he'll tell you where he is and we can tell the police where to find him.'

While Will fetches the duct tape, I quickly tap out a message and press send.

Thankfully, Fin buys it. A minute later, I receive his reply with an address near Växbo in Hälsingland. I can't believe it was that easy. The place is really close to my parents' lake cabin. I'll be able to find it, no problem.

'Got the tape,' Will grunts, walking back into the kitchen. 'I suppose I'm going to have to tie her up with it. I know what she did was unforgivable, but tying her up feels wrong.'

'That's because you're a good person, Will. Shall I do it?' I ask, getting to my feet, but feeling nauseous at the thought of going anywhere near Sian's inert body.

'No, it's okay. I can do it,' he replies.

'Sure?'

He nods but makes no move to go over to her.

'Once she's tied up, we can lock her in the spare room,' I say.

I give a start as Will's phone rings, wondering who it could be. He pulls his phone from his pocket and looks at the screen.

'It's the vet,' he says.

'Answer it,' I urge.

He does as I ask, and I have to wait for an agonising few seconds before Will gives me a thumbs up. I hardly dare hope that this means what I think it does. Will finally ends the call and exhales.

'Well?' I ask.

'The vet says Bo is going to be fine. He said he's tough for a dog of his age. Most puppies wouldn't have pulled through.' Will swipes a tear from his cheek.

'When can he come home?' I ask.

'Hopefully in a couple of days.'

'I don't know what I would have done if…' My voice cracks.

'Hey, it's okay, Anna. Bo is okay.' But there are still several feet separating Will and me.

I wrap my arms around my body.

Will looks at his watch. 'Look, Dad's supposed to be coming over in less than an hour. He was actually excited about coming away with us "on holiday". He thought it was some kind of wonderful surprise.'

I take a deep breath and try to concentrate on the matter in hand. 'You'll have to hide Sian before he gets here. We'll make it up to him. Take him somewhere after this is all over. If we're still… I mean, if you want to.'

Will doesn't reply.

I swallow down my disappointment. 'At least there's no danger to you or your dad now Fin's in Sweden and Sian's here.'

'Do you want to call the police while I tie her up?'

'Will, I'm not calling the police. I'm going to get Olivia. I'm sure Fin won't hurt her. She's his daughter, too,' I say, trying to convince myself it will all be straightforward. But a part of me isn't sure. Fin isn't all there. Maybe he doesn't even think of Olivia as his child.

'You can't go over there.' He stares at me like I'm crazy.

'I have to.'

'Give the address to the police. Let them handle it.'

'If the police go storming in, Livi might get hurt. It could turn into some kind of hostage situation.' Saying those words makes my head swim with how terrifying and surreal everything has become. 'Look, I think I can reason with him, convince him to let her go without any violence. Now he's finally away from Sian's poisonous scheming I might be able to get him to see sense.'

'I don't like it,' Will says, grim-faced. 'But if you're going over there, I'll come with you.'

I take a few more steps towards him, place my hand on his arm for a moment. 'No. Will, you have to stay here. Make sure Sian doesn't get away.' I flick a glance over to her inert body, wondering if she's still alive. 'And you'll have to keep an eye on your dad in case somehow Fin gets back here.'

'I can't let you go over there on your own.' He frowns and shakes his head slowly. 'You said it yourself – Fin isn't a rational human being.'

'I have to do this, Will. I have to stop him. I have to get my little girl. Anyway, if you come with me, it will only antagonise him.'

'I can't just let you waltz into danger on your own. What kind of a husband would that make me?'

I give him a grateful smile. 'You're an amazing husband. And I won't be in any danger. Trust me. Fin's the one out of his element. He's a townie in the middle of the forests and lakes of Hälsingland. That place is not hospitable in winter. I can use that to my advantage. And anyway, I know the area like the back of my hand.' I'm exaggerating a little. The region is massive and I certainly don't know all of it like the back of my hand, not by a long way. But I know it a damn sight better than Fin does.

'What if he has a gun, Anna? You may be Sweden's answer to Bear Grylls, but he could still shoot you.'

'He won't,' I scoff. 'Where would he get a gun? He's in a foreign country. He doesn't know anyone. He's not even expecting me to be there. He doesn't know that we know where he is.'

'I don't like it, Anna. Not at all.'

'Please.' I'm aching to walk over to Will and reassure him with kisses. To wrap my arms around him and run my hands through his hair, but we're still uneasy with each other. I can't presume that he would welcome my touch. And I couldn't bear his rejection right now. So, instead, I focus on the practical. On what needs to be done. 'I won't be more than a day or two. My flight's already booked for first thing tomorrow morning. I'll throw some things into a bag and go. Make sure I get there in plenty of time.'

Will chews his bottom lip and listens. His face drawn.

'You stay here,' I say. 'Guard Sian. Make sure your dad's okay. If things should somehow go wrong, and you don't hear from me by tomorrow evening, then you can call the police, okay?'

Will sets the duct tape on the counter. He comes towards me and takes me in his arms, holds me tight. An ache tears through my chest and I hug him back, breathing his scent, grateful for his touch and desperate for this nightmare to be behind us.

'I wish you hadn't lied to me, Anna,' he says, releasing his hold on me. 'I wish you'd trusted me enough to tell me about Olivia from the start. But I guess I can understand how things got away from you. You were trying to protect me and your daughter from Fin. So, I want you to know… when you get back, I'll still be here for you. And for Olivia, too.'

I'm so choked up by his words, I hardly know what to say. All I can manage is: 'Thank you. I love you, Will.'

He nods and takes my hand. Squeezes it once and then lets go.

'You'll be okay with…' I jerk my head over to where Sian is lying on the kitchen floor.

'Yeah. Go and pack, before I change my mind.'

CHAPTER TWENTY-FIVE

I realise it's up to me to fix this now. If I'd been honest with Will from the start, we could have reported Fin to the police after he killed his wife, and I could have told Will about Olivia. Now my daughter is in danger. And I have to save her. I never wanted to kill anyone, but I may not have a choice. As I drive to the airport, a rough plan is forming in my mind. It's risky but it's the only thing I can think of to keep Olivia out of harm's way.

Once I'm in the airport terminal, I find a quiet place to sit as the check-in desk doesn't open for another two hours. I take my phone out of my back and text Will:

Hey, I'm at the airport

Glad you got there safe. Dad's here.

Okay, great. Send him my love. And what about Sian?

She's okay.

Awake?

In the spare room. Not awake yet, no.

I'll text you again when I get to Stockholm.

Okay. Stay safe x

Thanks. Love you xxx

Love you too x

I'm pleased Steve is there with Will, but I wonder if he's told his dad about what's happened. Surely Steve will hate me for putting his son in such jeopardy. And what about Will? I know he said he would wait for me, but what if he changes his mind? He'll have plenty of time to dwell on things while I'm away from him. To think about all the trouble I've brought to his door. The secrets I've kept from him. And he'll have to guard Sian. What will happen when she wakes up? It'll just mean more stress for him. More pressure on top of everything else.

As I shift in my seat to try and get more comfortable, a call comes in... from my father. I should have called my parents already, but with everything going on, I haven't been thinking straight. I answer quickly.

'Pappa?'

'Anna. Oh, Anna. I don't know how to tell you. It's Livi…'

'It's okay, Pappa. I know where she is.'

'You know? How do you know? Is she with you? You should have told us. Oh thank goodness!' I hear him tell my mother the news that I know where Olivia is. 'We went to check on her before going to sleep, and her bed – it was empty! We didn't call you straightaway because we didn't want to worry you. But when we couldn't find her …'

'Don't worry,' I say, wishing I could take my own advice.

'So? Where is she?'

'Fin's got her.'

There's a pause, and then: 'Oh no. Not him. Is she safe?'

'It's okay. I'm on my way to fetch her.'

'You know where she is? I'll call the police.'

'No!' I cry, attracting the attention of an airport cleaner who's emptying a nearby bin. I lower my voice. 'No, you mustn't do that. Don't worry, I'm going to get her.'

'But—'

'You have to trust me, Pappa.'

'That boy! Your mother was right about him all along.'

'I know,' I reply.

'Where are you, Anna?'

'Heathrow Airport.'

'You're not even in Sweden?'

'It's okay. Livi will be asleep now. Fin won't hurt her.' I say this to reassure my parents, wishing I could believe it.

'What time's your flight?'

'6.40 a.m. I'll go straight to get her once we've landed. You should both get some sleep now. I'll call you once I've got Livi back.'

'Where's he taken her?'

'A cabin near Växbo.'

'That's not too far. Why don't I drive up there? I can be there before you. I'll have stern words with that boy. He must have broken into their flat. I don't know how.'

'No, please, Pappa. It'll be better if I go. He'll listen to me.'

But I'm not at all convinced that he will.

The business-class section of the plane is almost full, but I have a spacious, grey window seat, a private cocoon where I can lean back on the padded chair and stretch my legs. It's still dark out on the runway, but soon the sun will rise and today will begin. A day to end things... one way or another.

It's a short flight – only two and a half hours – so I should really try to get some sleep. I'll need every ounce of energy once I get there. I'll need a sharp brain, quick reactions. But I'm too wired, my mind buzzing with thoughts, images, pain, regret, simmering terror...

Instead of closing my eyes, I reach forward for my handbag and pull out Sian's phone. I open up the video, watching it with the sound down. At least Olivia seems content, playing with her doll, unaware of the situation she's in. But Fin isn't used to dealing with young children. She's only two and a half. She needs a bedtime story and a lullaby to get her to sleep. What if she gets upset, starts crying? Will Fin know how to soothe her? Will he become frustrated? Shout at her? Scare her? Hurt her? She needs her grandparents. No. She needs *me*.

Even though I told him to stay behind, I suddenly wish Will was here, telling me everything is going to be okay, giving me courage, his comforting presence by my side, my hand in his. A sob escapes my lips and I turn it into a cough in case anyone notices my distress. I don't need any sympathy from strangers – that would tip me over the edge. Instead, I focus on my outrage at Sian's betrayal. On Bo's attempted murder. On all the shit I've been dragged into by my ex and my so-called best friend. On the growing heat in my stomach, spreading to my limbs and causing a fire behind my eyes. I focus on my rapidly forming plan.

Hours later, I'm driving north in an olive-green hired Jeep to the forest lakes of Hälsingland, the early afternoon sun hanging low in a pale, blue sky. The empty roads are thick with brown slush, but pristine snow coats the grass verges and frosts the towering fir trees which line my route. The radio weather report forecasts more snowfall tonight and temperatures of up to minus 20 degrees Celsius. I shiver at the thought, thankful Fin didn't take Livi further north where the cold is even more severe.

Before leaving Stockholm this morning, I texted Will to let him know I'd arrived safely. Then I made a quick detour to my brother Theo's flat, just catching him before he left for his lunchtime shift at the restaurant. My normally quiet eldest brother was full of smiles and questions for me, but soon went silent when I told him I was there to borrow one of his hunting rifles. I don't have one of my own, and I couldn't very well ask my parents to borrow theirs as it would set off alarm bells.

I told Theo it was purely for protection as I was going into the forest on my own. I made out that I was nervous about the wildlife – the brown bears and wolves. But even I know that they are shy creatures, and the chances of spotting either are remote. Eventually, Theo gave in to my request, unlocking his gun safe and handing me his semi-automatic Ruger Mini-14 and a box of ammo, reminding me that it's illegal to travel with a loaded firearm. He told me this was a one-time thing. That we could both get in serious trouble if anything happened. That if I was going to make a habit of trekking alone, I would need to apply for my own gun licence. I placated him with gratitude and promises to catch up soon.

Two hours into my road journey and I spot a sign up ahead for an outdoors shop and café. I decide to pull over for a bathroom break and some lunch. I'd rather not waste any time, but I haven't eaten anything since breakfast on the plane – that croissant, fruit and coffee seem like days ago – and, as I haven't slept, I'll need food to keep me going, even though I'm not at all hungry. Indicating right, I pull off the main road and into a snow-covered car park, finding a cleared parking space near the café entrance.

As I open the Jeep door, chill air sweeps into the vehicle making me instantly more awake and alert. I step outside, zipping my parka up to my chin and pulling up my hood. But the cold seeps in, freezing my legs and working its way into the marrow of my bones. I pick my way through mounds of dirty snow onto the gritted path that leads to the café, my trainers already wet through. If I had been thinking straight, I'd have worn hiking boots.

The café is warm, thank goodness, rustic, with pine beams, sage-coloured walls, and a wood burner roaring in the corner. I take a seat by the window, and a middle-aged woman comes over to take my order. I scan the specials board and go for the moose stew. Pure comfort food. Something my mum used to make when we were growing up. Maybe I'll be able to force down a few mouthfuls.

After ordering, I head to the bathroom to freshen up. In the mirror, my face is pale, my eyes red-rimmed. I run a hand through my lank hair, gathering it up and tying it into a low ponytail at the nape of my neck. Then I splash icy water on my face, berating myself for not taking advantage of the two-and-a-half hour flight to get some sleep.

As I return to my table, the waitress approaches with my bowl of stew and a hunk of rye bread. Despite my earlier loss of appetite, I manage to polish off the lot in record-quick time, using my bread to mop up the rich juices. I thank the woman, pay and walk through a swing door into the adjoining camping shop.

Here, I stock up on everything I might need – a fleece, snow jacket, snow boots, base layers, thermal socks, gloves and hat, a lightweight rucksack, torch, hunting knife, various foodstuffs and other essentials I may need. I also buy Livi a set of outdoor clothing, as I doubt Fin thought to bring her any warm clothes. She's probably still dressed in her pyjamas. The thought of his selfishness makes me grit my teeth and want to scream. But I manage to keep it together and hand my credit card to the young guy at the counter

Behind the slatted door of the changing room, I strip off my impractical clothes and layer up with my new ones, finally pulling on a pair of felt-lined snow boots, feeling instantly more secure and prepared. While I'm in the changing room, I take the opportunity to pack the rucksack with my newly purchased provisions. I leave my old clothes and shoes behind in a neat pile, bid farewell to the sales guy, and head out into the cold, ready to complete the final part of my journey.

As I climb into the Jeep, my phone starts ringing. It's Will.

'Hey.'

'I've been calling you, Anna, why didn't you pick up? I was worried.'

'Sorry. I didn't hear your calls. The signal's patchy out here.'

'I left messages. How's it going?'

'I'm almost there. Only about an hour away. How are things?' By "things" I mean Sian, but I can't bear to utter her name.

'She woke up last night. Started going crazy at me so I had to gag her. I've tried offering her food and water, but she won't touch anything. Dad wants us to call the police and, quite frankly, I agree with him. I'm still not happy about you facing that lunatic alone.'

'Please just give me a few more hours, Will. Let me get Olivia back, make sure she's safe, then I'll call you and you can ring the authorities, okay?'

He doesn't reply.

'Will? Will? Hello?'

I look at my mobile to see that there are no bars – I've lost signal. So I quickly tap in a text asking him to hold off calling the police. I'll hit send once I get a signal again, but right now I have to focus on getting to Olivia.

I reach the outskirts of Växbo at just after 4 p.m., the sky bleaching white in preparation for the next snowfall. I pull into a layby and see that I have a signal once more so I send my text to Will. Then I punch Fin's address into Google Maps. The cabin is northwest of here, off the main road, down what looks like a single-lane track, and then deeper still into the forest. If there's any kind of road leading from the track up to the dwelling, it isn't shown on the mapping system.

I take Sian's phone out of my bag, unplug it from my portable charger, and text Fin to say I'll be there in around an hour – or rather that Sian will be there in around an hour. Then I wait until he replies:

Thank God. This kid is doing my head in. She won't go to fucking sleep and she won't speak any English.

I flinch at his words. How can he write so cruelly about his own daughter? I want to tell him to have some patience. To treat her gently. But, from Sian's previous texts, I know she would be as heartless as him. So, instead, I write:

> *Don't know what you think I can do about it. I'm not exactly Super Nanny xx*

> **Bring tranquilizer gun with you, lol.**

> *We better keep her safe, Fin. We need her in good shape or we won't get our £££*

> **Yeah, I know. Just a joke. Hurry up and get here. Want to screw your brains out.**

> *On my way xx*

That short exchange with Fin has reignited my fury, has reaffirmed I'm doing the right thing. I restart the Jeep and follow the directions that will take me to my little girl.

CHAPTER TWENTY-SIX

There's not much traffic on the road. The area is sparsely populated at this time of year, a wilderness of ancient boreal forests, rivers, mountains, meadows and over a thousand inland lakes. A place where city dwellers come for the summer months to relax in their wooden cabins and get back to nature. But in winter… it's desolate and wild, its lakes frozen over, the snowy terrain hard to navigate. The perfect place to hide a kidnapped child.

I wonder if I'm crazy coming out here alone. If maybe Will was right and I should have got the police involved. But I know Fin – he'd talk his way out of it, twist it. I wouldn't be surprised if he made out that he was doing it to spend time with his daughter, rather than for the money. And the thought of him and Sian being granted any kind of access to Olivia makes my skin crawl.

Google Maps is telling me to turn right off the main road onto a single-track lane. Snow-covered farmland stretches out on both sides and I see a couple of large timber farm buildings up ahead nestled into the treeline, their windows dark. Other vehicles have been along here recently – their muddy tyre marks ground into the snow. My Jeep handles the terrain well, but I go slowly nonetheless. I can't afford to have an accident out here.

Dead ahead lies deep forest. It seems as though my departure from the main road has signalled to the sun that it's time to leave. As the light dims, I flick my headlamps onto full beam. Once

I pass the farm buildings, the tyre tracks disappear along with Google Maps and WiFi. I'm entering a more desolate landscape.

I drive on, the Jeep crawling along the narrow lane for a couple of miles until I reach the final turn-off – a narrow track which will lead to Fin and to my daughter. But first I'll need to scope out the immediate area. I bring the Jeep to a stop, turn off the engine and kill the lights. Dusk hovers beneath a pale, snow-filled sky. I wonder when the first flakes will begin to fall.

Flipping on the interior light makes me feel even more vulnerable than before, although common sense tells me that no one is watching. With my pulse racing, I pull on my new snow jacket, hat and gloves. I'm sweating in the heated interior, but I know I'll need all these layers if I'm to avoid freezing to death out there. I open my door and gasp at the twilight temperature outside. It hits me like an airbag going off in my face. Even with my new gear, the cold is brutal. No time to dwell on that. I slide out of the vehicle, my new boots landing on virgin snow. Not too deep, thank goodness.

I check again, but there's still no WiFi here and only a weak phone signal. I'm on my own. I stand for a moment, my shallow breaths the only sound. It's the kind of silence that is impossible to find in towns and cities. But I can't hang around listening to my breathing all night, I have to get a move on.

I head to the rear of the Jeep and open up the boot. First I take the torch out of my rucksack, then I swing the pack onto my back and adjust the straps until it sits comfortably. Next I take my brother's hunting rifle out of its bag, check the safety's on and insert the loaded five-round magazine, locking it into place. I put the spare magazine and box of ammo in my left coat pocket, zip it up, sling the rifle across my chest, and set off down the track, keeping close to the trees.

We all hunted as teens, living off the land during summer family vacations in our cabin, but I haven't handled a gun in over a decade.

I still feel confident with it, but that doesn't mean to say I like the idea of having such a deadly weapon anywhere near my daughter.

I walk fast along the snow-covered path, the light from the sky not yet completely gone so I'll save my torch batteries for now. Occasionally, I slow my pace to look around, but there's nothing except narrow track ahead and behind, and snowy forest either side. Fin has selected this place for its isolation. That suits me fine. With what I've got in mind, the further away from civilisation the better.

After around fifteen minutes of brisk walking, the light has almost gone and I think about turning on my torch. But then I spy a faint glow up ahead. With a thumping heart, I slow my pace, the crunch of my footsteps amplified. I suddenly become hyper-aware of everything, my ears cocked for any sounds, eyes scanning for movement, the scent of snow and woodsmoke in my nostrils. As I draw closer, I see the glow is emanating from the hanging porch light of a forest cabin where I presume Livi is being held. A BMW 4x4 is parked off to the side beneath a rustic carport, its windscreen iced over.

The wooden cottage is small, traditional, painted red with white-framed windows and a snow-covered roof, dark smoke billowing out of the chimney. It sits at the back of a clearing, surrounded by dense forest like something out of a fairy tale. It takes all of my willpower not to race over to the building, fling open the door and snatch up my baby. Instead, I come to a standstill at the end of the track, and stare through the cold darkness, making a mental note of everything.

The curtains are shut but a dim light burns through the windows. I spot a slight movement and catch my breath as one of the curtains is twitched aside and I see someone peering out into the darkness – Fin.

I shrink back against the treeline, paranoid he's spotted me. Rationally, I know that's not likely, but the knowledge doesn't do anything to quell my racing heart.

I think about knocking on the door right now. Getting the confrontation over with. But it's too far and too cold to take Livi back to the Jeep on foot. I briefly consider the possibility of taking Fin's BMW, but I instantly dismiss the idea – I'd have to de-ice the windows, I don't know how full the tank is, or where the keys are. So – recce over – I stick with my original plan, turn around and make my way back along the track to the lane. I'll drive up to the cabin in my Jeep.

As I jog through the snow, the last of the daylight leaches from the sky leaving an eerie whiteness backlit by a hidden moon. I click on the torch and think about what lies ahead.

Back at the jeep, I stuff the torch in my right pocket and zip it closed. Then I sling my rucksack into the passenger footwell and lay the Ruger on the seat. Despite the fact my body is cold, a light sweat breaks out on my forehead. I'll be glad when I'm finally facing him. When I force him into giving me back my child.

I climb into the Jeep, start up the engine, flick on the headlights and begin the short journey back down the track.

I'm here.

Within seconds of my arrival, Fin steps out of the front door of the cabin, wearing jeans, hiking boots and a grey jumper. Judging by the happy expression on his face, he thinks I'm Sian, come to hide out with him. He holds the back of his hand to his eyes to block out the beam of my headlights, but I keep them pointed at him until I've shouldered my rucksack, grasped my rifle and chambered a round. I take a breath and finally turn off the lights and the engine.

As I step out of the vehicle and train my weapon on Fin's chest, I watch the smile on his face dissolve into utter confusion. He stays rooted to the spot under the porch light, his eyes darting around, trying to figure out what he should do.

'Anna,' he calls out, trying and failing to plaster the smile back on his face. 'What are you doing here?'

My footsteps squeak across the snow as I head towards him. 'What do you think? I've come to get my daughter.' I stop about twenty yards away.

'Why have you got a gun?'

'Because if you don't hand her over I'm going to kill you.'

His skin pales.

'There's no need for that, is there?' He takes a couple of steps towards me.

'Stay where you are,' I yell, my voice filling up the night air.

'Come on, Anna. This is crazy.' He takes two more steps in my direction and I grip the rifle tighter, my finger twitching over the trigger. All I have to do is squeeze and Fin Chambers will take a bullet to the chest. At this close range, it will make quite a mess.

'I mean it, Fin. Don't come any closer.' My palms are sweating, my fingers slick against the rifle. I wonder if I will actually have the courage to shoot him if he ignores my warning.

My heart pounds as he comes closer and closer still, moving away from the cottage. Sweat trickles down my forehead, stinging my eyes. I blink and lean forward, trying to wipe away the moisture with my cuff. I can't seem to think straight. Why can't I just shoot him? I realise now that the practice of shooting a person is quite different to the theory. What if Olivia hears the gunshot and comes outside to see Fin's blood-covered body. It could traumatise her. Not to mention the fact that I could go to jail. And, no matter what Fin has done, we did love each other once. Can I take his life?

'Bring Olivia to me,' I say, my voice high and thin.

'No,' he replies, with a taunting smile.

'Come any closer and I swear I'll kill you,' I say, my voice trembling now. I'm losing it. Please don't let me fall apart now.

'If you were going to kill me you'd have done it already.' His voice is calm, lazy, mocking.

I realise it's started snowing, tiny white flakes whirling and dancing through the night towards me. Maybe I don't have to kill him. I can just injure him. Shoot him in the leg, disable him. I aim the gun lower, at his left leg.

'Mamma!' Olivia's voice. I jerk my gaze towards the cabin to see her standing under the porch light, arms stretched out towards me. I notice her feet are bare. Bloody Fin. Why didn't he put her socks on?

'Livi! Stay there a minute,' I call out in Swedish.

Before I have a chance to turn my attention back to Fin, he is upon me. Pushing the gun barrel down towards the ground and wrenching the weapon from me in one fluid movement. I scream, but it's no good. He shoves me away so I fall sideways into the snow. *I've blown it.*

'Mamma!' Olivia is screaming now. She stumbles across the porch in her pyjamas.

'Livi,' I call out. 'It's okay. Mamma's here.' I push myself up onto my feet and stagger forward, but Fin has already backed up. Has already reached her. As he scoops Olivia up under one arm, I yell: 'Don't touch her!' But he yanks open the cabin door and shoves her inside, slamming the door. He locks it from the outside, then stuffs the key into his jeans pocket.

My baby's thin cries come through the cabin walls and, as much as I ache to press my lips to her soft cheek, I also want to smash my fists into Fin's face at his rough treatment of her. I howl in frustration, cursing myself for my earlier indecision. If I get the chance again, I won't hesitate to shoot the bastard.

'Let her go!' I cry with a choking sob. 'How could you just push her like that?' I stride over to where he's standing on the porch, not caring that I'm walking towards the barrel of a loaded gun. 'She's just a baby. She's your daughter, for Christ's sake! Touch her again and I'll kill you.'

'Yeah?' Fin sneers. 'Well you had the chance just now but you didn't take it, did you?' He points the Ruger at my head, stopping me in my tracks. 'How did you find me?' he barks. 'Where's Sian? She was supposed to—'

'That bitch?' I say through gritted teeth.

His face darkens. 'What have you done? You better not have hurt her, Anna.'

'That's rich,' I say with more bravado that I'm feeling. 'You can't lecture me about hurting people. You've done it all your life.'

'Tell me! Or, I swear I'll kill that squalling brat in there.'

I shake my head in disbelief. 'You value that evil cow's life over the life of your own daughter?'

'How do I even know she's mine?'

'Oh, give me a break, Fin. How can you even doubt it? We were living together. I told you I was pregnant. I was working and studying all the hours of the day and night. When would I have had time for an affair? And anyway, I was in love with you. More fool me.'

'Whether that kid has got my DNA or not, it doesn't matter. I love Sian.'

'Just give me my daughter and let us go. I never want to see either of you two psychos again.'

'That's not going to happen,' he says, starting to shiver, his sweater no match for a Swedish winter's night. 'You're going to go back to England and you're going to get rid of your husband and father-in-law. It'll be easy – car accident, food poisoning – I dunno, use your imagination. Then you'll transfer your inheritance over to us and we'll hand you the kid. If you deviate from this in any way – call the police, try to save her, whatever, then baby gets it, okay?'

'You're such a cold bastard,' I hiss, shaking my head. 'I can't believe I wasted so many years with you.' My predicament hits me in the solar plexus. I've screwed this whole thing up royally. I had the opportunity to save my child and I blew it. Why the hell didn't I shoot Fin in the leg when I had the chance? I can still hear Olivia's cries – softer now, but more heartbreaking if that's possible. 'Even if Olivia wasn't yours,' I continue, 'how can you even think about harming a two-year-old child?'

'Easy,' he says. 'I'd do anything for Sian. She's the one I should've been with all along. Me and her, we're the same.'

'Psychotic, you mean.'

'Call it what you want, Anna. You may have a beautiful face, but you're spineless. Boring as fuck, if you must know.'

I wince at his words, despite the fact that I'd rather be boring than be anything like Sian.

'Sian is more of a woman than you'll ever be,' he adds. 'I'd do anything for her.'

'Really.'

'I just said so, didn't I?'

'Well that's fortunate for me,' I reply as it suddenly occurs to me that maybe I do have a shot at getting Olivia back tonight.

'What do you mean?' he says, eyes narrowing.

I start to unzip my coat pocket.

'What are you doing?' Fin takes a step towards me, thrusting the rifle down towards my chest.

I raise my hands in the air. 'Careful with that, Fin? Do you even know how to use a gun?'

'I'm guessing this trigger has something to do with it.' His voice drips with sarcasm.

'I'm just getting my phone out of my pocket,' I say. 'I've got something I want you to see.'

'Slowly,' Fin orders.

I push my fingers beneath the rubber torch in my pocket and locate my phone, drawing it out of my pocket. Once Fin sees I'm true to my word, that it's just my mobile, his shoulders relax.

I bring up the video I took before I left England. It's a short clip of Sian, tied up, unconscious on the kitchen floor.

'Shit.' Fin's face falls and then flushes with anger. 'Is she…'

'Dead? No. But she deserves to be. She's just a bit tied up at the moment.' I shouldn't provoke Fin – not while he has a gun pointed at my chest – but I'm so mad, I can't censor my words.

'You're pissing me off, Anna. I'm this close to putting a bullet in you right now.'

'That would be unfortunate for Sian.' My voice has begun to tremble again – fear, cold, anger, all of the above.

'Call Will,' Fin hisses. 'Get him to release Sian. No more games.'

'No,' I reply, squaring my shoulders. 'Give me my daughter first.'

'I told you, you don't get the kid until we get the money.' His teeth are chattering now, his hands shaking, almost blue with cold. 'Call Will. Right now.'

'No,' I repeat.

'Okay then, I'll kill you, and then I'll kill your brat. And then I'll go to England and kill your husband and your father-in-law.'

'That's a lot of dead people to hide,' I say, trying to buy some time. Trying to come up with a plan. 'I'm pretty sure the police will work out it was you.'

'Yeah, well, you won't be around to find out,' he says. And then his voice changes, becomes more determined. 'Turn around.'

This is it. He really means to kill me.

'You do realise that rifle's not even loaded,' I bluff.

'What?' He glances down for a nanosecond and as he does so I shove the gun up and out of his hand. It goes off with a boom into the night sky, reverberating in my gut, paralysing us both for a moment, eyes wide, ears ringing.

And then I run.

CHAPTER TWENTY-SEVEN

I don't look behind me. I sprint towards the trees as fast as I can, hoping to draw him away from the cabin, away from Olivia. She'll be okay in there by herself for a short while, won't she? She knows not to touch the woodstove, doesn't she? Don't think about that. Think about reaching the trees. Fin is more of a danger to her than anything in the cabin. Hopefully, she'll curl up on the bed and cry herself to sleep.

My feet pound the snow, my breath comes in ragged gasps. The thought of Olivia being hurt threatens to drain my energy. I'm one step away from throwing myself onto the ground in surrender. From begging Fin to save her. But then my resolve kicks in. Must stay strong for Olivia. For Will. Must hold my nerve. Must keep going. I'm no good to anyone if I'm dead. I have to stay alive until I can figure out how to rescue her.

'Anna!' Fin yells. 'I'm going to kill you!'

I ignore his taunt and concentrate on getting to cover. I make a snap decision to head northwest into the forest, rather than towards the road. There's more cover. Less chance of being hit by a bullet. If I can lose him, maybe I'll be able to double back, grab Olivia and make our escape. If only it can be that easy.

I run flat out, expecting a bullet in the back of my head at any moment. But I'm slowed by the uneven carpet of snow, by my new boots, stiff and heavy, by my rucksack, a dead weight on my shoulders. Sucking frigid air into my lungs, I finally reach the treeline. I weave my way through the trees, just a little way in, then I duck behind a thick fir to catch my breath. To risk a glance back at Fin.

He strides towards the trees, not running and not aiming the rifle in my direction. Instead, he's fiddling with the gun, and I realise he's clueless about what to do. He has four bullets left, but he needs to figure out how to get the next one from the magazine to the chamber. I allow myself a tiny moment of relief before continuing on into the dark forest.

Fin is wasting time. If he stopped to think for a moment, he'd realise he doesn't need to fire the gun to stop me. He simply needs to catch me and tackle me to the ground, whack me over the head with the rifle stock. Instead, he's letting me have a crucial head start.

Maybe he's finally wised up, as I suddenly hear his thudding footsteps drawing closer, merging with the thudding of my heart.

I wind and weave my way through the forest, brushing the soft, low branches, accidentally knocking snow from the trees, so it falls over me in random showers, onto my shoulders, down my neck. I pull my hood up over my hat and push on, my eyes barely able to see in the snowy gloom, keeping ahead of him but making just enough noise so he can follow me – I have to keep him away from the cabin until I figure out what to do.

A shot rings out, a dull crack dampened by the snow, the splinter of wood as the bullet hits a tree. *Shit*, he's worked out how to chamber the bullets. I can't go any faster – it's too dark, the ground too uneven, the cold air making it hard to catch my breath, my lungs squeezed. I can't even use my torch as that would act as a beacon for Fin to target me. I desperately need to put some more distance between us. It wasn't a threat – he really does mean to kill me. I cringe as another shot whizzes past, hitting a bough just up ahead to my right. Too close.

As I duck low-hanging branches and weave through the dark tangle of firs, I try not to think about Olivia in the cabin, alone.

About the fact that I'm heading away from her when every part of me is screaming out to run back and scoop her up in my arms.

'I'm gonna get you, Anna!' In the hush of the snowy forest, his voice sounds hoarse. He's panting hard. I think he's falling further behind. But I don't dare hope. Fin has two bullets left. I tense up ready for the next crack of the gun, praying he doesn't manage to hit me. I suck in more air and push myself harder, taking longer strides despite my throbbing leg muscles and the strain in my chest.

The gun goes off once more. My brother's rifle in the hands of a madman. I should never have brought it with me. As my boots pound the snow and I weave through the trees, I can't help wondering what it would feel like to have a bullet bury itself in my head. Would I realise it instantly? Or would there be a delay in the pain? Maybe I wouldn't feel a thing – my life extinguished in a millisecond. I try to push the thought away, to ward off the panic. I'm still alive. Still unhurt. Yet I can't stop the images flashing up in my head – the bullet piercing my skull, a bloom of red staining my blonde hair, matting it together, a mess of brains and bone and blood.

But the chances of it happening are decreasing. He now only has one bullet left.

My shoulders begin to ache, the weight of my rucksack slowing me down, but I can't toss it. I may need its contents. They could very well save my life if I get stuck out here for too long. At least my peripheral vision is starting to kick in now, my eyes adjusting to the dark.

As kids, we spent long summers learning how to navigate so we would never get lost out here. But that was a long time ago, and Pappa's lessons are not so fresh in my mind. Snippets of information glimmer and fade. And I'm realising that navigating at night is harder than in daylight, navigating in winter is harder than in summer. Natural features are less distinct. Landmarks smoothed over by carpets of snow. Boundaries between land and frozen water trickier to spot. Shapes blurred. Vegetation covered. Everything looks the same. Everything is white. And while the snow still falls, our footprints are erased. Our route back to the cabin is disappearing flake by flake.

As I move deeper into the forest, I begin to snap small, dead limbs off the trees. Once I have a decent handful, I drop them in a pile to my right. Then I do it all over again, leaving little markers behind. Even if they become covered in snow, I can use my torch to try to spot the regular mounds on my way back... if I get the chance. The other benefit to leaving these markers is the noise I'm creating, snapping the dead branches – it means Fin can follow me more easily. And now the moon has begun to glow through the snow clouds, its eerie light bright enough for Fin to follow my fading footprints.

I still hear him, the dull thud of his footsteps on the snowy forest floor, the crackle of twigs, the swish of branches as he tries to catch up with me. It's a fine balance, though – I need him to keep following without actually reaching me. Without seeing my shape to aim at. Occasionally, I hear him swear or cough, signs that he's tiring, weakening, starting to feel the cold. We go on like this for a while.

'Anna!' His voice comes from further away now. I can no longer hear his footsteps behind me, but I keep going, slowing my pace only slightly. 'Anna, wait! You're going to get lost out there!'

What he really means is *he* is going to get lost out here. Me, I should be able to find my way back, as long as he doesn't catch me. I don't reply. Don't give him the opportunity to latch onto my voice and find me.

'Anna, come back! Look, I promise I won't hurt you.'

I don't believe him for one minute.

'You can take Olivia,' he calls, his words turning into a wracking cough. 'I'm going back, okay? It's too cold out here. You'll freeze to death if you keep going.'

Why is he suddenly telling me I can have Olivia? It must be a trap. He hasn't been able to catch me, so he must be trying to lure me back instead. But I'm not falling for it. I won't show myself so he can use his last bullet on me.

I stop and turn, squint through the gloom, past the spinning flakes of snow and the needle-covered branches, but I don't see him. I'm panting hard, my lungs grateful for the respite. I remember that Fin isn't even wearing a coat. No wonder he says he's cold. I have the opposite problem – now that I've stopped, I realise how warm I've become. That I'm in danger of sweating through all my layers. So I push down my hood and remove my hat. Unzip my coat and my fleece to let the air cool me down for a moment. Pappa always told us that if we sweated outside in the winter at night, we could end up freezing to death as our warm sweat would eventually become cold.

'Anna!' Fin's voice sounds even further away now. 'I mean it! I'm going back.'

I wonder if he'll be able to find his way to the cabin from here. He might just do it, and I can't let that happen. I can't take the risk of him hurting Olivia. But what can I do? I can't stop him; he still has the damn gun.

I listen out for any sounds. Branches snapping, footfalls, a cough. But the forest has fallen quiet. Just my breath, my heartbeat and the silent snow filtering through the gaps in the trees. I move like a hunter now, calling on my childhood lessons of how to blend with nature – becoming part of the landscape, trying to remember how to move like the animals, like the trees, like the wind. Mindful of that last bullet.

'Anna?' His voice is faint. Distant.

I follow the sound. Heel to toe, heel to toe, I move silently, tracking him. If he really is heading back to the cabin, I'll need to work out how I'm going to get to Olivia before he does.

As I draw closer to his position, I realise I don't need to worry about losing him – he's louder than a stampeding herd of elk. Thanks to his noisy progress, I'll have time to check my compass, to make absolutely certain where he's going. I stop, ease off my rucksack, and open the top strap with fumbling fingers. I extract my compass from the inside pocket and then, as an afterthought, I take out my brand-new hunting knife, close and re-shoulder my pack.

Holding the compass in my gloved hand, I click on its built-in light and take a moment to find true north. To get to the cabin, he should be heading southeast. I hope and pray he's going in the wrong direction, but my prayers aren't answered. *Damn.* He's heading southeast, back to Olivia.

I shove the compass in my pocket and unsheathe the knife, gripping it in my right hand, feeling a little more secure now I have a weapon, even though it's no match for a gun. I pick up his trail once more, close enough to hear his progress, but far enough away to be out of danger. Starting to feel the chill again, I zip up my fleece. With every step he takes towards the cabin, my chances to stop him are becoming more and more limited. We're probably an hour or so out given the slow rate at which he's moving. I need to act now.

With a sinking stomach, I realise I only have one option – to creep up on him from behind, stab him in the kidney and try to grab the gun. The thought of doing it makes me nauseous, sets my pulse racing.

Thing is, I don't really think I have a choice. Not if I want to keep my daughter safe.

I need to get much, much closer without him hearing me. I'll have to be almost on top of him to give me the element of surprise.

Okay, I'm going to do it. Have to do it.

Clutching my knife, I increase my pace, my heart lurching when I finally catch sight of him up ahead, a dark bumbling shape weaving through the trees, his arms wrapped around his body, the Ruger hanging loosely from his right shoulder.

I match his steps to mask any sounds I might make. When he steps with his left foot, I use my left foot. When he steps with his right, I use my right. But I make sure to step a fraction earlier than he does as sound travels differently, and there's a delay between his visual step and the sound of his step. We move like this for a while, I can't say for how long. Time seems suspended one minute, racing forward the next.

The snow has stopped falling, the clouds are clearing, temperature dropping fast. Fin is slowing down even more now, muttering to himself. Slowly, slowly, I'm catching up to him. My heart clatters so loudly, I'm convinced he'll hear it, turn around and see me here, almost upon him. A cloud moves to reveal a half moon, illuminating him completely. His hair is covered in crystallised drops, his shoulders coated with snow. It's now or never. I need to gather my courage and make my move. I grip the knife handle and hold the weapon out in front of me, its lethal blade glinting in the moonlight.

But before I get the chance to act, Fin yells my name, almost giving me a heart attack. I freeze. Does he know I'm here? Has he seen me? I step back and duck behind a tree clamping my lips together to stop myself from whimpering in fear, almost dropping the knife. Do I wait here to be discovered, or do I make a run for it?

CHAPTER TWENTY-EIGHT

I decide to stay put behind the tree. Breaking my cover could give him a clear shot, but if I stay where I am, I can use the knife on him as soon as he gets close enough. I take a breath and hold it, listening hard.

'You bitch!' Fin shouts.

I flinch and risk a peek. Sweat breaks out on my forehead as I see him swing around, pointing the rifle in all directions. I'm still holding my breath, not daring to breathe, convinced he's about to uncover my hiding place and drag me out so he can shoot me. I need to be ready to act.

'Where the fuck are you?' he cries.

Did he hear me creeping up on him? Or is this simply a random outburst of fear and anger?

'Bitch,' he mutters. 'Leading me out into this pissing, freezing shit hole of a forest. Where the fuck is she? I'll fucking kill her when I find her.'

I don't dare peer out again. I press my back hard against the tree trunk, wishing I could disappear into it. Hoping he doesn't choose to head over this way. I stay where I am for what seems like forever, listening to him shuffle around, muttering and swearing. My core temperature is dropping again. I need to zip up my coat, but I'm scared it will make too much noise.

I keep telling myself that it's okay. I know this place. I know it. Fin is way out of his depth. Okay, yes, he has a gun, but a gun is no good if you can't find your prey. And right now I'm pretty sure he doesn't have a clue that I'm only a few yards away listening to him lunge around in shambolic circles.

After an interminable amount of time, there is no more muttering or shuffling so I take a chance and peer out at where he was last standing. I think he's gone, but I can't be sure so I look out from the other side of the tree. No, he's definitely not there.

I zip up my outer coat and pull on my woollen hat once more, revelling in the new warmth over my ears. Then I leave my hiding place and study the ground. His footprints are going in the wrong direction, heading west towards the lake. It looks as though he might have lost his bearings.

This could be my chance. I could run back to the cabin now. All my maternal instincts are screaming at me to head back there and check on my daughter. But then my paranoia kicks in. What if Fin is watching me? My scalp tingles as I realise it could be a trick to lure me out of my hiding place so he can follow me out of the forest. But I really don't think so. Fin was a shivering mess when I last saw him, I don't believe he's capable of thinking rationally out here. I can't chance it, though. I need to find him, to check for myself.

It doesn't take me long to catch him up. He's inching along at a painfully slow pace, stumbling in all directions, shaking with cold. I settle in behind him at a distance, tracking his every move, still holding my knife, just in case.

Fin has been moving in meandering circles for a while, now. But despite his circuitous route, he's also moving further and further away from Olivia, deeper and deeper into the wilderness. Winter has begun to bury its way into my clothing. It has chilled my skin and is attempting to penetrate my flesh. Goodness only knows what levels of cold Fin is experiencing without a coat. I can't believe he's still upright, still ploughing onwards. It must be safe to leave him. I think I can finally head back to Olivia without fear of him following me. I'll wait just ten minutes more to ensure he's well and truly lost.

I'm walking without thinking now, mesmerised by our slow progress. By the soft squeak of our boots in the snow. By the muffled hush of the forest at night. By the insistent cold biting into my body. But then something jolts me out of my hypnotic state. I hear it off in the distance. A noise I haven't heard for years – the howl of wolves.

Fin stops dead in his tracks, cocking his ear.

I bite my lip and step behind a tree as he turns around slowly, three-hundred-and-sixty degrees, trying to determine the source of the sound. The pack is likely to be miles away, but Fin doesn't know that. He's probably shitting himself, probably thinks they're hunting him. Swedish wolves are shy creatures and haven't attacked humans in the wild for over a century. But Fin doesn't know that, either.

As if on cue, the howling starts up again, like something out of Twilight.

'Fuck!' His voice is hoarse, almost a sob. Fin scrabbles to get my brother's hunting rifle from his shoulder, aiming in front of him as he spins around in every direction, probably terrified that a wolf is going to leap out and sink its fangs into his neck.

'Anna!' he hisses. 'Anna! Are you there? Please be there.'

His footsteps draw closer and I shrink back, hiding myself within the bushy branches of a Norway spruce. Seconds later, I see his dark shape ploughing through the trees towards me, clutching the rifle, his fair hair covered in frost, his face ashen, ears red, eyes wide with terror, tears freezing on his cheeks. I almost feel sorry for him. Almost. But not quite.

He blunders, unseeing, past my hiding place, calling out my name, praying to a god he doesn't believe in to save him. I let him go. Watch him stagger and swerve northwards, deeper into the woods, heading away from civilisation, away from the lake towards miles and miles of ancient wilderness. No, Fin doesn't need to worry about the wolves. It's the cold night forest that will kill him.

At that moment, I realise he's probably not going to make it. He'll likely die out here if I don't help him. I may not have been able to kill him in cold blood earlier with the gun or with the knife, but I realise I'm quite capable of leaving him out here in the wild to die. I'm pretty sure we're far enough into the forest for him to never find his way out again. Hypothermia will get him before that ever happens.

The chill is deepening. Winter's fingers have found their way to my bones. I've been living in the city for too long. My body has grown soft. More acclimatised to central heating than to this subarctic climate. My brain is slowing, but I'm lucid enough to know that I have to get back. That Olivia has already been on her own for far too long.

First I need to boost my energy or I'm not going to make it. Stiff-limbed, I pull a power bar from my rucksack, tear open the wrapper with my teeth, and cram half the bar into my mouth. It's almost frozen, but not quite. I chew carefully, making sure I warm it up in my mouth before swallowing. Then, still chewing, I check my compass, and turn and head back towards the cabin – or at least, to where I *think* the cabin is. I can't afford to second-guess myself. I need to be decisive or I'm going to end up dead out here. And if I die, then what will happen to my baby girl?

As I take my first steps back, my heart pounds with uncertainty. Is this the way? Am I lost, too? Don't panic, stay calm. Sweat breaks out on my upper lip and on my back beneath my rucksack. The more I try to calm myself, the more I panic. I unzip my coat and fleece, trying not to lose control, trying to remember all my wilderness training. Panicking is the worst thing I can do out here. I'm tempted to dump my backpack so I can move more freely, but that would be a mistake. Don't do it. Keep it on.

Images of my daughter flash through my mind. How she's all alone in the cabin, crying, terrified, worse... Don't think like that. Don't think about how long she's been on her own. I need to put these thoughts out of my head or I'll end up going crazy, making mistakes. No. I need to take deep breaths, slow my breathing. Look out for landmarks. Keep checking my compass. Keep moving forward. Not long now. Not long now... is it?

As I pick my way through the gloom, the wolves continue to howl mournfully, sometimes sounding distant, other times close by, the air playing tricks on my hearing. Several times, I lose my footing, stumble forward over tree roots and other obstacles hidden beneath the snow. But I push myself back up onto my feet and keep going, alternately clenching my fists and flexing my gloved fingers to try to keep the circulation going in my hands.

After a while, I'm trudging on autopilot, my legs aching but my mind distanced from the pain, my thoughts still with Olivia. Desperation keeps me moving. Right leg, left leg, right leg, left leg. There are no features I recognise on my route. Just snow on the ground, dark sky above, trees all around. Always the same. Keep checking my compass. Don't cry. Don't panic. Don't think about being lost. Think about getting back to my baby. Keep breathing. Keep going.

I realise the wolves have stopped howling. Perhaps they're hunting. A twisted part of me hopes they're hunting Fin. Hopes they rip him to shreds. I give a short laugh that sounds strange to my ears. I sound like a wild animal.

Am I going to die out here?

As soon as I have that thought, I see it – a small mound of dead twigs. *My* twigs. My marker. I stop walking and stare at the twigs. Relief is like a warm blanket around my shoulders and I start to cry. But then I sniff away my tears, dab at my cheeks with my scarf and set my mouth in a hard line. I'm going to make it. I'm going to get back to my daughter.

I walk faster now, my mind more alert knowing I'm almost there. My heart leaps as I see a light ahead of me through the forest. The cabin porch light! No. I can't have reached the cabin already. I'm guessing it will take me at least another half hour, maybe more. I stop dead as I hear the crackle of branches ahead, the sound of a person or large creature moving through the woods. And then I see that the light is moving. And it's heading my way.

CHAPTER TWENTY-NINE

I stand rooted to the spot. Ahead of me the trees themselves appear to be moving, the branches swishing and crackling. I see the flicker of lights. What's going on? My first thought is to run and hide. Has Fin managed to somehow get back here ahead of me? No that can't be possible.

Then, from my right:

'Anna!' A deep voice calling my name.

'Anna!' Another voice dead ahead.

More voices calling out my name. Am I hallucinating? The whine of a wolf, or a dog, and then a volley of barks. And I see them emerging through the trees like a dream – police officers in high-vis jackets with sniffer dogs and torches.

I don't even have enough energy to call out. I simply stand where I am, letting my backpack slide to the ground in a shower of snow and relief.

Within seconds, an officer has come over to me, propping me up as I lean into his solid shoulder.

'Anna Blackwell?' he asks.

'Yes,' I croak. 'My daughter…'

'Olivia is fine,' he says, speaking English. 'We got to her over two hours ago. Nothing to worry about. She's safe. Completely unharmed, okay?' He smiles, his blue eyes, kind, sympathetic.

I finally allow myself to relax. To breathe. But my body is shaking. I'm quivering from head to toe. I can't stop it.

'Was anyone else with you?' another of the officers asks. 'Anyone still out there?' He gestures with his hand to the forest beyond me.

I pause for a moment. Do I want them to rescue Fin? No. No, I don't. But even if they do manage to find him out there, I can't imagine how he could possibly still be alive. Maybe I need the police to find him so I can see his frozen, dead body. It would be good to have that closure. So, I answer the officer: 'Fin. Fin Chambers. My ex-boyfriend. He's still out there. He kidnapped Olivia.' My teeth are chattering so much I can hardly speak. 'He was trying to kill me. He wanted to kill us both so I ran into the forest to get him away from my daughter.'

A woman in uniform comes over and wraps a thick blanket around my shoulders, starts asking me questions about how I'm feeling. But I don't answer. I'm too desperate to see my little one. 'How far are we from the cabin?' I ask.

'About forty minutes,' the woman says, taking my temperature. She checks the thermometer. 'You have mild hypothermia, but you'll be fine. You're extremely lucky.'

'I know,' I reply, chewing my lower lip. 'Thank you for coming to find me.'

She inclines her head and smiles. 'We'll put you on a stretcher, keep you insulated. I have some sweet tea for you in this thermos.' She reaches into her bag and draws out a flask, unscrews the lid, pours out the tea and holds it in front of my lips. 'Small sips,' she says.

Sweetness floods my mouth before the hot liquid slides down my throat, warming my body from the inside. 'Thank you,' I say again. Then I turn to the officer: 'Can we go back now? Olivia will be so scared.'

'It's okay. Her grandparents have just arrived,' the officer says. 'But yes. We'll go. I'll keep a team out here searching for Mr Chambers.'

The woman and her colleague, who I'm guessing must be paramedics, are telling me to lie on the stretcher. I do as they say. I'm not in any state to continue walking. My legs have turned to jelly.

'How did you know where to find me? How to find the cabin?' I ask the officer as I ease myself down, the paramedics covering me with layers of blankets. It's heaven to be off my feet. I gaze up at the inky sky, at a myriad of stars, realising the snow clouds have completely dispersed. The paramedics lift the stretcher and it's like I'm floating.

'Your husband got in touch with the British Police earlier this evening,' the officer explains, his voice deep and steady. 'He was worried when you failed to answer your phone. He told them everything that's been happening to you over the past few weeks. About Mr Chambers and Sian Davies. Their alleged plans to extort money, and the possible homicide of Mr Chamber's wife. Your husband gave us the address where your daughter was being held.'

'Will,' I say, closing my eyes for a second and picturing his face.

'You should never have come out here on your own,' the officer says. 'Very foolish. Dangerous.'

'I was just trying to keep my daughter safe,' I explain.

'Okay. Well, we'll talk about it back at the station.'

I blink in acknowledgement, realising I'm going to have an awful lot of questions to answer.

'In which direction would you say the suspect was headed when you last saw him?' the officer asks.

I look up at him. 'North,' I reply. 'But he must be miles away by now.'

'And he has a weapon?'

'A hunting rifle,' I reply, neglecting to tell them that he got it from me. That it belongs to my brother. 'I think he only has one bullet left.'

'Okay. Well. You'll be fine now.'

'Thank you,' I say.

He smiles and rests a hand on my blanketed shoulder for a moment. Then he turns to his colleagues. 'Let's go.'

I allow myself to close my eyes. To thank God that Olivia is safe. That I will get the opportunity to make it up to her. To finally be her mother.

CHAPTER THIRTY

Six months later

'Do you want an iced coffee?' I poke my head through the open French doors and smile at the sight of Will stretched out on a teak sun lounger by the pool. It's Saturday afternoon, one of those rare hot days where there's no trace of chill in the air. Just a warm southerly breeze that ripples across bare skin like a trail of kisses. Will is engrossed in one of my chick-lit novels – one that he recently mocked me for reading. 'Enjoying your book?' I ask.

'It's okay,' he says grudgingly. Then he grins. 'Actually, it's hilarious.'

'I knew you'd love it.'

He rolls his eyes. 'Know-all.'

'That's me. Anyway, as I was saying – do you want an iced coffee?'

'Yeah, please, that would be great. It's roasting out here.'

'Why don't you put the umbrella up?'

'Can't be bothered.'

Now it's my turn to roll my eyes. 'How are they doing?' I ask.

'Having an absolute ball.' He sits up and shields his eyes, gazing down the garden.

I follow his line of sight to see Olivia and Bo playing on the lawn. The two of them are inseparable. Bo made a full recovery after his ordeal, and has really helped Olivia to settle in.

Olivia had nightmares for the first few weeks with us in England. My parents stayed for a couple weeks to help get her settled, but when they finally left, she missed them terribly, and cried for them at night. It made me feel so guilty that I haven't been there for her. My mum and dad have been her main caregivers throughout her short life so far so I guess it was only natural for Olivia to miss them. But there's no point regretting the past. I simply have to do my best to make up for those two lost years. Gradually, by spending all my time with her, I'm managing to win her around. And she's had Will wrapped around her finger from day one. He's an incredible parent. She already calls him Daddy. Hopefully, she'll forget any memories of the brief time she spent with her biological father.

No one has seen or heard from Fin since that awful night. Will was the only person I told about the truly terrible physical state Fin was in. That he was suffering from chronic hypothermia. That there was no way the search party could have found him in time. They never recovered his body so I guess he ended up being food for wolves.

Sian was extradited to Barbados where she's just started serving a twenty-five-year prison sentence, convicted of both *murder* and *conspiracy to commit murder*. It seems that during a winter holiday to Barbados with Remy, she took a little side trip on her own and paid two locals to drive the speedboat which killed Fin's wife. She lied to me – It wasn't actually her who committed the murder, although it may as well have been. And if Fin were still alive, he would have gone on trial for murder, too.

Remy is naturally devastated by Sian's disgusting betrayal. But Will and I are helping him through it. Spending lots of time with him. And Olivia loves her Uncle Remy.

I shade my eyes, watching Olivia and Bo play for a moment. Bo has a length of twisted rope in his mouth and Olivia is zigzagging across the grass trying to take it from him, but the little scamp is far too speedy. My daughter is giggling so hard I'm worried she's going to pee her pants.

'Okay, coffee,' I say to myself, heading back inside to the shade of the kitchen, loving the feel of the cool marble floor beneath my bare, swollen feet.

'Want an iced coffee?' I ask Suzy, who's Will's cousin and Olivia's nanny. She's sitting at the kitchen island reading one of her textbooks. I didn't want a nanny. I wanted to look after my daughter myself, but after Olivia started having nightmares, Will suggested we get some short-term help as I wasn't getting any sleep. We lucked out and managed to hire Suzy, who is also a child psychologist studying for her Doctorate. Olivia is going to be one of her case studies and Suzy is helping us to make sure Olivia isn't suffering any ill effects after her abduction. In return, we're providing Suzy with her bed and board and a wage to help out with her uni fees.

'I'll make it.' Suzy jumps up, eager to help.

'No, sit,' I say, motioning to her to stay where she is. 'Carry on with your studying.'

'Ugh, it's too hard to concentrate with all that crazy sunshine out there. I'll take Livi down to the beach in a bit.'

'Ooh, yes, I'll come, too,' I reply, pressing the ice button on the fridge and watching as the frosty cubes clatter into the tall glass. I pop a couple of ice chips in my mouth, savouring the icy burn on my tongue. 'I could do with a bit of sea breeze. I feel like I'm carrying a hot water bottle around with me.' I pat my stomach, marvelling once again at its evolving shape.

'Bet you'll be glad to see the end of August,' Suzy says.

I smile. A little bit of heat and discomfort is nothing compared to the excitement I'm feeling at carrying Olivia's baby brother. I can't quite believe I'm already seven months pregnant. I didn't even realise my condition until I was four-and-a-half months gone. I just assumed my body clock had been disrupted after everything that had happened back in Sweden with Fin. It was quite a shock when I found out, but now Will and I can't wait. And I think Olivia is excited, even though she's not entirely sure what it's all about.

'Mamma!' I hear her calling me from the garden.

'Back in a sec,' I say to Suzy. I waddle outside again, past a lazy bee who's frenziedly bashing itself against the glass in one of the French doors. I waft it away and watch as it buzzes off across the terrace towards the climbing rose bush.

Will is already on his feet, heading down the stone steps. I follow him, holding onto the stone balustrade for support.

Olivia is pointing down the garden. 'Daddy, I can't find Bo. He runned through the wall.'

'He ran through the wall?' Will says. 'You mean the fence, down there? He can't get through. It's okay. It's safe.'

'No.' Olivia sticks her bottom lip out and points at the fence. 'He runned through there.'

Will replaced the broken fence panel back in March. We also checked every other panel to ensure they were all sound, with no holes or gaps. A structural engineer came out to re-examine the garden to make sure the unfenced area wasn't in danger of collapsing. He gave us the all clear, saying that as long as we didn't go past the fenced area, we were in no danger.

As I glance at Will over the top of Olivia's head, a whooshing starts up in my ears. I know I'm being ridiculous even thinking what I'm thinking. But I see it in Will's eyes, too. The doubt. A menacing déjà vu.

'Can you take Livi inside,' Will says. 'I'm just going to check that Bo's okay.'

'Bo down there.' Olivia points again.

I take her warm, pudgy hand and we walk up the steps together, my legs trembling. 'Shall we see if Suzy's got any ice cream in the freezer?' I say, my voice unnaturally bright.

'Yes pweese.'

We walk into the kitchen to see Suzy standing over by the coffee machine. 'I finished making Will's coffee,' she says, turning around with a smile. 'Shall I take it out to—'

'Can you take Olivia?' I interrupt. 'Keep her inside? And can you make sure all the doors and windows are locked.'

Suzy's face pales, her mouth falls open.

'I'm sure everything's fine,' I add. 'It's just to be on the safe side.'

'What's happened?' she asks, coming over and taking Olivia's hand.

'Probably nothing. I'm just being paranoid.'

'Ok-ay.'

'Bo might have got himself into difficulty,' I explain, slipping my feet into a pair of flip flops. 'He might have got through the fence at the end of the garden. We're just going to check, that's all.'

But my face must have given away some of the panic I'm feeling as I see traces of fear etch themselves across Suzy's face, too.

'If I'm not back in ten minutes, call the police.'

She blanches and then nods. 'Sure.'

'Thank you,' I add, before turning and leaving the cool sanctuary of the kitchen, closing the French doors behind me.

As I walk back out onto the terrace and down the garden steps, the hairs on my arms start to prickle and my heart begins to race.

CHAPTER THIRTY-ONE

Will beckons me down to the end of the garden, to the boundary where the fence sits. I want to call out and ask him what's wrong, but something stops me. I'm wary of raising my voice just in case... *Just in case of what?* The thoughts flying around my head are too ridiculous to entertain so why am I even thinking them?

As I draw closer to the fence, Will points to a gap at the bottom of one of the panels where two of the wooden slats are missing, creating a hole large enough for a small dog to wriggle through – just like last time. Will and I stare at one another and I try to bite back the tears that are threatening to come, my nerves raw, recently buried fears suddenly racing to the surface. If Bo has been poisoned again, I don't know what I'll do. And Livi will be devastated.

'Can you see him out there?' I ask, looking over the fence, scanning for any signs of his dark fur. But it's such a summer wilderness of trees and overgrown shrubs, a whole football team could be hiding out there and we wouldn't be able to spot them from here.

Will pushes a hand through his hair. 'Maybe his fur's caught on a bush. Or he's behind a tree or something.'

Neither of us says what we're really thinking – that he could have found a piece of poisoned meat. Or he could have gone over the edge of the cliff.

'I don't want to think the worst,' he says, 'but this is all too much of a coincidence.'

I nod, biting my lip. 'What should we do? Shall I call the police?'

'Just let me go and check down there, first. We could be over-reacting. It might be nothing.'

'No, Will. No way! It's too dangerous. I love Bo, but you can't risk your life like last time.'

'I won't risk anything,' he says. 'I'm just going to take a look, that's all.'

'Then we'll go together,' I reply.

'Anna, you're pregnant,' he says sternly.

'Don't worry, I won't go near the edge.' I give him a stare to let him know I won't take no for an answer.

'No,' he says, ignoring my stare. 'Absolutely not. If something has happened to Bo, I don't want you seeing. I don't want you stressed.'

'Well, there's absolutely no way you're going out there alone, Will. What if it's him? What if he didn't die?'

'It won't be him. The police said his chances of survival were about five per cent.'

'But what if it is him?' I don't honestly believe Fin can be in our garden. I saw the state he was in back in Sweden. I can't imagine how he could have survived that. But I also know that there's no way I'm letting my husband walk out towards the cliff edge on his own. 'I'm coming with you, Will, whether you like it or not.'

He shakes his head slowly. 'Okay. But if it is him, I want you to go straight back to the house—'

'I'm not leaving you out there.'

'In case you need to get help,' he adds.

'Okay.' I nod, hoping and praying our fears are unfounded.

Will unlocks and opens the gate. We go through, stepping from our manicured lawn to the wild tangle of grasses and shrubs. Will takes my hand and we walk together, picking our way over brambles, the long grass brushing our bare legs. I keep my eyes peeled for Bo, scanning the bushes for his brown fur, listening out for a whine or a bark. But all I hear are the crickets chirping and wasps buzzing, the sound of the sea beyond, and of children's laughter drifting up from the beach. However, all sounds fade away when I see a figure step out from behind a tree at the cliff edge.

I grip Will's hand harder, and he squeezes mine back. My heart pounds and I rest my other hand on my bump, trying to calm the little one down. He's picking up on my rising terror, shifting and turning, making his discomfort known.

'Go back,' Will whispers.

'No,' I reply.

We keep going, walking forward as though in a dream. Or a nightmare.

The man on the edge is unkempt with a patchy beard. Dishevelled, like a homeless person. He's wearing filthy cut-off jeans, a torn, stained, blue t-shirt and hiking boots that are falling apart. His hair is dirty blond, matted and greasy. He's grinning. And in his arms, he's holding Bo.

I exhale, let go of Will's hand and come to a stop. Will steps in front of me, trying to shield me from view, but I move forward to be at his side once more.

'You shouldn't stand there,' Will calls out to him. 'It's not safe.'

'Thanks for your concern, but I think I'll be okay.' Fin's voice is scratchy, raw, weak.

I have no idea what to do. How we're going to get Bo back from this psycho. Despite the queasiness in my gut, I start walking towards Fin. Confident strides. Will steps past me, trying once more to put himself between me and Fin, hissing at me to stop, that it's not safe to go on, that we don't know if Fin has a weapon. I barely hear his words.

'What do you want, Fin?' I call out. 'How did you—'

'How did I what? Survive?' He loses the smile.

I come to a halt, Will stops a little way in front of me. We're only a few yards away from Fin, now. Close enough to lunge forward and shove him over the edge. But I can't risk hurting my baby and, besides, Fin has our dog. How could we harm Bo?

'You're having another brat, then.' Fin jerks his chin in the direction of my bump. I cover it with my hands, protectively, as though Fin's attention has the power to hurt my unborn son.

'How did you get out of Sweden?' Will snaps. 'You're on a *wanted* list.'

'Yeah, I know,' Fin replies. 'Managed to stow away on a ferry from Gothenburg.' He's stroking Bo's fur. Our dog seems okay for now, but God only knows what Fin is planning.

'You left me out in that wilderness to die, Anna,' he says softly, sadly.

'Can you blame me?' I cry. 'You tried to kill me. Threatened to kill Olivia. You and Sian—'

'You took Sian,' he growls. 'You ruined everything.' He stops stroking Bo and shifts him so he's now in the crook of his left arm. Then he sticks his right hand up in the air. 'Look what you did,' he cries.

'Oh!' I clap my hands over my mouth. My baby jumps at my cry, a painful, jagged movement inside that makes me catch my breath.

Fin's hand is red and swollen, but worse than that, all the fingers are missing. Only his thumb remains. The rest are stumps.

'Fucking frostbite, Anna. That's what you did to me. Three of my toes, too.'

'How did you find your way out of the forest?' Will asks.

Fin scowls at my husband. 'Not that it's any of your business.' Fin turns his attention to me once more. 'I was lucky,' he says. 'I ran into these three outdoorsy blokes. Going ice fishing or something. They warmed me up. Fed me. Saved my life. Anyway, fun as it is to catch up, I'm here for a reason.'

'What do you want, Chambers?' Anger radiates off Will. I put a hand on his arm to try to calm him down. I don't want him doing anything stupid. Anything risky.

'You still owe me money, Anna,' Fin says. 'And you left me for dead in that forest. I'm owed some compensation for that. I think it's only fair. I need cash to get away.'

'Money?' I sneer. 'After everything you put us through, you have the nerve to come back here for money.'

'How much do you want?' Will asks.

'No!' I turn to Will. 'You can't give him—'

'Shh,' Will says. 'It's okay, Anna. It'll be worth it to get rid of him.'

'Smart man,' Fin says.

'Ten grand,' Will says. 'I can get it for you now.'

'In your dreams, Blackwell. Two hundred thou and I'm gone.'

'Don't do it,' I murmur to Will out of Fin's earshot. 'He'll keep coming back for more.'

'Stop whispering!' Fin says.

Will takes a step towards Fin, keeping me back with an outstretched arm. 'Two hundred grand and you disappear. You don't contact any of us. I never want to see or hear from you again.'

Fin nods. 'In cash.'

'Deal. Now give me my dog.' Will takes a step closer. There are only about two arm lengths separating them now.

'No,' Fin warns. 'Don't come any closer. You don't get the dog until I get my cash.'

I flinch as Will takes another small step towards Fin.

'One more step and I'll throw the little poochie over,' Fin says. He takes Bo by the scruff of his neck with his good hand and holds him out to the side.

Bo whimpers and I clench my fists.

'To have a poisoned puppy is unlucky,' Fin says. 'But then to have it fall off a cliff? I think you might be getting a visit from the

RSPCA soon.' He laughs and glances behind him, taking a tiny step backwards, holding Bo right out over the edge.

'Please, Fin!' I cry out. 'Will says you'll get your money. Don't hurt him.'

'That cliff edge is unstable,' Will warns. 'You're going to go over if you're not careful.'

Fin takes a tiny step to his right and another to his left, in a little dance to show how unafraid he is. As he does so, he dislodges some earth which skitters down the cliffside. 'Whoah,' Fin says with a nervous smile, trying to appear unruffled. He swings Bo back over solid ground and steps closer to Will. 'Yeah, I see what you mean. It's pretty dodgy out here. Dangerous place to live.'

'It's only dangerous for some people,' Will says, with ice in his voice. 'People who threaten my family.' As he speaks, Will suddenly lunges forwards and makes a grab for Bo with both his hands.

I give a squeal of alarm, tensing and splaying my fingers wide over my bump. I'd help Will, but I can't risk hurting my baby. And I daren't run off to fetch help, either, unwilling to leave Will alone with Fin. They both have hold of Bo, now – Fin still has him by the scruff of the neck, and Will has his hands around Bo's midsection – and neither will let go. It's killing me to see our dog yelping and crying in terror.

'Look out, Will!' I yell.

My heart is in my mouth. They're both about to topple over. But somehow, they manage to keep their balance. I exhale with relief until Fin brings his right elbow down, smashing it into Will's face. I scream at the sharp crack of bone on bone. Will grunts in pain, but still he won't let go of Bo. Fin goes in again for another elbow, and I know I can't stand by any more and watch this. I'm going to have to do something to help. I glance around for a stick, a fallen branch, a rock… anything, my eyes constantly darting over to Will.

Before I can act, Bo turns his head and sinks his needle-sharp teeth into Fin's chin, making him howl in pain and let go of his neck. At the same time, Will kicks him hard in the shin. This is enough to unbalance Fin who stumbles backwards, dislodging part of the ground behind him, sending earth slithering down the cliff.

With Bo safely under his arm, Will backtracks towards me, taking my hand and pulling me further away from my crazy ex, further away from the edge, while Fin wavers, trying to right himself, one hand over his bleeding chin, the other reaching for the wind-blown pine to his right. But he has no fingers with which to grip and the branches are too high for him to hook his elbow over. With his face screwed up in desperation, Fin turns his face towards me. We stare at one another for a moment, until, with a low rumble and hiss, the ground beneath his feet gives way and Fin disappears. One second he's there, the next second he's gone.

Where Fin's shape once stood, there is now nothing but clear, blue sky, and a dissipating cloud of dust.

Screams and cries fly up from below as crowds on the packed beach witness a man fall from a hundred-foot cliff.

Instinctively, I move forward to peer over the edge – a knee-jerk reaction – fearing that Fin might make another of his miraculous escapes. But Will tugs me back and pulls me close.

'It's okay, Anna,' he says. 'It's over. We're safe.'

'Are you sure?' I pull back from Will and stare into his eyes, not daring to believe it. 'How do you know?'

He presses his lips together and hands Bo to me. 'Stay here,' he says. 'Don't move.'

'What? Where are you going?'

'I'll be back in a minute,' he calls, already sprinting away across the wild garden towards the house.

Suddenly exhausted, I do as he asks, sinking down into the scratchy grass with Bo on my lap, not daring to let him go.

As the seconds tick by, sounds still filter up from the beach. The summer crowds, the gentle ocean, jet-ski engines, motorboats, a helicopter's blades whirring. And then… the sound of sirens.

Minutes later, I hear the thud of footsteps rushing towards me. I heave myself to my feet. Will has returned, his face red, his forehead slick with sweat.

'He's gone,' Will says, out of breath, his eyes a little wild. 'Fin is dead.'

'You saw?'

He nods. 'Someone covered him with a beach towel. Not just his body, they covered his face, too. Can you hear the sirens?'

'He's really gone, then.' I exhale.

'He's really gone.' Will's voice sounds thick like he has a cold.

'Are you okay?' I ask.

'Yeah,' he nods. 'But I think he might have broken my nose.'

'Oh no! We better get you to a hospital.'

'Shh. I'm fine,' Will says, taking Bo from my arms and kissing my forehead. 'We're safe, Anna. And so is this little one.'

We gaze at our bundle of fluff, his button eyes bright, his nose quivering.

'You did good, Bo,' I say, stroking his head. 'You bit that nasty man.'

Bo sneezes in response, and Will and I smile at one another.

'Come on.' He takes my trembling hand and leads me back through the garden, across the emerald lawn and up the stone steps.

I see Suzy, pale and drawn at the kitchen window, her face relaxing slightly as she spots us approaching. I give her a small wave and point to the French doors, making a key-turning motion with my hand.

Suzy opens the doors and my daughter bursts gleefully out onto the patio.

'You got Bo!' Olivia cries, her cheeks flushed, eyes sparkling.

'Yes, sweetie,' Will says. 'He's okay. Look.' He places our beloved dog into Olivia's outstretched hands and scoops the two of them into his arms.

'Still want that iced coffee?' I ask my husband.

He smiles. 'Yeah, why not.'

I gaze at my family, my heart swelling with love, hardly daring to believe that everyone is safe. That the nightmare is finally over. *No more secrets.* As I kiss Livi's round cheek, Will bends to kiss my forehead and run his palm over my belly. With this new life comes a new start. For all of us.

A LETTER FROM SHALINI

Thank you for reading *The Millionaire's Wife*. It was enormous fun to write, and I do hope you enjoyed it. If you would like to keep up-to-date with my latest releases, just sign up at *www.bookouture.com/shalini-boland* and I'll let you know when my next novel comes out.

I'm always thrilled to get feedback about my books, so if you enjoyed it, I'd love it if you could post a review online or tell your friends about it. Your opinion makes a huge difference helping people to discover my books for the first time.

I do love chatting to readers, so please feel free to get in touch via my Facebook page, through Twitter, Goodreads or my website.

Thanks so much!
Shalini Boland x

 ShaliniBolandAuthor

 @ShaliniBoland

 shaliniboland.co.uk

ACKNOWLEDGEMENTS

Thank you to the wonderful team at Bookouture for taking my book and giving it a fabulous reboot. I'm especially grateful to my amazing editor Natasha Harding, to the incredibly lovely Peta Nightingale, and to the mighty Oliver Rhodes. And also to Emily Hayward-Whitlock at The Artists Partnership.

Thank you to the talented Emma Graves for such a beautiful cover. I love it! Thanks to Lauren Finger, Ellen Gleeson, Kim Nash, Noelle Holton, Natalie Butlin, and Alex Crow, you have my undying appreciation for being such hard working and wonderful people. The voodoo magic is strong with all of you.

Massive thanks to my husband Pete for giving great feedback and suggestions. And for making the kids' dinner when I 'just have to finish writing this bit.' It wouldn't be the same book without you.

Thank you to my original editor, Jessica Dall from Red Adept. Your notes were detailed and insightful. My favourite parts are the smiley faces :)

I'm thankful for my beta readers Julie Carey, Amara Gillo, Maryjo English and Suzy Turner, whose feedback and typo-spotting was invaluable.

I'd also like to mention Tracy Fenton and Helen Boyce from *The Book Club*, and David Gilchrist and Caroline Maston from *UK Crime Book Club* who have all been instrumental in spreading the word and with feedback and support. Their members are wonderful and I feel privileged to be part of such a lovely, bookish family. Thank you!

Other people I'd like to thank for their support and wonderful words of encouragement: Neil Nagarkar, Sarah Dalton, Mandy Cowley, Jaz Hunt, Kelly New, Bev Price, Sarah Mackins, Dan Boland, Billie Boland and my woolly writing companion Jess. Finally, to all my readers and reviewers, love and thanks always.

Lightning Source UK Ltd.
Milton Keynes UK
UKHW020344230819
348428UK00016B/311/P

9 781786 815989